THE CAREGIVER

An unputdownable psychological thriller with
a breathtaking twist

N.L. HINKENS

Joffe Books, London
www.joffebooks.com

First published in Great Britain in 2024

Cover art by Nick Castle

ISBN: 978-1-83526-580-2

For my readers,
who opened up a window of opportunity
for my books to enter the world.

CHAPTER 1

Morgan

By the time the police arrive at the house, I'm hyperventilating. *My mother is missing.* How does an eighty-one-year-old woman, barely weighing ninety pounds soaking wet, who hasn't left her bedroom — let alone the house — without assistance in months, simply vanish into thin air? I'm trying not to freak out at the thought of her wandering the neighborhood, lost in a maze of confusion.

"Finally! I mean . . . thanks for coming so quickly," I stammer, extending my hand to the wiry, sallow-skinned female detective who greets me when I yank open the front door. "I'm Morgan Klein, Pamela's daughter. I'm the one who reported her missing."

"Detective Kumar," the woman replies, her dimples accentuating a reassuring smile.

I lead her inside and gesture for her to take a seat at the kitchen table.

"When did you last see your mother?" she begins.

"About one-thirty. I fed her lunch and then put her down for her — Sorry!" I slap my forehead. "I have four-year-old twins. I meant to say she *lay* down for her afternoon nap.

1

I popped next door for a coffee with my neighbor, Andrea, and, when I came back, my mother was . . . gone."

It sounds terrifying when I say it out loud — like she's no longer with us, *a dearly departed*, relegated to an ancestral photo album. An image of myself in black mourning attire flashes to mind, and a cold front of fear envelops me. I hate the way my mind leapfrogs over the most obvious explanations to the worst possible scenarios. She's fine, I know she is. Everything's going to be all right — just like Will assured me when I spoke with him on the phone earlier. All I need to do is find her.

Will, my husband of seven years, is my rock when I start gyrating like a propellor. He has an uncanny ability to calm me down enough to allow me to function. He even offered to cut short his business trip and fly home tonight, but I told him to wait a couple of hours in case Mom shows up unharmed. The truth is, telling Will to come home means admitting I think she might not.

I rub my fingers over my forehead, my brain firing off in every direction. No one abducts the elderly, do they? Not unless the victims are rich enough to be ransomed. But they do get mugged on a regular basis — people are such callous brutes nowadays. My thoughts continue their march of doom, pondering the latest report I saw on the evening news about a suspected serial killer on the West Coast. Three women's bodies have been found so far, all abducted and battered to death in a similarly gruesome manner. My lungs feel as though the air is being vacuumed out of them as I picture my elderly mother facing off against some unhinged thug wielding a skull-crushing weapon. She's not in any condition to fend for herself — mentally or physically.

"She has dementia, you know that, right?" I say to Detective Kumar. I made that clear to dispatch when I filed the missing person's report, but who knows if they pass on all the information.

Kumar gives a definitive nod. "Yes, ma'am."

I'm fascinated by her expressive eyes — chocolate with a hint of maple syrup. She seems caring, but is she competent?

I'm not in need of a social worker — I want one of those marines who barks out orders and makes things happen. Someone who can set up roadblocks at every exit, if need be. Panic surges up inside me and I squeeze my hands into fists, trying to quell the emotional rollercoaster before it takes off with me on board. I'm twitching in a thousand places, like I'm fighting off a swarm of mosquitos. I'd rather be doing something concrete right now — knocking on doors, reaching out on social media — anything but sitting here relying on strangers to find my mom. I take a deep breath and try to rein in my turbulent thoughts. *Trust the process, Morgan. The police know what they're doing.*

Kumar pulls out a notebook. "Can you give me a description of what your mother was wearing when you last saw her?"

I mentally run through the protracted daily operation of getting her dressed, beginning with laying out the day's outfit for her approval — always the same one. I bought it in triplicate, so she doesn't get upset when it's in the laundry.

I blink, forcing myself to refocus on Kumar's question. "Uh . . . she was wearing a pink twinset and black pants. My mother's a stickler for looking put together, even though she can't remember how to dress herself." I reach for the photo I printed out a few minutes before Kumar arrived. "This is a recent picture. That's pretty much all she wears anymore."

"Airdrop me a copy, please." Kumar slips the printed photo between the pages of her notebook. "I'll put a BOLO out to our patrol officers."

"What's the first step in finding her?" I ask, already tapping on my screen.

"We'll go door-to-door and canvass the neighborhood. Due to your mother's age and vulnerability, she's considered a critical missing person."

I stare at the dark, elfin curls on Kumar's forehead, inwardly mouthing the words, *critical . . . missing . . . person.* I've grown used to repeating things in my head. It keeps me on task. If it wasn't for my housekeeper, VV, I don't know where I would be. Her real name is Veronica Valdez, which makes her sound like an exotic supermodel, but at a pudding-shaped five-foot-one, with a wiry bob streaked with gray, nothing could be further from the truth.

Kumar's radio crackles, startling me out of my reverie. "Be right back," she mouths, stepping out of the room.

I chew doggedly on my nail, as I check the time on my phone. I need to pick the twins up from preschool soon. My innards rapidly knit themselves into a knot. How am I going to juggle two spirited four-year-olds while trying to track down a missing eighty-one-year-old? Maybe I should have caved and told Will to catch the next flight home, after all. But I don't want him to think I'm on the verge of another breakdown.

"Good news," Kumar announces, bouncing back into the room. "A woman in the adjacent subdivision just reported finding an elderly woman matching your mother's description inside her garage. Apparently, she told the homeowner she was waiting on her daughter to unlock the door for her."

I leap to my feet but Kumar gestures for me to sit back down. "I've already dispatched an officer to pick her up. They'll be here any minute."

"I can't thank you enough." I sink back down in my seat like a deflated balloon and pass a shaking hand over my brow. "I feel like I've just run a marathon." It's a stupid thing to say, as I've never come remotely close to running a marathon, but relief has me rambling. I close my eyes and let out a long, shuddering breath. "To tell you the truth, I was bracing myself for the worst-case scenario, with that report on the news of the West Coast Killer striking again last week. Mom must have woken up from her nap and wandered outside. I didn't know she could open the door with her arthritic fingers. I feel like a neglectful daughter."

Kumar pockets her notebook, her voice softening. "It's hard staying one step ahead of a wandering mind. I'm glad your mother's okay."

* * *

"You gave me a terrible scare, disappearing like that," I chide Mom, as I'm getting her ready for bed later that evening. "Where were you going?"

She cocks her head at me quizzically, her rheumy eyes drifting past my shoulder to the pseudo world she inhabits. "Didn't you take me somewhere?"

I let out an aggrieved sigh, reminding myself to be patient. Will is so much better with her when she gets like this. "No, Mom, I didn't. You can't wander off like that without me. We've talked about this before, remember?"

"I suppose so," she says, a vacant expression settling in the quilted folds of her face.

"Never mind." I hug her skinny frame close. "No harm done. I'm just glad you're home safe."

After helping her into bed, I throw her black pants into the laundry basket. A crumpled piece of paper falls from the pocket, and I reach for it to toss it in the trash. My breath catches in my throat when I see what's written on it.

I know where you live.

CHAPTER 2

I'm at our local park with Sam and Ella, enjoying a welcome respite from the monotony of hanging around the house keeping an eye on Mom while the walls close in on me like a shrinking crypt. Andrea has volunteered to watch her for the next hour or so, which is good of her as she's busy with the bookkeeping business she runs from home. I need to find a more permanent solution than roping in friends and neighbors now that Mom's dementia has gotten so much worse — a live-in caregiver would be ideal. I could put them up in the detached guest studio at the bottom of our garden, so we could still retain our privacy — something that's very important to Will.

My thoughts drift to the unsettling note I found in Mom's pocket. It plays on a loop like a dirge stuck in my head.

I know where you live. I know where you live. I know where you live.

I've lost several consecutive nights of sleep and chewed my way through most of my remaining nails worrying about it. I wanted to run it by Detective Kumar, but Will convinced me it's probably just something Mom picked up and pocketed — which isn't beyond the realms of possibility.

She's forever finding random items and stashing them in her clothing. Along with the note, I found a candy bar wrapper, several elastic bands, a child's sock, and a lollipop stick. Still, the note was odd — ominous even. It's had me looking over my shoulder ever since. I keep getting the feeling someone's watching me when I go to the mailbox. I wish I hadn't tossed the note into the fireplace. Being impetuous by nature has led to more regret than I care to admit to.

"Everything okay? You look like you're lost in thought," a vaguely familiar voice asks.

I glance up to see Dana Becker peering down at me, her pale brow crinkled in concern. We've chatted at the park a couple of times in passing. She's new to the area, helping out with her sister's kids, Patrick and Esther, while she looks for something more permanent. I don't know her all that well, but that's never stopped me from spilling my guts before.

"It's my mom," I say, with a weighty sigh. I direct my gaze to the twins playing contentedly on the toddler slide. "She's eighty-one and has dementia. She wandered out of the house a few days ago and got lost. It was full-on drama in the neighborhood. I ended up calling the police and reporting her missing. Thankfully, some woman on Pine Street found her sitting on a cooler in her garage. Mom thought she was home. She was waiting on me to unlock the door and let her in."

Dana pulls down the corners of her lips and shoves her oversized glasses up her nose. "I'm so sorry. That must have been very frightening — for both of you."

"Yeah, I was pretty freaked out. She could have been run over, or mugged, or died of hypothermia — anything could have happened. It didn't help that I'd just watched that report on the news about the serial killer striking again." I let out an awkward bark of laughter, aware that I'm sensationalizing my mom's neighborhood jaunt. "I'm not ready to institutional-ize her yet, but I'm considering hiring a live-in caregiver to help out. I have a fantastic housekeeper, VV, who comes three mornings a week, so we manage to stay on top of laundry and stuff, but it's overwhelming trying to keep up with the twins and Mom. VV's been like a surrogate mother to me. I'd never have made it through those harrowing early months after the twins were born without her. Most days, I'm hovering somewhere between a Category Five meltdown and a Class X breakdown." I almost add that it wouldn't be the first time, but I manage to bite my tongue on that unflattering sliver.

Dana flashes a faint smile. "What about your husband — does he help out?"

"Will travels for work, so he's gone during the week. He's the Chief Investment Manager for a national company."

"Sounds like you could definitely use some help," Dana says, waving to her sister's kids, who are gleefully chasing each other around the climbing frame.

"Hey, just a thought," she goes on. "I'd be interested in applying for the position. My sister doesn't really need me — she's just doing me a favor paying me a few bucks to help out with the kids and random stuff around the house until I find something else."

I gawk at Dana. "But . . . I thought you were looking for an administrative job."

She shrugs. "I considered it, but I don't have any experience. To be honest, I've only ever worked as a nanny. Sitting in an office all day isn't really me anyway."

"It would be a live-in position," I say, thinking out loud, as I sweep a critical gaze over Dana's appearance. She's young — always a hazard where husbands are concerned. But with her bushy brows, clunky glasses, and dark hair pulled back severely from her face, the risk of an amorous entanglement is negligible. Hope begins to flutter amid the turmoil in my belly at the serendipity of bumping into her today. This could actually work. The voice of reason, which I rarely lend an ear to, is telling me not to make an impulsive offer I might regret, but I'm desperate for help, and help is currently staring me in the face.

Dana beams back at me. "That would be perfect! I'm tired of sleeping on the couch at my sister's."

I nod slowly, turning the logistics over in my mind. I know what my commonsensical husband will say if I consult him first — *don't be rash, go through an agency, check her references.* Sound advice, but that could take weeks. Dana's here now, she's available, and she has experience with kids, which is a bonus — I could use an extra set of hands in that department, too. "Can you get me some references?" I blurt out, before I can second-guess myself.

A wide grin breaks across Dana's face. "Absolutely! I'll bring them by tomorrow, if that works for you. You must be close to Pine Street, right?"

I know where you live. I suck in a sharp breath, hesitating for half a heartbeat before nuking my last chance to retract my offer. "Uh, yes. I'm at 1207 Cagney Creek. It's a two-story white house with a stamped gray concrete driveway."

I walk home with a lighter step, one twin trotting along on either side of me, chattering over one another as they discuss their new friends, Patrick and Esther. My mind is elsewhere. If Dana's references check out — and why wouldn't they? — my only problem will be convincing Will to let someone move into our studio. He's always been dead set against renting it out to strangers. Nothing a little exaggeration of the extent of my *friendship* with Dana can't overcome.

"Looks like the fresh air did you some good," Andrea remarks when I arrive back at the house, flush with anticipation. "Your mom was no trouble at all. She's napping in her rocker right now."

I thank her profusely as she slips her laptop into her bag. I'm tempted to tell her about my conversation with Dana, but she wouldn't approve of me hiring someone I met at the park any more than Will would. Number crunchers are all the same — uptight and paranoid. *Are you crazy? What if she's a homeless bum? The West Coast Killer disguised as a nanny?* Admittedly, it is a bit spontaneous on my part, but I'm a firm believer in embracing opportunity when it comes knocking.

When Dana drops off her references the following morning, I waste no time reaching out to the people she has listed. The vote of confidence is unanimous — at least from the two women I manage to get ahold of. Both of them rave about her being kind-hearted, reliable, honest, and a hard worker — checking all the boxes on my short list of requirements — *available and breathing.* There's a very low likelihood she's lurking at the park posing as her sister's nanny for nefarious purposes. I'm itching to call her the minute I get off the phone and tell her she's hired.

First, I have to convince Will that letting a stranger move in is a necessary step for my sanity.

CHAPTER 3

A deep groove forms on Will's forehead when I present the idea to him Friday night after dinner. "I don't want a stranger living with us, Morgan. It's intrusive."

I huff in frustration as I wipe Sam's mouth and help him down from the table. Will's been in a bleak mood ever since he got home. He found out today that one of his high school buddies passed away from pancreatic cancer a couple of months back. I don't know why it's affecting him so badly — it wasn't even someone he kept in touch with. I'm trying to be understanding, but my patience is in short supply with everything I'm already juggling. "You're gone all week, so what does it matter? Besides, she won't be living with us. She'll stay in the studio when she's not working. She'll only be in the house weekdays to help out with Mom and stuff."

Will clamps his lips together in a thin line. "The studio's not set up for long-term stays. She'll be in and out of our house constantly, using the kitchen and laundry room, evenings and weekends too. She might as well be living with us. Never mind the fact that you barely know this woman. I've never even heard you mention her name."

To be fair, I have exaggerated that part — painting a picture of a friendship that blossomed over a period of several

11

months rather than a couple of weeks. Thankfully, the twins are too young to contradict my inflated timeline.

"*Please* can Dana come live with us, Daddy?" Ella begs, tugging on his arm.

"Please, Daddy," Sam chimes in. "Then I can have play dates with Patrick all . . . the . . . time." He jumps up and down, emphasizing each word. Will grabs him and begins to tickle him. I can't help but smile at the rapturous expression on Ella's face as she looks on, waiting for her turn. Distraction is one way to avoid bringing closure to the topic, but I'm not about to back down. I need to make this happen before I lose my mind. I stack the plates as noisily as possible in an attempt to reclaim Will's attention.

"The bottom line is I need help, and I need it now. I can't leave Mom alone anymore, and I can't take her with me everywhere I go. She could have been abducted, or raped, killed even." Will throws me a reproving look, and I lower my voice before continuing. "It's going to take some time to research a suitable memory-care facility for her. There might be a waiting list to contend with after that. So, unless you're willing to pack in your job and work closer to home so you can be around to take the kids to preschool and practices—"

"Fine! Hire her. On a probationary basis." Will tosses Sam onto the couch and grabs a squealing Ella. "Just make it clear to her, I don't want her in the house when I'm here."

When I deliver the news to Dana on Saturday morning, she throws her arms around me and hugs me effusively. "Thank you so much, Morgan! This is perfect! I already love your kids and I can't wait to meet your mother. I'm sure she's darling!"

"It's only a minimum wage position," I say, laughing as I extricate myself from her surprisingly strong grip.

"With room and board thrown in, it's enough for me to live on," she assures me.

"Don't forget, it's only for the short term," I add. "I'm going to start looking for a memory-care facility for Mom."

Dana gives an emphatic nod, still beaming. "Of course. Understood."

"Good. In that case, talk to your sister and figure out when you can start. We'll try a sixty-day probationary period and see where we're at after that."

I invite her to bring her stuff over at her convenience and do my best to mute my shock when she shows up later that afternoon. I hadn't expected to see her until next week at the earliest.

I accompany her to the studio and unlock the front door. "I'm surprised your sister was willing to let you go at such short notice."

She shrugs as she steps inside. "She's just happy I've found a real job. Wow! This place is awesome. I love the decor — all natural wood, greenery, crisp, white linens. It's like a spa in here." Her gaze flicks to me, a sly grin on her lips. "I might never want to leave."

An uncomfortable tingling sensation travels down my spine. Something about the way she said that makes me think she wasn't joking. I brush the thought aside — I'm sleep deprived and paranoid. It was a perfectly harmless thing to say; she was complimenting my taste.

"There's not a lot of closet space or storage," I tell her.

"Not a problem. I didn't bring much with me." She gestures to her lone suitcase. "I left most of my stuff at my sister's. No sense moving it all."

I give an approving nod, relieved she's gotten the message that the position won't last indefinitely. "I can have VV clean the studio one of the mornings she's here, or you can do it yourself, if you prefer. You don't have a washer or dryer, or a kitchen per se — just a microwave and mini-fridge — so you'll have to use the facilities in the main house. We can work out a schedule for the laundry room. You'll be eating your meals with us during the week, so the only inconvenient part will be weekends when you're off and my husband's home."

I make a point of emphasizing that last part for Will's benefit.

She raises a playful brow. "Don't worry. I'll make sure to give you and Will plenty of space. Believe me, I'm no stranger to a microwave meal."

I laugh along with her, feeling more confident in my decision. I make a mental note to add *accommodating* and *good sense of humor* to Dana's glowing résumé. "Let me show you Mom's room next and go over her routine with you. She's never had a caregiver other than me before, so it might take her some time to warm up to you. I'll introduce you later when I've had a chance to explain the new arrangement to her."

Dana follows me into the main house, and I lead her down the hallway to the guest room where Mom sleeps. "I usually bring her coffee around seven in the morning. So when you get here at eight, you can help her shower and dress. That will give me time to get the kids ready and off to preschool."

"Easy enough," Dana says. "Anything else I should know?"

I grimace as I open Mom's closet. "Dressing her can be tricky. I always ask her what she wants to wear, and she picks out the same outfit every day — this pink twinset and black pants."

Dana arches an amused brow. "I'm guessing that's why you have multiples." She runs a hand over the other items hanging in the closet. "What a shame to see all these beautiful clothes go to waste!"

"This was Mom's favorite outfit." I pull out a blue silk wrap dress and drape the bottom half over my arm. "She wore it at her seventieth birthday party."

"It's stunning!" Dana's voice drops in awe as she fingers the fabric.

I smile, recalling better days. "I can't talk her into putting it on anymore. Dementia has changed her, it's shrunk her world to a microcosm of what it used to be."

Dana throws me a pitying look from behind her thick glasses. "It must be painful watching the disease wreak havoc on someone you love. At least you have your twins to brighten your day." She lets out a fluttering sigh. "I love looking after children, but it's hard not having a family of my own."

14

I hang the dress back up and close the closet door. "Trust me, when you have your own kids, you'll be wishing you'd enjoyed your freedom more when you had it."

* * *

It's been four weeks since Dana moved in, and she's proven her references right in every way. For her part, Mom seems to be under the mistaken impression that Dana is her younger sister — which has made her more accepting of the arrangement than I anticipated. She scolds her for random things that happened in their childhood, which Dana and I have a good laugh about afterward.

There have been one or two small issues — VV's reaction being one of them, which bothers me because I respect her opinion. She never says a bad word about anyone, but something about the reproachful way she seals her lips every time Dana walks into the room makes it clear she dislikes her. I'm choosing to dismiss it as a territorial dispute, easily resolved by making sure Dana is out of the house with Mom or the kids when VV comes to clean.

Will is still miffed about the live-in arrangement. He claims I strong-armed him into it. But he has to admit it's given me a lot more flexibility to focus on the kids, now that I'm no longer in imminent danger of falling apart.

What irks me most is that Sam — who jumped up and down in excitement when I told him we were hiring Dana — has soured on her. He doesn't run up to hug her anymore when she shows up for work in the mornings. In fact, he does his best to avoid her. When I asked him if anything was wrong, he just shrugged his shoulders. All I could get out of him was that Dana gives Ella more ice cream than him.

I'm choosing to ignore it as a fit of childish petulance on Sam's part. Ella, on the other hand, is besotted with Dana. She tries to dress like her and talk like her and follows her around like a puppy the minute she gets home from pre-school. They spend a lot of time doing art projects together.

Just the other day, Dana bought her a seventy-two-color washable marker set.

"Our names both have four letters and end with the letter *a*. Isn't that cool, Mommy?" Ella says, when I tuck her into bed that night. "Dana said we're twins, just like me and Sam!"

I give her a tight smile as I kiss her goodnight. "Not quite, but it's fun to pretend."

After turning on a nightlight, I pull the door partially closed behind me. *Twins?* What next? Last week Ella started calling Dana *Auntie D*, which I put a stop to. Dana's not family, and I don't want Ella thinking of her that way. She doesn't understand that Dana is only with us temporarily. Still, no sense in bursting Ella's bubble. Maybe the novelty of having Dana around will wear off in another couple of weeks.

* * *

When I climb out of bed the following morning, a somber stillness pervades the house. I can't put my finger on what's wrong, but something is off. An unsettling sensation creeps through my bones. I pull on my robe and belt it tightly around my waist. Maybe a bad dream has left me shaken.

I peek in on the twins on my way to the kitchen to make Mom's morning coffee. They're both sleeping soundly, cheeks flushed, cherubic lips parted, puffing soft breaths. I smile contentedly and continue down the hall.

Mug in hand, I make my way to Mom's room to wake her. When I push open the door, the *Best Grandma Ever* mug slips from my fingers and shatters on the hardwood floor, the heady scent of coffee mingling with the sickly tang of blood.

CHAPTER 4

My mother lies in a crumpled heap of limbs on the floor by the bed. I fall to my knees at her side and cradle her slack head in my arms. "Mom!" I scream, over and over again, as though the sound of my voice will somehow bring her back to me. But I can't reach her where she is now. She's cold in my arms, and there's a patch of matted hair where blood has congealed on the side of her head. My thoughts careen in a thousand directions. This can't be happening — not here in my own house where I was supposed to keep her safe from all the hazards of the outside world.

I frantically dial 911. My brain splinters as I struggle to make sense of what's happened. She must have tried to get out of bed by herself in the middle of the night and fallen. Why didn't she use her pager to call me like she usually does? It's right where it always sits on her bedside cabinet.

I'm still on the floor rocking my mother's body gently back and forth in my arms, racked by juddering sobs, when the emergency services arrive. The urgent hustling and bustling wakes the kids, and they trot down the hallway in their footed pajamas, puffy-eyed and rosy with sleep.

"What's wrong with Nana?" Ella asks, removing her thumb from her mouth with a loud slurp.

My lips quiver as I search for a way to explain this rude awakening to my children's day. I'm never usually at a loss for words, but nothing could have prepared me for this — a moment in time that has come too soon, and too abruptly. *Nana's sleeping? She's sick?* But that would only delay the inevitable. I could tell the kids that she died in her sleep, but I know how they are. They'll worry they might be next. That was Will's concern, too, when I called him to give him the news. He's getting the next flight home and then we'll tell the kids together.

My agonizing internal struggle must be playing out on my face because a friendly paramedic kneels down next to Ella. "Your nana's singing with the angels, honey, just like my nana."

The ambulance has just pulled out with Mom's remains when Dana barges through the back door in her sweats, hair uncombed, glasses askew. "What's going on?" Her eyes swivel from me to the kids, sitting around the kitchen table. "Is everything all right? I was getting out of the shower when I heard all the racket. Was that a siren outside?"

"Nana's singing with the angels," Sam announces, his chubby hands circling his blue plastic tumbler. A half-moon of orange juice lines his upper lip.

"With the police lady's nana," Ella says, leaning over to poke Sam. "You forgot to say that."

"The police?" Dana's brows shoot up.

"She means the paramedic." I choke back a jerky sob as I pull Dana aside. "Mom fell getting out of bed and hit her head."

Dana claps a hand to her mouth. "Is she . . . all right?"

I shake my head, then brush the back of my hand over my eyes to catch the tears poised to fall from my lashes. "She was cold when I found her. She must have been lying there for hours. I feel like the worst daughter in the world. I didn't hear a thing. I had no idea she'd fallen."

"Oh, Morgan, I'm so sorry." Dana steps forward to hug me, but I'm afraid I'll collapse in her arms and blubber incoherently, so I turn away and swiftly scoop up the twins' tumblers. "You two can go play on your iPads for a bit," I say, forcing an unnaturally bright tone into my voice.

"But will we be late for preschool?" Ella pins me with a solemn gaze that mirrors her father's.

"You're not going to preschool today," I tell her. "Daddy's coming home early this week."

"Yay! Daddy!" Sam squeals, pumping his fists in the air.

I manage a wan smile as they tear out of the room like tandem tornadoes. "They haven't made the connection, yet, that my mom just died."

Dana slides into a seat at the table. "The dementia made that difficult for them. You were more like a caretaker than a daughter in their eyes, at least before you hired me."

"There's some truth to that." I reach for a tea towel and absentmindedly wipe the counter before turning to face her. "I feel bad about where this leaves you, Dana. I was hoping hiring you would have allowed me to keep Mom at home for another six months, a year even. I'm sorry it's ended so soon." I fish out a tissue to blow my nose, waiting for her to respond.

Shock detonates over her face as she catches my drift. A thick silence descends between us.

"Morgan, I don't have anywhere else to go," she says at length, her voice small and wheedling.

"What do you mean? What about your sister?"

"They moved to Florida last week for her husband's job. I was only giving her a hand with the kids for a couple of weeks while she packed up the house. All my stuff's in storage now."

I thread my hands awkwardly through my hair. I was hoping Dana would offer to move back into her sister's place right away. We'll need the studio for family coming into town for the funeral. "Maybe you could join her in Florida?"

"I can't afford to move." A hint of panic hitches Dana's voice up a notch. "Can't you let me finish out the probation period? I was counting on being here at least that long."

I rub a hand over my brow, trying to hide my irritation at how much she's focused on herself right now instead of my loss. I can't deal with her problems as well as my own — I'm in too much pain. "I'm sorry. I really am, but we don't need you anymore. This was unforeseen, but there's nothing I can do about it."

Dana promptly bursts into tears. "Please, let me stay," she wails. "I could help out with the kids. Ella adores me. And I'll win Sam's heart too, if you give me a chance. It's going to take time to find another place to live. There's nothing available. If you turn me out, I'll be forced to sleep in my car."

My mouth drops open. She can't be serious. Doesn't she have anything else to fall back on? A friend she could stay with? A plan B? Any savings at all?

She throws me a pleading look, eyes red-rimmed and glistening.

I grit my teeth, the words sticking to my tongue. I can't exactly ask her to leave from one day to the next if she has nowhere to go. I was desperate to have her move in, and I'm not heartless enough to turn her out on the street now that she's here. Much as Will is going to hate the thought of her living with us for another month, at least my clamoring conscience will allow me to sleep at night.

"Fine," I concede, sucking in a ragged breath. "You can stay until the sixty days are up. You can help out with the kids, maybe do some light housework on the days VV's not here."

Her tragic expression vanishes faster than the speed of light. She clasps my hand and squeezes it so hard, it feels as though she's going to crush my bones. "Thank you, Morgan. You won't regret this. I'll finish getting ready and be back in a few minutes to help you." She springs to her feet and exits through the back door.

A discomfiting shiver crosses my shoulders. Did I imagine it, or did I glimpse a self-congratulatory glint in her eyes as she waltzed by me?

I might never want to leave.

CHAPTER 5

It's the morning of Mom's funeral, and Will and I are still arguing about my decision to let Dana stay on in the studio.

"What was I supposed to do — tell her to sleep in her car?" I fume. "What do you think the neighbors would say if we kicked her out on the street with nowhere to go?"

Will scowls as he buttons up his shirt. "I wasn't suggesting kicking her to the curb. You could have given her a few days to find someplace else. Now we're stuck with her for another month, *and* we're still paying her — for what?"

"I told you already. She's going to help out with the kids and do some housework."

"I thought *you* wanted to spend more time with the kids. And we have VV to look after the house — she's a rockstar. We don't need Dana."

"I don't want to argue about this now," I say, dabbing powder over my face. "I need to get the kids dressed for the funeral."

"I suppose *she's* coming too," Will grumbles, adjusting his tie.

"Of course she's coming. She was Mom's caregiver. She's going to catch a ride with Andrea."

On the drive to the funeral home, the twins chatter incessantly to one another, while Will and I scarcely exchange two words. I've chewed my thumbnail down so far it's throbbing, but the pain is a welcome distraction from the tightness in my chest. I've barely slept in two days. That stupid note I found in Mom's pocket is haunting my every waking thought.

I know where you live.

Was it really a random item she picked up, or was it intended for her? Was her sudden death a coincidence, or could there be more to it? She thought I had taken her somewhere the day she went missing. Is it possible someone lured her out of the house? Am I crazy for even thinking like this? The coroner ruled her death an accident. How could it have been anything else? She was alone when it happened. Old people fall all the time. I dig my fingertips into my aching temples. I'm being irrational — reading into things too much, making connections where there are none. I just need to take a few deep breaths and let my emotions simmer down.

It's not only grief I'm struggling with, it's anger, and resentment, too. I'm mad at Will for making things more difficult than they need to be by picking on me when I'm already plagued with self-doubt over my snap decision to let Dana stay on in the studio. She sounded desperate, and I caved in the moment. But something about the situation feels off, and I can't put my finger on what it is exactly. I'm pretty sure her tears were manufactured to cajole me into giving her what she wanted. I should have told her I would talk it over with Will first. I jumped the gun — again. This is how I get myself in trouble every time.

Tears bubble up inside me as we pull up outside the funeral home, and the reality of Mom's death hits me afresh. Despite her dementia diagnosis, I never expected to be saying goodbye to her this soon. I'd pictured a slow decline over several years. I'm going to miss repeating myself a thousand times a day and chuckling over random objects I find in her pockets.

Inside the funeral home, we make our way up to the casket to pay our respects in private before the service begins.

Mom looks almost regal in her immaculate black pants and pink twinset, her lifeless face expertly made up, masking the dementia that ravaged her in the end. After a few moments of quiet reflection, I kiss her cold forehead and proceed to the office to go over a few final details with the funeral director regarding the service.

When the first mourners arrive, we take our seats at the front of the room. As soft music is piped through the space, I struggle to keep my composure. I'm vaguely aware of the seats behind us filling up, but I don't dare turn my head. I know I'll fall apart the minute I lock eyes with a familiar face. It will be enough of a challenge greeting everyone afterward.

Despite plying Sam and Ella with mints, they have a hard time staying seated for the duration of the short service. When the final prayer concludes, I rise from my seat with a sense of relief and move to the front of the room, the twins clamped to my legs like mollusks. I take my place next to Mom's coffin, comforted by the arm Will slips around me.

The next few minutes are a blur of mechanical motions — exchanging hugs with friends and neighbors, shaking hands with acquaintances, and murmuring appreciative responses to the steady stream of mourners as they weave their way to the front of the room and file past my mother's coffin. I'm touched to see that VV has taken time off work to be here. She kisses me squarely on the cheek. "*Lo siento mucho*, Mrs. Morgan. Your mother was a good lady."

Andrea steps up after VV and squeezes me. "My condolences, Morgan. I'm so sorry. I can't believe she's gone."

I choke back a sob. "It was hard not being able to say goodbye. I didn't expect to lose her like that — so suddenly."

Andrea gives a sad shake of her head. "She was a sweet lady. Please let me know if you need help with the kids or anything."

"Thanks. I'll—"

Whatever I was about to say evaporates on my lips the minute Dana comes into view. I blink to make sure my watery eyes aren't deceiving me, but there's no mistaking what I'm looking at. Instead of her usual ill-fitting attire, she's decked out in my mother's blue silk dress, fully made up. She steps toward me, long, dark curls bouncing down her back, and wraps me in a fierce hug before I can remove myself from her reach. I recoil beneath her touch, my arms frozen stiff.

"I'm so, *so* sorry, Morgan," she purrs as she releases me. "I didn't know Pamela all that long, but I'm going to miss her terribly."

I narrow my eyes at her. My lips wobble, but I can't bring them together to form a response.

Will nudges me gently, and I blink at the line of people waiting, suddenly aware that everyone can see me staring daggers at Dana. I force myself to focus on greeting the remainder of the waiting mourners, while seething inwardly at the audacity of Dana donning my mother's favorite dress — without permission — to wear at her funeral service.

The minute we climb into the car in the funeral home parking lot, I explode. "Did you *see* what she was wearing?"

Will's eyes are fixed on the backup camera as he reverses out of our spot. "Who are you talking about?"

"Dana! Who else?"

Will rumples his brow. "To be honest, I wasn't really paying much attention to what people were wearing."

"She had on my mother's blue silk dress — the one she wore for her seventieth birthday! She must have gone into our house and taken it out of Mom's closet after we'd already left for the funeral home."

Will's forehead creases. "How do you know it was your mother's dress?"

"Because I showed it to Dana a couple of weeks ago and told her it was Mom's favorite outfit. There's no way she owns the exact same dress. I can't believe she borrowed it, without even asking, and wore it to the funeral. It's downright disrespectful."

"Dana looked pretty, Mommy," Ella pipes up from the back seat.

I let out an irritated humph. "Shh, Ella! Mommy's talking to Daddy right now."

Her lips droop and she turns and presses her nose against the window.

"Maybe we can talk about this later." Will throws me a meaningful look. "No sense arriving at the graveside with everyone upset."

I press my lips together. I'm outraged at Dana's stunt, but Will's right. This is going to be a long day for the twins, and an emotionally charged one for all of us. I need to calm down and take things one step at a time. I can deal with Dana once I get home. Thankfully, the burial is for immediate family only, so I won't have to look at her glowing at the graveside in Mom's dress as they lower the casket into the ground.

There's an odd atmosphere in the house when we return later that afternoon. It's eerily empty and still, and yet the space feels violated. I picture Dana walking from room to room, fingering our possessions, trying things on, grinning to herself with that smug look that sometimes comes over her. I shudder at the thought. Why did I ever invite a stranger into my home?

In the kitchen, Will pours me a glass of water and kisses the top of my head. "Good job, honey. You held it together. I know this was a hard day for you."

I sniffle into his chest. "*She* made it worse. I still can't believe she pulled that stunt."

"This might be a good time to tell her it's not going to work out after all — give her twenty-four hours to pack up and leave."

I give a faltering nod. "You're right. It's for the best, after what happened. I'll tell her after I put the kids down for the night."

I take the twins upstairs and tuck them in to bed.

"Mommy's sorry for getting angry with you in the car today," I say, smoothing Ella's soft curls away from her forehead. "I was feeling sad because Nana's not with us anymore."

She pulls out her thumb and pats my head. "It's okay, Mommy. Dana said we don't have to be sad, because she's part of our family now."

25

CHAPTER 6

I thump my way back down the stairs, reeling with shock and anger as I flop down on the couch next to Will. "You're not going to believe what our daughter just told me."

"Hmm?" he mutters distractedly, his eyes flicking back and forth across his laptop screen.

I wave a hand five inches from his face. "Hello? Did you even hear what I said?"

"Sorry, just catching up on some correspondence. What's up?" He sets his laptop aside and gives me his full attention as I proceed to fill him in.

"Maybe Ella misunderstood what Dana said," he suggests, rubbing his hands over his face. "Or it could be wishful thinking on Ella's part. You know how obsessed she is with Dana."

"Ella wouldn't make up something like that. Dana's manipulating her. How dare she toy with my kids' emotions like that! First, she shows up at the funeral in Mom's birthday dress, now she's trying to replace her as a family member. It's time we had it out with her and sent her packing."

I pull out my phone and shoot off a text asking Dana to return Mom's dress.

Five minutes go by before she responds. *Just stepped out of the shower. Can it wait?*

I tap furiously on my screen. *No, we need to talk, now!*
K, be there in a few.

I pace across the floor, one hand on my hip, rehearsing what I want to say as I wait for Dana to make an appearance.

"Do you want me to break it to her about moving out?" Will asks.

I fold my arms across my chest. "No! I'm the one who hired her, I should be the one to fire her. I just want you here to back me up in case she throws another fit."

"Fair enough. Give her until the end of the day tomorrow. It's too late tonight to make her leave."

At the sound of the back door rattling open, I lock eyes with Will before hurriedly resuming my seat on the couch next to him. A moment later, Dana glides into the room and throws my mother's dress over the back of a chair. I freeze, my well-rehearsed lines instantly fizzling out at the sight of her. For the second time today, I'm rendered speechless at her appearance. She tosses her head and takes a seat opposite us, glistening hair tumbling down her back. The suggestive ivory-colored negligee and matching robe she's wearing leave little to the imagination. Gone are the ugly glasses, and her face is fully made up, complete with false eyelashes — a far cry from the homely look she's been cultivating until today. I shift uneasily in my seat. Will is getting an eyeful. Is this for his benefit, or was she getting ready to go out somewhere? I quash a flicker of resentment at the thought of my mother's caregiver going out bar-hopping the night of her funeral.

Will clears his throat, prompting me into action.

"Thanks for bringing Mom's dress back, Dana."

I cringe as the words leave my lips. It sounds all wrong, like she's the one doing us a favor. She's taken advantage of us in the worst possible way — intruding in our lives, emotionally and physically, violating our privacy. I clench my fists and start over.

"Look, I'm just going to come right out with it. I'm appalled that you showed up at my mom's funeral in her favorite dress. You completely overstepped every boundary

27

— first, by entering our house when we weren't here, and second, by helping yourself to Mom's clothes without my permission."

Dana blinks her spidery lashes at me, a puzzled expression forming on her impeccably made-up face. "I don't understand, Morgan. You said I could borrow something for the funeral. I only brought casual clothes for the job when I moved in." She gives a sheepish shrug. "I'm sorry if the dress I picked out was your mother's favorite. I can understand now why you got so emotional over it."

I gasp in disbelief at the multiple lies batched into one smooth delivery. Not to mention the fact that the getup she's wearing now could hardly be labeled *casual*, but that's beside the point. "I never gave you permission to wear my mother's clothes to her funeral."

She tinkles an apologetic laugh. "Oh, Morgan! You've probably forgotten with all the stress. Don't feel bad about it — I know you're overwhelmed." She arches a knowing brow in Will's direction. "When you showed me your mother's clothes, you said I could borrow anything I wanted as she wore the same thing every day anyway." She leans forward with a conspiratorial glint in her eye, cleavage on full display. "We laughed about you having to buy multiple outfits to keep her happy, don't you remember?"

I half-rise out of my seat. "Of course I remember telling you she wore the same thing every day, but I never—"

"It sounds to me like it was a simple misunderstanding," Will cuts in, pulling me back down.

I turn and glare at him. Is he actually falling for her pack of lies? Or is he trying to appease her so she agrees to leave quietly?

Before I can say anything more, she glances at her watch and lets out an exclamation of surprise. "Is that the time already? I'm meeting a friend for a drink in a few minutes, and I have to finish getting ready. Was there anything else you wanted to discuss with me?"

So she *is* going out. Heartless cow!

"As a matter of fact, there is something else. I think it would be best if you moved out as soon as possible. We can give you until the end of the day tomorrow."

I watch as she runs her fingers provocatively through her hair from root to tip, blinking coquettishly in Will's direction. "You might have forgotten this too, Morgan — perfectly understandable, given the circumstances — but you and I have a verbal agreement that allows me to work out my sixty-day probation period. As I'm sure you're aware, verbal agreements are binding. Of course, I'm happy to help out with the kids and housework, as you requested."

I open my mouth to protest, but Will grabs me by the elbow and squeezes firmly.

"That's fine, Dana," he says congenially. "That gives you four weeks to find alternative accommodation."

A satisfied smile stretches across her lips as she gets to her feet. "I'm so glad you and I are on the same page, Will." She walks to the door, then spins to face me. "My condolences again on the loss of your mother. I miss her already. What a tragic turn of events!"

I stare at her, dumbstruck, as she sashays out of the room. When the back door clicks closed behind her, I punch the couch cushion next to me and groan. "Why did you capitulate to her demands, Will? You're the one who didn't want her here to begin with!"

"Do the words *binding verbal agreement* mean anything to you?" he asks grimly. "She was clearly indicating her intent to pursue legal action if we try to force her out. Unless you want a lawsuit on your hands, which will drag this out even further, we have no choice but to let her live in the studio until the sixty days are up. Don't blame me for how this is playing out. You're the one who invited her to move in."

I squeeze my nails into the flesh of my palms as it slowly sinks in that we're stuck with a squatter, at least for now. I have a bad feeling about this. All indications so far are that Dana Becker gets what Dana Becker wants. The question is, what does she want next? Something she said is bothering me: *It's hard not having a family of my own.*

I lay awake for hours, haunted by my little girl's words playing on a loop inside my brain: *We don't have to be sad, because she's part of our family now.*

CHAPTER 7

On Friday, VV arrives to clean as usual and immediately envelops me in a heartfelt hug. "So sorry, Mrs. Morgan," she says, enunciating each syllable. "*Y los niños.* They miss their nana, no?"

I give a glum nod as I slump down on a bar stool at the kitchen counter. I'm still furious at Dana for trying to slither her way into my daughter's affections like a venomous viper replacing her nana. Of course she'll insist Ella must have misunderstood what she said if I confront her about it.

"Sit down for a minute, VV." I pat the stool next to me. "I need to explain the situation with Dana to you. Obviously, we no longer need her services now that Mom is gone, but she was counting on this job for its accommodation — she's telling us she has nowhere else to go. She got very upset when we asked her to move out, so we've reluctantly agreed to let her work out the remainder of her probation. She's going to help me with the kids, and I was thinking maybe she could help with some housework too, on the days you're not here. Or even when you're here. You could direct her on what needs to be done."

VV juts out her lip. "*No la necesito.*"

"I know you don't need her, but maybe you could give her something to do."

"I work alone. I like best."

I heave a sigh, knotting my hands in my lap. She's dug in her heels and nothing I say is going to make her change her mind. "Sure, I understand. I'll keep her out of your way."

VV reaches for her bucket of rags, then hesitates. "Be careful, Mrs. Morgan. *Entiendes*?"

I frown. "Of what?"

"Just be careful. I no say more." She waddles off down the hallway and disappears into a bathroom, turning up the volume on her Spanish-language podcast.

Be careful. Is she warning me about Dana? Or something else? A shiver ripples across my shoulders. My mind goes back to the note that fell out of Mom's pants. Am I crazy for thinking it had some connection to her death? Is my family in danger? I feel like I'm beginning to fall apart at the seams. I still can't shake the feeling that someone is watching me at times. I need to get a grip and think this through rationally. VV's English isn't the best — I might be misunderstanding what she means by *careful*.

"Ella! Sam!" I call up the stairs. "Time to go!"

My hand flies to my chest when Dana suddenly materializes at my side. "Hi, Morgan! I'm ready."

I grimace, trying to conjure up an air of civility. I dread being stuck with her all morning, but I can't give her a reason to pick a fight with me. The last thing I want is for this to devolve into an ugly lawsuit that drags out even longer than the sixty days I'm sentenced to endure her. "You don't have to come, Dana. I'm just dropping the kids off at preschool."

She wags a finger at me, a ghost of a grin on her lips. "Nuh-uh! I'm not going to let you talk me into taking advantage of you. I want to earn my keep. If I'm going to help out with the twins, I need to know where they go to school. Besides, I wouldn't want to get in the Queen of Clean's way." She wiggles her newly tinted brows at me. "She can be a little temperamental."

I give a stiff nod, resigning myself to the unwelcome idea of spending the morning with her. "Okay. I need to run a few errands after I drop the kids off — post office, groceries, that kind of thing."

Dana flashes me an ingratiating smile. "Maybe we can grab a coffee afterward — get to know one another a little better now that I'm no longer housebound looking after your mother."

I don't bother responding. A coffee tête-à-tête isn't going to happen. Dana and I may have started out on friendly terms, but it's strictly business from here on out, as far as I'm concerned. She's my employee, and I don't intend to give her an opportunity to blur those lines, especially not after her scantily clad appearance in front of my husband. She's underestimated me if she thinks she can get whatever she wants for the next four weeks. I'm fully capable of defending my territory.

"What do the kids like to do in the afternoons?" Dana asks, on the drive to the grocery store. "I can take them to the park, or the library, do crafts, whatever."

"They love the park. But most afternoons they have scheduled activities. Tuesdays and Thursdays, Ella has dance and Sam has judo, and they both take swim lessons on Mondays."

Dana eyes me dubiously. "That's a lot for four-year-olds, don't you think? And so much driving for you. No wonder you're stressed out all the time."

I grip the steering wheel a little tighter, the hair on the back of my neck rising. "The kids enjoy it. They'd rather be busy than bored."

"Well, you're their mother. I'm sure you know best," Dana replies, her words appeasing, her scathing tone anything but.

"Speaking of the kids, it was kind of you to buy Ella those washable markers, but Sam felt left out. It would have been better to have asked the kids to share them."

Dana looks deflated. "I'm sorry. I wasn't intentionally trying to upset Sam. I'll find a way to make it up to him. In fact, why don't I get him some paint and paper while we're out shopping this morning? I have an idea for a fun project he and I can do together."

33

I throw her a sidelong glance, momentarily taken aback. I was expecting pushback, not contrition, but there's nothing disingenuous in her expression.

"Sam would like that," I say, pasting on a smile. I might as well do my part to make things go as smoothly as possible for the next few weeks — for everyone's sake.

* * *

Sam's face lights up when he sees the paints. And true to her word, Dana spends the afternoon working on a project with him in the playroom, while Ella and I bake cookies together. Maybe I was too harsh, asking Dana to move out immediately after the funeral. I can hardly blame her for being upset about it. After all, she did take excellent care of Mom. And maybe I had given her the impression I didn't care if she wore Mom's clothes. I was so strung out at the time, I can barely remember what I said on any given day. As for the negligée I was so ticked off about, I have only myself to blame. Dana made it clear she'd just stepped out of the shower. I was the one who insisted she come up to the house right away.

When Will walks in later that evening, he's greeted with the delighted shrieks of the twins, eager to show him their respective creations.

"Sam and I can finish our project some other time," Dana says, nodding a cool greeting to Will. She tidies up the paints and makes a discreet exit.

I'm thankful she's respecting our boundaries regarding family time. She may have convinced Ella that she's family now, but nothing could be further from the truth.

After pizza and a movie, Will carries Sam and Ella to bed and tucks them in. I pour myself a glass of wine and turn on the crime show we're halfway through the second season of. Will frowns when I top my glass off a short time later, but I ignore him. He always goes on about how his father's alcoholism ruined his childhood, but that doesn't mean I'm traumatized too. It bugs me that he never wants to socialize on the weekend. He says he feels awkward when everyone around him is drinking, but he's just making excuses. He doesn't like getting close to people. We used to joke about opposites attracting, but sometimes I think we're just neutralizing the best parts of each other. I'm sick and tired of sitting in front of the television every Friday night. By the end of the second crime show episode, I've polished off the entire bottle of Cabernet.

"Time to hit the sack," Will says, pointing the remote at the TV. I stifle a yawn as I turn off the lights and follow him to bed.

I'm running across endless miles of white, sandy beach in my dreams when a blood-curdling scream wakes me.

CHAPTER 8

Will and I sit bolt upright in bed, struggling to untangle ourselves from the sheets through a haze of sleep. I'm the first to reach our bedroom door, and I wrench it open to find Ella standing there in her mermaid nightgown, clutching a floppy-eared rabbit my mother crocheted for her.

"Sweetheart! What's wrong?" I cry. Will reaches past me and swoops her up into his arms.

She blinks solemnly at me, snuggling her rabbit beneath her chin. "When I waked up, Sam was dead, just like Nana."

The air is instantly sucked from my lungs like an industrial vacuum. A moan emanates from a pit of pain deep inside me as I sway back and forth on my feet. *No! No! No!* I clutch the wall for support and pinch myself to make sure I'm awake and not in the throes of some sickening nightmare. *This can't be happening!*

Will springs into action first, triggering my own delayed response. The pounding of our feet on the hardwood floor in the hallway echoes through my brain like gunshots shattering the peace of what should have been an ordinary Saturday morning filled with chocolate chip pancakes and kids' laughter. My heart feels like it's about to burst out of my chest, desperation to reach my son propelling me forward.

We burst into the kids' bedroom and come to an abrupt halt at the foot of Sam's bed. I gasp at the sight that greets us — both beautiful and horrifying, all at once. Sam is sitting up, covered in what appears to be blood, tears tracking a scarlet path down his cheeks. "Ella sc-sc-scared m-m-me," he sobs.

Heart thudding mercilessly, I dash to his side and frantically check him out. "He's okay!" I shoot a reassuring glance in Will's direction. "I think it's just paint."

I draw Sam into a tight embrace, too relieved that he's alive to care about the gaudy red color staining my pajamas. "It's okay, baby," I whisper to him, rocking him gently in my lap.

Out of the corner of my eye, I catch sight of the tub of paint Dana bought him lying on the floor next to his toy box. He must have snuck it into his room last night after Will tucked him in to bed.

"Ella didn't mean to scare you. She thought you were hurt, that's all." I lock eyes with Will. The relief on his face mirrors my own.

Once Sam's sobs subside, I pick him up and carry him into the bathroom. Ella tags along behind, watching my every move as I fill the tub and grab a washcloth from the towel rack. "Sam's not 'lowed paint in the bedroom, is he, Mommy?" she asks, eagerly watching my face for confirmation that Sam has been naughty — now that he's no longer dead.

"Mommy will talk to Sam about that," I say firmly. "Why don't you and Daddy make us some pancakes while I'm getting your brother cleaned up?" I gesture to Will, and he dutifully snatches Ella up and strides out of the room.

I help Sam out of his pajamas and lift him into the bath water. I'm shocked at how much paint he's managed to get on himself — it's all through his hair and over his face. He scrunches his eyes shut while I soap him up and begin rinsing. Thankfully, it's only poster paint and washes out easily enough. I stare uncomfortably at the ruby-colored water, shaken to the core, but thankful it isn't my son's blood I'm rinsing off. Ella's pronouncement cut me like a sword. *Sam was dead, just like Nana.* It made me think of that creepy note again. Ever since

Mom died, I've been fearful for our safety. I couldn't have handled burying another family member, especially not my child. I inhale a calming breath before turning my attention to the situation at hand. I don't want to come down too hard on Sam, but he needs to know that what he did was wrong.

"Sweetheart, remember Mommy said no painting except in the playroom?"

He nods, reaching for a plastic boat in the drawstring bag suctioned to the tile above the bathtub. I grab his wrist to stop him from becoming distracted. "Sam, look at Mommy. Why did you bring the paint into your bedroom?"

"I didn't," he huffs, eyes fixed longingly on the plastic boat just out of reach.

"Sam," I say in a softly scolding tone. "You mustn't tell lies."

"I'm not . . . telling . . . lies!" he insists, slapping the water in frustration.

A fist-sized clod of bubbles lands on me. I count to three — ten's always been too much of a stretch for me — and try again. "Okay, so who painted your face? The tooth fairy?"

"No."

"Then who?"

He shrugs his skinny shoulders. "Nobody."

"Sam, look at this red paint in the water. It was all over your face and in your hair."

He sighs dramatically. "I'm hungry. Can I have pancakes now?"

"Not until you tell me the truth about how the paint ended up in your bedroom."

He slaps some suds between his palms, laughing delightedly when they shoot upward.

"Sam, are you listening to me?"

He looks away and whispers something to the tile wall, but I can't make it out.

I tap him on the shoulder. "What did you say?"

He cups a sudsy hand to my ear and whispers, "Ella . . . did . . . it."

38

I frown down at him. "That's not true. Ella was scared when she woke up and saw you. She thought you were . . . hurt." I almost said the d-word, but I don't want to spook him.

"Are there any hungry pancake monsters in this house?" Will calls down the hallway.

"Me!" Sam shouts, standing up in the tub and flapping his arms excitedly.

I sigh as I wrap a towel around him. I'll talk it over with Will and decide what to do about it. We can't allow Sam to get away with lying about the paint — not when the evidence of his guilt is sitting right next to his toy box.

During the course of the day, Will takes a couple of stabs at getting him to confess, but Sam stubbornly refuses to cave. Nothing we say can persuade him to admit to what he's done. In the end, we settle on revoking his painting privileges for a week and drop the topic.

When Monday morning rolls around, Dana shows up bright and early, eager to finish her project with Sam. "We're going to have to postpone it," I tell her. "Sam took the paint into his bedroom over the weekend and made a huge mess, then lied about it. He's lost his painting privileges for the week."

Dana's smile falters. "Oh no! I'm so sorry. I feel responsible for buying him the paints to begin with."

"It's not your fault. And it wasn't the mess that bothered us as much as the lying."

Dana nods thoughtfully. "Yes, I notice he has a tendency to lie."

I throw her a sharp look. "What do you mean? What else has he lied about?"

She shrugs. "Little things, for the most part, like telling you I give Ella more ice cream than him. It's a trivial example but, my point is, I think you're doing the right thing. It's best to nip it in the bud."

She stretches her lips into the semblance of a smile. "Men just become more proficient liars over time. You can never really trust them."

CHAPTER 9

Tuesday morning, I leave Dana watching the kids while I pop next door for a quick coffee with Andrea. I haven't seen her since the day of the funeral, and I've been meaning to thank her for helping out when Mom passed away. I'm lucky to have her as a neighbor. She and her husband, Tom, have invited Will and me over for dinner on multiple occasions, but Will always makes an excuse. I've more or less accepted the fact that we're never going to socialize with them as a couple, but that doesn't mean Andrea and I can't be friends.

"I didn't get to thank you properly for letting my aunt stay with you the night of Mom's funeral," I say, following Andrea into her kitchen. "That was a huge help."

"She's a sweet lady. She reminded me of your mom before the dementia got ahold of her." Andrea sets a steaming mug of coffee in front of me. "You look tired." She pulls out the chair opposite me and sinks into it, sliding her fingers around her own mug. "Are you sleeping okay?"

I flinch at the memory of waking up to a blood-curdling scream. "As much as any mother of four-year-old twins sleeps. Ella woke me up early on Saturday morning to tell me Sam was dead."

Andrea's jaw drops open. "No! What was that all about?"

I give a wry grin. "False alarm, thankfully. Sam snuck some red paint into their bedroom and got it all over his face and hair. When Ella woke up, she took one look at him and thought he was splattered in blood. She came screaming into our bedroom." A knot throbs in my throat at the memory of it. "It was awful. I've never been so relieved in all my life when I realized it was just paint. I couldn't even bring myself to be upset with Sam about the mess."

Andrea shakes her head slowly. "Sounds like a terrifying way to wake up. That little rascal!"

A strained smile flickers over my lips. "The worst part is that he wouldn't admit to doing it. He tried to pin it on Ella."

"Funny how kids instinctively try to pass the buck. Mine did the same."

"I'm worried it's becoming a pattern with him. Dana said he's been lying about her favoring Ella — I think he's jealous of how close she and Ella are."

Andrea presses her lips flat. "I wouldn't put too much credence in anything Dana tells you."

I set down my mug with a thunk. "Why's that?"

Her forehead wrinkles in thought. "From what I've seen, she doesn't always treat Sam fairly. The other day, I was outside weeding when they were in the backyard. Dana was pushing Ella on the swing, and Sam kept begging her to push him, too. She told him to man up and pump his own legs. He was upset, of course, and she called him a crybaby. I thought it was mean of her. I don't know if she tries to pit them against each other, or if she just doesn't like him." She lifts her mug to her lips. "I don't know why she wouldn't. He's such a fun little guy!"

I nod, unsettled by Andrea's observation. "He was excited about Dana moving in, at first, but he never took to her after that. Ella bonded with her from the get-go — too much in fact. It started to creep me out a little."

Andrea frowns. "What do you mean?"

"She started calling her *Auntie D*, until I put a stop to it. I didn't want Ella getting overly attached to someone who wasn't going to be around for long. Then it got weirder. Dana told her not to be sad when her nana died because *she* was part of our family now."

Andrea's face registers shock. "That's completely out of line. She's virtually a stranger. And I hate to think she favors Ella over Sam."

"I've spoken to her about that, and it's gotten better — especially now that she's helping out with the kids."

Andrea looks up sharply. "I thought she was moving out?"

"Not soon enough." I stare into my coffee. "Her sister moved to Florida, so now she has nowhere else to live." I pluck at a thread in the sleeve of my shirt. "Will doesn't want me discussing the situation with the neighbors so I'm telling you this in confidence — Dana's refusing to leave until her probationary period is up."

Andrea rumples her brow. "But the job she was hired to do no longer exists. You have every right to fire her."

I heave out a sigh. "It's complicated because it's a live-in situation. She says she'll have to sleep in her car if we kick her out. Will's afraid she might park right outside our house and make a scene in front of the neighbors. We've agreed to let her stay until the sixty days are up. It's only another few weeks."

Andrea swallows a mouthful of coffee. "I can't believe the nerve of that woman."

"She can be very manipulative," I agree. "I confronted her about showing up to the funeral in Mom's dress. She maintained I told her it was fine to borrow it. She even managed to convince Will that I'd forgotten what I'd said and that it was all a misunderstanding." I pick at a ragged fingernail. "To be honest, I've been so sleep deprived, I can't be sure what I said. I remember joking around with her about Mom wearing the same outfit day in and day out, but I don't recall Dana asking to borrow anything."

"Sounds like she's trying to pit you against your husband, and Sam against Ella. If you ask me, the sooner you get rid of her, the better." Andrea peers at me over the rim of her mug. "I wasn't going to mention this, but she came over here last Saturday in a leather mini skirt asking if Tom could take a look at her car. I told her to call AAA, and I warned him to steer clear of her. Next thing you know, she'll be claiming he assaulted her and suing for compensation."

I frown, shifting in my seat. "You might be right. Will and I asked her to come up to the house for a talk the night of the funeral, and she showed up in her negligee."

Andrea's brows shoot up. "I'd have sent her straight home to change — totally inappropriate."

I grimace. "In a way, it was my fault. She did let me know she'd just got out of the shower, but I insisted we meet right away."

Andrea snorts. "She could have thrown on some sweats. Don't kid yourself — she knew what she was doing."

"I'm beginning to think she had devious intentions all along. But, as Will reminds me, I'm the one who invited her in. And now she won't leave." I swirl the dregs of my coffee around in my mug. "I think she wants more than a place to live — I'm afraid she wants my family."

CHAPTER 10

Four Weeks Later
Will

Today is Morgan's forty-fifth birthday. I've taken the day off work so she can kick back and enjoy a few hours at the Sculpted Soul Spa with the gift certificate I surprised her with. The kids skipped preschool and helped me make her breakfast in bed. They presented her with handmade cards, complete with misshapen stick figures and misspellings, which she dutifully oohed and aahed over before heading into town for her appointment. My only task until her return is to make sure the kids get to their 12.30 p.m. swim lesson on time. Once Morgan returns, we'll spend a few hours at the zoo before going out to dinner at her favorite Italian restaurant.

I've given VV and Dana the day off — not that Dana does much other than play with the kids or help shuttle them around to their various activities. The funeral fiasco and its aftermath has faded to an unpleasant memory, and it's been smooth sailing for the past couple of weeks. Morgan seems to appreciate having the extra help, and Sam has finally warmed up to Dana. Still, I can't deny I'll be relieved when she moves out at the end of the week. There's something about the way her eyes drill into me at times that makes me uncomfortable. I can't tell if she's smoldering with desire or seething with hatred — almost as though she knows what I did. But that's impossible.

Thankfully, I'm gone all week, and she has weekends off, so I rarely run into her. When I do, I make a point of never being alone in the house with her. I don't trust her after the stunt she pulled to stay on in the studio. I was afraid she would resort to legal action if we kicked her out, but she could easily accuse me of much worse. I've managed to keep a low profile for thirty years. The last thing I need is cops looking into my life.

When I take the trash out, I notice Dana's blue Honda Civic parked in the carport next to the studio. She must be planning on having a lazy day at home instead of making the most of her day off. I don't feel the least bit guilty about excluding her from our plans, even though she helped the twins bake a chocolate cake and dropped numerous hints about celebrating with us. We've been careful to keep our relationship strictly professional since the funeral, and not give her the impression she's one of the family. I think that's why she resents VV so much — she's jealous of our relationship with her.

I finish loading the dishwasher and set it to run before heading down to the kids' room to pack their swim bags. When I'm done, I open the window and call out to them as they chase each other around the play equipment in the backyard. "Ella! Sam! Time to get dressed!" They ignore me for as long as possible before racing each other to the back door. At the last minute, Sam pulls ahead. Ella cries out in frustration and skids to a halt, tripping on a loose paver in the process. Her subsequent scream pierces the air like a razor to my heart.

I toss the swim bags aside and dart through the house and out to the yard. Dana beats me to it, dropping to her knees next to Ella and gathering her into her arms.

"I'm bleeding, Daddy!" Ella blubbers, a look of sheer terror in her eyes.

I lift my daughter from Dana's arms and carry her into the house, blood pouring from her mouth. Setting her next to the sink, I do my best to clean her up so I can assess her injuries. "It's okay, baby," I soothe. "Let Daddy take a look."

"Is Ella going to die like Nana?" Sam asks, wide eyes glued to his sister.

Dana places her hands on his shoulders and squeezes them. "No, of course not. Ella's going to be just fine."

Gingerly, I dab the inside of her mouth with a paper towel, only to discover she's knocked out a tooth and chipped another. Not what I'd hoped to find, but at least they're only baby teeth. I don't want to alarm her, but I'll need to have her dentist take a look.

After I've cleaned her up, I give her a popsicle to soothe her gums while I have a quiet word with Dana. "I'm going to try and get an emergency dental appointment for her. Can you keep an eye on them both for a minute?"

Dana rests a hand on my arm. "Of course, Will. Go make your call."

I give an awkward nod of thanks and beat a hasty retreat from the room, my mind flashing back to the night Dana showed up at the house in that provocative nightwear. Morgan blamed herself, but I'm not buying it. I suspect Dana got herself gussied up for my benefit.

After several minutes on hold, I finally get through to the pediatric dental clinic. The sympathetic receptionist promises to squeeze Ella into the schedule as soon as we get to the office.

"I can take Sam to his swim lesson, if you like," Dana offers. "He'll be bored hanging out at the dentist's."

I give a distracted nod. "That would be a big help, but I don't want to interrupt your plans for your day off."

She gives an abashed shrug. "I didn't make any."

"In that case, I'll take you up on it. Sam's swim bag is packed and ready to go."

I waste no time bundling Ella into the car, and quickly reverse out onto the street. I consider texting Morgan to tell her what's happened, but she'll have a million questions and I don't have any answers, yet. No sense making her cut short her spa day — she could use a few hours of being pampered. Losing her mother so suddenly was difficult for her. She's still struggling with guilt over it, even though it wasn't her fault.

I grimace as I pull up outside the dental office. I can't believe JT is gone either. He was only a few months older than me. It shook me to the core, but I'm doing my best to hide it from Morgan. I don't want her sympathy, and I don't want to talk about things that could dredge up too much dirt from the past — some things are best kept buried.

Dr. Patel, the pediatric dentist, has Ella smiling within minutes. He uses his tiny mirror to unobtrusively check the inside of her mouth, delighting her with a steady stream of humor. "Tell me, Ella, do you know why the donut went to the dentist?"

She shrugs, wide-eyed as she waits for the answer.

"Because he needed a filling."

Ella giggles, looking to me for reassurance that the punchline merits her response. I'm pretty sure she doesn't understand the joke, but the idea of a donut going to the dentist is funny enough to distract her.

After setting up an appointment for later that week to extract the broken tooth, I walk Ella back out to the car with the promise of ice cream to make up for missing her swim lesson.

I'm surprised to see Dana's Honda in the carport when we get back — I hadn't expected her to beat us home. I toss my keys in the bowl on the kitchen counter. "How was the swim lesson?" I glance around the room but there's no sign of Sam.

"Um . . . it could have gone better. Sam had a little mishap. He's okay though," she says, raising her palms defensively.

I frown. "What happened?"

"He swallowed some water and got into difficulty. I had to dive in and pull him out. The instructor and the lifeguard were distracted by another child who'd fallen on the pool deck and knocked himself out."

"Where is he?" I demand.

"In his room, just chilling." Dana flashes me a self-assured smile. She kneels down next to Ella. "How's my girl? Let me see those teeth."

While Ella's preoccupied, I stride down the hall to the kids' room to find Sam sitting on the floor surrounded by a mob of plastic dinosaurs.

"Hey, buddy!" I crouch down next to him. "I heard you had a bit of a rough time at your swim lesson. Good thing Dana was there to help you."

Sam gives a defiant shake of his head. "She didn't!"

I raise my brows. "What do you mean? She said she dove in when she saw you were struggling."

He glowers up at me from beneath his brows, clutching a plastic Tyrannosaurus Rex in one hand. Without warning, he rams it down on top of a Velociraptor with such ferocity that I sway back on my heels. "She jumped on me, and I couldn't breathe!"

CHAPTER 11

I close the door to my office and place a call to Sam's swim instructor, Tyler Goodwin. I want to hear what he has to say before I confront Dana. Something about the situation doesn't sit right with me. It's possible Sam misinterpreted her attempts to save him, but he's insisting he wasn't in any difficulty when she jumped into the pool. Is he too embarrassed to admit he was struggling? He has been lying about things lately — like blaming Ella for the paint incident. Did Dana misread the situation and panic? I run a hand through my hair as I wait for Tyler to pick up. I never could have imagined the crazy turns this day would take when I sent Morgan off to the spa with a birthday kiss and my reassurance that I had everything under control. I don't like it when things become unmanageable.

"Hey, Will! I've been trying to reach you," Tyler says, in his usual genial manner.

"Yeah, sorry about that. It's been a wild morning. Sam probably told you Ella took a spill in the backyard and knocked a tooth out."

"Ouch! Poor thing. Sam did mention she'd fallen but I didn't realize it was that bad. I'm sure Dana already told you what happened at the pool this morning."

"Yes, she did, and I talked to Sam about it too. There seems to be some confusion about how it all went down. I wanted to get your take on it."

"To be honest, I didn't see anything before I heard the splash of Dana jumping into the water. One of the kids had just slipped on the pool deck and knocked himself out cold. The lifeguard and I were attending to him, and it happened in the few seconds we took our eyes off the water."

I scratch the stubble on my jaw. "So, you didn't hear Sam crying out for help, or any splashing sounds before Dana jumped in?"

"No. Sam was doing great this morning. He's one of our strongest swimmers in that age bracket. I can see him swimming competitively in another few years."

"What about the lifeguard? Did he see anything?" I ask.

"She. And no, she didn't see what happened either. We were focused on the kid who'd cracked his head. Maybe that's what distracted Sam, and he swallowed some water or something."

"It's possible, but he's adamant he wasn't in any difficulty. He says Dana jumped on him and that's when he began struggling to breathe."

"Hmm . . . he might have thought that's how it went down. I'm just thankful she had eyes on him." Tyler is silent for a beat. "I don't want to speak out of turn here, but I don't think Sam's overly fond of Dana. He's told the other kids things about her before — silly stuff about her being mean to him, ignoring him and such."

"Yeah, Sam and Dana had a bit of a rocky start, but I thought he was over all that."

"Maybe so. Anyway, I need to get going, Will. I have a class to teach. Sorry again about what happened. For the record, it didn't dim Sam's enthusiasm one iota. He won the race the kids had this morning after his little mishap."

"Thanks, Tyler. Appreciate it."

I end the call and stare through the window at the studio at the bottom of the garden. Is it a coincidence that Sam got into difficulty at the very moment the other kid fell and distracted Tyler and the lifeguard? What if Sam was telling the truth and Dana jumped on him, causing him to swallow a bunch of water? If she genuinely thought he was in difficulty, she should be commended for her quick thinking. The alternative — that she deliberately jumped on him, then rescued him — is beyond the realms of credulity. Why would she do something like that — to look like a hero, hoping we'd keep her on? If that's the case, it's a misguided attempt that almost went horribly wrong.

Whatever her strategy is, it won't work. Friday's a hard deadline, and it can't come quickly enough, as far as I'm concerned. I sigh as I get to my feet and pocket my phone. It won't accomplish anything to confront Dana with Sam's version of events. Without witnesses, other than a bunch of squirming four- and five-year-olds, it's a he-said-she-said tug of war. Sam's physically unharmed, which is all that matters. And Dana will be gone by Friday. No sense stirring the pot if it can be avoided. I make my way back to the kitchen, thank her for her help, and send her on her way.

A little over an hour later, Morgan arrives back from the spa, radiant and relaxed — more like her old self. Her carefree, outgoing nature is what attracted me to her from the outset. Maybe I actually believed back then that she could counteract the darkness in me. The truth is, she only high-lights it. It bothers her that I don't want to get close to other people, but it's hard when you're a fake. I can't destroy my kids' lives with the truth.

"You look fantastic, babe! How was it?" I ask, whipping up a smile.

Morgan lets out a blissful sigh. "Soft strains of Peruvian windpipes instead of a cacophony of shrieking kids, trickling water instead of splashing limbs, the hint of cucumber and citrus in the air instead of chlorine burning my nostrils — what's not to love? How was your morning?"

I shake my head. "Where to begin? The good news is that both kids are alive. The bad news is that they're a little worse for wear."

51

Morgan quirks a brow. "O-kay. So what happened?"

After I fill her in, she leans back in her chair and exhales loudly. "Selfishly, I'm glad it was you who had to deal with the drama, for once."

"What do you make of the pool incident?"

"You know how Sam is. He likely got distracted when the kid fell. Dana panicked and thought he was going under. And he was embarrassed because she jumped in to help him, so he lied about it."

I rub a hand over my jaw. "Yeah, you're probably right." I slip an arm around her shoulder and kiss her glowing forehead. Why spoil the rest of her birthday by sharing how uncomfortable I've become around Dana and what I'm interpreting as her thinly disguised attempts to get my attention? By the end of the week, it will be just the four of us again, and Dana will be nothing but a thorny memory from the past.

The rest of the day passes uneventfully, and we enjoy a fun couple of hours at the zoo, followed by dinner at Luigi's Ristorante, just as I had planned.

I head to the airport the following morning, eagerly anticipating the coming weekend, the first one in months free of Dana hovering in the background.

My elation is short-lived. When I arrive home late Friday afternoon, I can almost see the steam coming off Morgan. She pulls me into the family room out of earshot of the kids and leans back against the wall, arms folded. "Brace yourself. Dana's still here. She's refusing to move out — *again*!"

CHAPTER 12

"She can't stay," I reiterate. "Today's the deadline. I'll talk to her."

Morgan tosses her head. "Good luck with that. I gave it my best shot. She told me we can't legally turn her out on the street without written notice."

I grimace. "Sounds like she's well versed on her rights. If she digs in her heels, we might have to formally evict her."

Morgan groans. "That could take weeks — months if she knows how to work the system."

I scrub my hands over my face, not wanting to believe this is happening. It's far from the peaceful start to the weekend I was anticipating. I need to fix this. "I'll have a word with her, see if I can talk some sense into her."

I head down to the studio and knock on the door. "Dana, it's Will. Can I talk to you?" I'm half-expecting her to ignore me entirely, but almost immediately the door swings open. Before I get a word out, a tear-stricken Dana throws herself at me. "Will! I'm so glad you're back! Nothing I ever do is right in Morgan's eyes. I only asked her for a little more time, and she threatened me with bodily harm if I didn't vacate the premises today. I don't know why she hates me so much. I've bent over backwards to keep her happy these past few weeks, but all Morgan does is criticize me. She even scolded me for jumping into the pool to save Sam. Can you believe it? The kid was choking on chlorinated water and couldn't breathe and—"

"Okay, okay, calm down," I interrupt, gently pushing her away from my chest. I'd like nothing more than to give her a good shove, but I need to tread carefully so she doesn't get her hackles up. The last thing I need is an arrest for assault on my record. "We very much appreciate you saving Sam, but that doesn't change the fact that we agreed you would vacate the studio today."

She sniffs, a hard, worried line between her eyes. "I know we talked about it, but I didn't agree to anything. I have nowhere else to go."

I clench my fists, quietly trying to curb my frustration. "You've had an extra month to find something else. We've been extremely patient and understanding of your circumstances, but we have no need of live-in help anymore. We made that clear to you."

Dana pulls out a tissue and dabs at her eyes. "You can't just throw me out from one day to the next."

"It's been sixty days."

She blows her nose and narrows her eyes at me, her voice taking on an undercurrent of steel. "I'm your tenant, Will. I have rights. Don't threaten me like your wife did."

A tendril of dread curls in my stomach. "What do you want, Dana? Why don't you quit playing around and come right out with it."

A wolfish smile curves over her lips. "No need to rush things. We can take it slow. I'm not going anywhere." I open my mouth to respond, but she suddenly slams the door in my face. I sway backwards on the steps, stunned by the dramatic turn of events. I stand there for a minute or two, tempted to kick the door down and drag her out. But that might be what she's angling for so she can call the police on me. I can't play into her hands. I need to keep my cool and do this the right way. Fists clenched, I stomp back to the house. Despite

54

all our attempts to pacify Dana, it's clear she never had any intention of moving out. I have the disconcerting feeling that she enjoys subjecting me to her demands.

"Well?" Morgan says, the minute I step back into the kitchen where she's busy setting the table for dinner.

I pour myself a glass of water and slump down on a stool at the island.

"She's dug in her heels. She's griping about having nowhere to go. Now, she's claiming she's our tenant. We might have to resort to going through the court system to evict her. I have a bad feeling she's going to try and drag this out as long as she can."

Morgan puts a hand on her hip. "She's not our tenant. She's never paid a penny of rent."

I rub a weary hand over the back of my neck. "I know that, and you know that, but we might have to prove it before we can evict her. There's a process that has to be followed."

"What kind of a process?"

"I'm not sure of the details. That's what I need to find out." I'm already scrolling through my phone. "By the way, she said you threatened her with bodily harm. Please tell me she's lying."

Morgan rolls her eyes and stomps over to the stove to give the pan of chicken stir fry she's cooking a vigorous stir. "It was *hardly* a threat — more like an off-the-cuff remark. Of course I wouldn't actually physically haul her out of there and throw her into her car."

I groan. "You said that?"

"Don't start on me and my big mouth!" Morgan waves her spatula around, splattering oil on the counter. "I was just trying to spur her into getting a move on packing up her stuff and clearing out before you got home. I know how much you've been looking forward to our first weekend without her."

"You might have made things a whole lot worse. Let's hope she doesn't retain a lawyer. I'll call Andy at work and see what he says. He's got a bunch of rentals. He's more familiar with the legal side of things."

I put the phone on speaker and sip on my water as I wait for him to answer.

"Hey, Andy. Got a bit of a situation here and I need some advice. How do you handle a tenant who refuses to move out — well, not exactly a tenant, per se?" I feed him a few more details about Dana and answer his questions until he's up to speed on what we're dealing with.

"Technically, that is her residence, so tenancy rules apply," he explains. "You'll have to go through the eviction process — tape a thirty-day notice to quit on the studio door and wait her out."

I grimace. "Thirty days? Why so long?"

"Be thankful it's not any longer. If she'd been there a year or more, you'd be looking at sixty days."

Morgan's expression darkens. She turns away and attacks the stir fry with the spatula once more.

"What if she still refuses to move out after that?" I ask.

"You'll have to take her to court." Andy clears his throat in an apologetic manner. "My advice, Will, tough as it is to swallow, is to offer her some relocation funds and hope she bites. It sucks, I know, but it'll be cheaper than hiring a lawyer, and quicker than the courts."

"Can't we just wait until she goes out one day and then change the locks?" Morgan asks. "It's not as if she's paying us rent."

"Don't even think about doing anything like that," Andy warns. "That's considered an illegal lockout. It's exactly the kind of stunt she's hoping you'll pull. The minute you do, she'll hit you with a lawsuit for punitive damages. Trust me, if you want to get rid of her, with your life as you know it intact, you need to do everything by the book from here on out."

CHAPTER 13

I end the call with Andy, my mind whirring with all his warnings. Morgan crosses her arms and glowers at me. "I'm not going to stand around and do nothing for the next thirty days while she squats in our studio. We need to find a way to get her out before that."

"I think we should try doing what Andy suggested — offer her some relocation funds." I rub my chin thoughtfully. "If this is about money, she'll jump at the chance to milk us for a few hundred bucks. At this point, it would be worth it just to see her gone."

"That's grossly unfair," Morgan fumes. "She doesn't deserve another dime. We've already bent over backwards to help her out. She's saved a fortune on rent by living here for free. Enough is enough."

I grab her wrist and pull her onto my knee. "I get your frustration, babe, but Andy's right. We need to follow the letter of the law, or we might end up with a worse mess on our hands."

"Fine!" She pushes herself up from my lap and marches back over to the stove. "Put the eviction notice on the studio door. But I don't want her in our house anymore. Tonight will be the last meal she eats with us — if she dares show her face. And I don't want her anywhere near the kids either. We'll give her the new terms of her stay and see how she likes it."

"Fair enough." I get to my feet and retrieve my laptop from my briefcase. "I'll print that form and fill it out right now."

Morgan slams another pan onto the stovetop and stomps over to the refrigerator. "Dana may think she has the upper hand, but she's underestimated me. I'm going to do my level best to make life as miserable as possible for her until she packs up and leaves. Without all the free meals and other perks, I bet those relocation funds are going to look more and more enticing."

I frown across at her, increasingly worried we're going to end up with law enforcement knocking on our door. I can't let things get messy. There's too much at stake. "Promise me you won't do anything stupid."

"If by stupid you mean illegal, then no. Everything else is on the table."

I bite back a response that will only fire her up even more. I finish filling out the eviction notice and wave it in the air. "All done. I'll post it after dinner."

"Do it now! We need to get the ball rolling."

She watches me like a hawk through the kitchen window as I make my way down the garden to the studio. I knock on the front door and step to one side, out of arm's reach. I'm not sure if Morgan has noticed the unsettling habit Dana has of laying her hands on me every chance she gets. I shift impatiently in place. I don't know why I even bothered knocking — it's not as if I'm delivering a warrant. All I have to do is tape the notice to the door. I wait for another minute or two and then do exactly that.

We're almost done with dinner when the back door bursts open and Dana steps into the kitchen, a cool smile frosting her lips. "Nice of you to let me know dinner was ready."

"You're supposed to be gone by now," Morgan says through bared teeth.

Undeterred, Dana saunters over to the counter where the leftovers are cooling in a Tupperware container. "Smells good. What are we having?"

"Chicken stir fry." Morgan's eyes glitter dangerously. "Enjoy! It will be your last meal at my table."

Undaunted, Dana helps herself to a plateful of food, grabs some silverware, and winks at Ella as she takes a seat next to her. "Room and board was the deal."

"*Was*. The deal's off," Morgan snaps.

Dana sets down her plate and flutters her eyelashes at me. "Your wife seems a little tense tonight, Will."

I frown and stab my fork into a piece of red bell pepper, sending it skidding across the table. The twins guffaw in delight and set about trying to make their vegetables follow suit.

"That's enough, you two!" Morgan yells, slapping her palms down on the table. "Go get ready for bed while Daddy and I talk to Dana."

"You're scaring the kids, Morgan," Dana coos in a ridiculously silky tone. "They're just having fun."

"Go!" Morgan repeats, shooing them away from the table.

They slide down from their chairs and scuttle out of the room, casting furtive glances at Dana as they go.

"Are you okay, Morgan?" she asks, spearing a piece of chicken on her fork. "You seem very stressed — the stir fry's excellent, by the way."

Morgan rolls her eyes. "What exactly are you playing at, Dana? What's your end game? The agreement was that you would move out today."

She chuckles apologetically. "*I* didn't agree to anything. You came up with that arbitrary deadline all on your own."

I clear my throat. I need to intervene and defuse the situation before Morgan erupts. "Dana, we're willing to offer you some relocation funds — a few hundred dollars you could put toward a deposit — if you move out this weekend."

She sighs dramatically. "Oh, Will, I wish I could oblige, but it's not that easy to find a place to live. It's going to take time. As your tenant, I'm entitled to proper notice if you wish me to vacate the premises."

I squeeze my fists beneath the table, trying not to imagine them around Dana's throat. "I take it you saw the eviction notice I taped to the studio door."

She raises a scolding eyebrow. "Such a dirty move. We could have handled things in a much more civilized manner — sat down and worked out a timetable that suited both parties."

Morgan tosses her silverware on the plate with a clatter. "The timetable's set in stone now, and the free ride's over. From here on, you're responsible for feeding yourself, and you're not to set foot in our house again unless we invite you in."

A delicate frown forms on Dana's forehead. "I'm afraid that's not going to work for me. I need access to a freezer to store my food, and I'll still need to use the laundry room."

Morgan arches a contemptuous brow. "You can take your clothes to a laundromat. And you'll have to make do with the mini fridge in the studio."

A nerve flinches in Dana's neck. She shoves her plate aside and jumps to her feet. "I can't believe you're turning on me after everything I've done for you and your family. You're a cold-blooded cow!" She clutches at her throat, faking a sob as she turns and runs from the kitchen.

Morgan stands and starts stacking the plates scattered around the table. "Pathetic! If there were a best scammer award for squatters, she would win hands down."

I twist my lips. "She sure knows how to turn the water-works on and off."

I head down the hallway to tuck the kids into bed, leaving Morgan to clean up the kitchen and take out her frustration on the dishwasher. After reading the twins a bedtime story, I make my way to our room to change into some sweats.

The wail of an ambulance turning onto the street distracts me, and I hurry to the family room window to see which of my neighbors has an emergency brewing. My jaw drops when the ambulance rolls to a stop outside our place. Two paramedics climb out and wheel a gurney around the side of our house and down the driveway to the studio. A cold ripple of panic goes through me. Did Dana fall or something? "Morgan!" I yell.

She hurries into the room and joins me at the window. "What's going on?"

"I think it's Dana," I say in a hoarse whisper, as the paramedics wheel the loaded gurney back to the waiting ambulance.

Morgan grips my arm. "It doesn't look good. She's not moving."

I blow out a heavy breath. "I'd better go out there and find out what's going on."

I'm halfway down the hall when the doorbell rings. I grimace as the sound echoes through the house — the kids are never going to sleep through all this ruckus.

I pull open the door to reveal a somber-looking Detective Kumar standing on the front steps. My heart slugs against my ribs.

Is Dana dead?

CHAPTER 14

"What's going on?" Morgan asks. "Is Dana all right?"

Detective Kumar's brows bunch together. "Mind if I come in?"

A cold sweat prickles along my hairline. I don't like strangers in my house at the best of times, let alone the police. They belong in another life I keep locked away. I fight to keep my expression neutral as I step aside and lead the detective through to the kitchen.

"Can you please tell us what's happened?" Morgan repeats, making no attempt to mask her irritation.

"That's what we're trying to determine." Kumar pulls out a notebook and consults it. "Emergency services got a call from a Dana Becker, requesting an ambulance." She looks up and glances questioningly between us. "She's your tenant, I believe?"

I exchange a loaded look with Morgan. "Not exactly," I answer. "It's complicated. She's been staying in our studio, rent-free. We hired her to look after Morgan's mom who passed away after a fall a couple of months back."

"I'm sorry to hear that," Kumar says, looking shocked. "Did she wander off again?"

"No. She fell getting out of bed in the middle of the night and hit her head." Morgan's voice drops an octave. "I . . . didn't find her until the following morning."

Kumar scribbles something in her notebook. "That must have been a shock. My condolences."

"Thank you." Morgan brushes a hand over her cheek to catch a stray tear.

"Does Dana still live in the studio?" Kumar directs her question at me.

I give a tight nod. "She was upset when we told her we didn't need her services anymore and she'd have to move out. She kept saying she had nowhere to go, and she'd have to sleep in her car. We felt pressured into agreeing to let her stay for the full sixty-day probation period, on the condition she vacate the premises when the time was up — which was today. When she refused, I posted a thirty-day eviction notice on the studio door."

Kumar's gaze bores further into me, almost as though she's reading her way back through the years to the secrets I've buried. "How did she react to that?"

"Not well," I admit. "We told her she was no longer welcome in the house. Up until today, she ate all her meals here during the week, and she had full use of the kitchen and laundry room — anything she needed. As you can imagine, she wasn't too happy when my wife told her she'd have to take her clothes to a laundromat from now on."

Morgan leans forward in her chair. "You haven't told us, yet, if she's okay. She didn't try to harm herself, did she?"

Kumar's face remains expressionless. "We'll get to that. Will, can you tell me about your interactions with Dana Becker today? I need to establish a timeline."

"I wasn't here for most of the day. I got back from a business trip around four-thirty this afternoon."

Kumar turns to Morgan. "What about you?"

She frowns in concentration. "Dana showed up around eight this morning and ate breakfast with us. I picked the twins up from preschool at noon, and we took them to the mall. They needed new shoes — they're growing like weeds."

Detective Kumar gives a ghost of a smile — a polite reminder that our kids' remarkable growth spurt is irrelevant. "And after that?"

"We came home. I gave Dana the rest of the afternoon off to pack up her stuff. Not that she needed it — she only brought one suitcase and a small duffle bag."

"What time was she supposed to move out?" Kumar asks.

"I asked her to drop the key off at four and say goodbye to the kids on her way out, but she never showed up. So, I went down to the studio to see if she needed any help. That's when she told me she wasn't leaving." Morgan turns to me. "Will arrived home shortly after that."

I nod. "When I got home, Morgan was upset, naturally, so I went down to the studio to try and reason with Dana."

"How did she respond?"

"She tried the tears tactic first of all, claimed Morgan was being cruel to her, and whined about having nowhere to go. When that didn't move me, her demeanor changed. She told me she had rights, started referring to herself as our tenant, then slammed the door in my face. That's when I realized she was going to be trouble."

Detective Kumar raises her eyebrows. "That must have been frustrating for you. Was there a physical altercation?"

I give a vigorous shake of my head, not liking the direction the interrogation is taking. "No. I walked away. What else could I do at that point? I came back up to the house and called a friend who has a bunch of rentals for advice. He suggested offering her cash to relocate. Failing that, he said we had no choice but to post a thirty-day notice to quit and wait her out."

"Did you speak to Dana at any other time today?"

I scratch the back of my neck. "She showed up at the house when we were finishing dinner. She made herself a plate of leftovers and sat down at the table as though nothing was—"

Kumar holds up a hand. "Just to be clear, you didn't serve up a plate for her — she helped herself. Is that right?"

Morgan nods. "Yes. The leftovers were in a Tupperware container on the counter."

Kumar glances around the room. "Where is that container now?"

Morgan frowns. "In the dishwasher. It's running. Why?"

Kumar jots something down. "Never mind. Let's get back to Dana. What happened next?"

"I told her she had a nerve, showing up uninvited after everything that had gone down," Morgan rants. "I made it clear she wasn't welcome in our house anymore. She stormed out, feigning tears and sounding off about how cruel I was."

"Did either of you threaten her at any point?"

I resist the temptation to look at Morgan and stare instead at Detective Kumar with a suitably dumbfounded expression. "Is that what she's telling you? That's ridiculous! Dana was the one threatening us with legal action if we didn't comply with her demands."

Morgan jumps to her feet and paces across the floor, vibrating with rage. "That woman is trying to destroy our lives. She'll stop at nothing. Whatever she's told you is an outright lie! She's a bloodsucking squatter and she's not going to stay here one more night, eviction notice or no eviction—"

"Morgan! Honey, sit down!" I urge, silently willing her to quit talking before she incriminates herself.

She catches herself mid-breath when Detective Kumar slides a piercing gaze in her direction.

"Did Dana *say* we threatened her?" I ask.

"Yes." Kumar braces her elbows on the table in front of her, her expression grim. "She also told the 911 dispatcher that you poisoned her."

CHAPTER 15

Morgan

Dana actually had the gall to call and ask if I could pick her up from the hospital this morning. I told her to get an Uber, then hung up before she had a chance to respond. I would have chewed her out on the phone if I could have been sure she wasn't recording our conversation — she's devious enough to try and goad me into saying something threatening. After Kumar's visit, I have no doubt that's her intention.

I strongly suspect she deliberately took some substance to make herself violently ill. I was tempted to search the studio for evidence last night, but Will talked me out of it. If she ever found out we had invaded her privacy in her absence, we'd be in even worse trouble than we are already. The police are looking at us with suspicion after all the lies Dana fed them. Thankfully, there's no evidence to back up her claims.

I'd felt an instant connection with Kumar when I met her a few weeks back. She had exuded nothing but compassion when she was helping me search for Mom, but I didn't get the same warm and fuzzy vibes when she was eyeballing me last night — especially not when I suggested that Dana might have made herself sick on purpose. "We can't trust her," I explained. "Even my housekeeper warned me to be careful of her. She's out to get us." I went on to describe the incident with Sam in the pool, but Kumar dismissed my concerns as unrelated to her investigation. I took that to mean Dana's not the one under suspicion.

A car rumbles to a stop in the driveway, interrupting my thoughts. I run to the window, my chest tightening when I catch sight of Dana climbing out. Moments later, the back door rattles open and she steps into the kitchen. I steel myself for trouble. Will took off for the gym earlier this morning so I can't enlist him to help me deal with her. I'm not sure I can trust myself to control my temper. The thought of bringing the full force of a cast iron pan down on her head is immensely appealing.

"Ugh. I'm so dehydrated," she groans, throwing herself down in a chair. "Be a dear and fix me a cup of peppermint tea."

"Do I look like a waitress to you?" I square my shoulders and glare at her. "Why did you lie to the police?"

She presses a hand to her chest. "Me? You're the one who lied to the police."

"About what?"

She wags her finger at me. "For starters, you weren't exactly honest about the threats you've been making. Threatening to throw me out on the street, starving me, denying me access to basic needs like a refrigerator and laundry facilities." She gives a theatrical sigh. "All items that were part of our rental agreement to begin with."

"*What* rental agreement? You haven't paid a penny of rent since you moved in!"

Dana flaps a hand dismissively through the air. "Rental, verbal, call it what you will. The point is, we agreed on the terms and now you're reneging on the deal."

I let out a snort of disgust. "I'm not going to waste time arguing with you. I've already resigned myself to the fact that we're stuck with you for the next thirty days. But you still haven't answered my question. Why did you tell the police we tried to poison you?"

"I told them I had food poisoning. I'll leave it to the experts to figure out whether it was intentional or not." She smirks at me. "Maybe you're just a terrible cook."

"Well, you won't have to endure my cooking any longer. You're responsible for feeding yourself from now on."

"Actually, that's what I'm here about," she replies, blinking demurely up at me. "Now that you've arbitrarily changed the terms of our agreement, I'm going to need a food allowance, in addition to my stipend. You've left me with no choice but to eat all my meals out." She frowns and taps a finger on the side of her cheek. "I don't want to gouge you. Fifty dollars a day ought to do it." She tinkles a mocking laugh. "You wouldn't want to be accused of starving me after trying to poison me, would you, Morgan? I can't imagine what the neighbors would say to that."

I grit my teeth, shaking with rage. "Let me get this straight. You don't want to gouge me, but you're refusing to leave the studio after I generously let you live there for free. You've scored another whole month rent free while the eviction process runs its course and, in addition to that, you want *me* to pay *you*?"

Dana shrugs. "It's either me or a very expensive lawyer who will cost a whole lot more than fifty dollars a day. I'll leave you to do the math. You're a reasonably intelligent woman, when you don't let your emotions get in the way."

I toss my head. "You're unbelievable."

She gives a self-deprecating laugh, as though I've just complimented her. "Oh, and there's one other thing."

"Let me guess. You'd like eggs Benedict on a silver tray with a bud vase in the mornings."

Dana chuckles, and the sound grates across my chest like sandpaper. "I wouldn't turn it down if you're offering. But as food seems to be off the table — no pun intended — I wanted to bring up a more serious matter." She pauses and kneads her brow. "I'd like to move into the guest room now that your mother's no longer using it. I'm nervous sleeping alone with that serial killer still on the loose. The windows in the studio aren't very secure. It would be easy for someone to break in, and no one would hear my screams back there."

I'm not usually rendered speechless, but her request is so outrageous that it takes me a moment to string together a rational thought. I glare at her, hands on hips. "Over my dead body! If you don't feel safe in the studio, I'd suggest you redouble your efforts to find somewhere else to live. Speaking of which, you should jump on it as you have exactly twenty-nine days left to make it happen."

"In that case, you'll have to install a security system in the studio." Dana narrows her eyes at me. "I wouldn't want to encounter any intruders — serial killers, or anyone bent on poisoning me."

"I'm sure you'll do a fine job of scaring them off yourself," I hurl after her as she makes her exit.

I watch her stroll down the garden to the studio like she owns the place. When she disappears inside, I pick up my mug and throw it across the room. I stare at the coffee dripping down the wall, wishing it was Dana's blood instead.

CHAPTER 16

The minute Will returns from the gym, I corral him in the kitchen.

"Our squatter's back from the hospital. You're not going to believe the nerve of that woman. She actually asked if she could move into Mom's old room. I told her over my dead body. I haven't even begun to clean out Mom's stuff, and I'm certainly not letting Dana sleep there. Now, she's insisting we install a security system in the studio. She says she's scared of the serial killer." I throw up my hands. "*Seriously*? Last I heard, he's in the Bay Area — not prowling around our sub-division. That witch will say anything to get what she wants. *And* she's demanding a fifty-dollar daily food allowance now that we've banned her from using our kitchen. I put my foot down on that one too. She's not getting another penny out of us!"

Will runs a hand distractedly through his hair, avoiding my scrutiny. "Maybe we should try and keep her satisfied as best we can until she leaves — so she goes quietly. It's not such a big deal. I say we pay her the money. And it might not be a bad idea to install a simple security system in the studio — that way we can download the app on our phones and keep an eye on her comings and goings." He turns and heads for the door. "I need to get out of these gym clothes and shower up."

My mouth falls open. "That's it? That's all you've got to say? You're just going to lie down and let her walk all over us like this?"

A thin crease splits his forehead. "Not now. Please, Morgan."

Something about his tone halts the torrent of words about to erupt from my mouth. "What is it? What's wrong?"

He presses his lips tightly together. "I got more bad news today."

Guilt surges through me. I should have picked up on how dejected he looked when he walked in, but I was too busy unloading my own frustrations on him.

"I'm sorry. This whole Dana thing has me going out of my mind. Sit down for a minute and tell me what happened."

I pull him toward the table, and he reluctantly flops down in a chair. "Another buddy of mine from high school passed away."

A pit forms in my stomach. "Was it . . . cancer, too?"

"No." His voice sounds thick, as though he's trying hard not to break down. "Accidental drowning. He was found floating in his pool. He'd been drinking."

"When did it happen?"

"A week or so after JT died. I just found out about it." He rubs a hand across his jaw. "It's thrown me for a loop, losing two classmates back-to-back."

I slide my chair closer and wrap him in a hug. "I'm so sorry, Will. That's rough. Did he have a family?"

"I think he had a son. He and his wife split up years ago."

"What was his name?"

The twins come hurtling into the room before he can answer.

"Mommy! Can we go play in the treehouse?" Ella asks.

I flash her a smile. "Sure thing. I'll call you in when it's time for dinner. Just be careful on that loose paver. Daddy's going to fix it this weekend."

Will frowns. "Thanks for reminding me. I'll take care of it. I still don't understand how it worked itself loose."

"It might have been Sam's fault. You know how he's always digging." I plant a kiss on Will's cheek and get to my feet. "I'm going to make us some toasted sandwiches. How does roast beef and provolone sound?"

"Great," he answers, his brow knitted in a worried frown.

I plaster on a smile as he exits the room. I dread to think how this is going to affect him. He was shaken enough when he heard about JT passing away — he's been more withdrawn than usual ever since.

While he showers, I set the table for lunch and call the twins inside. They wash their hands at the sink, disheveled curls plastered to their sweaty foreheads. I pour them each a glass of juice, then place their sandwiches and some chopped up fruit in front of them. Will joins us a moment later, wet hair slicked back from his pale face.

"Mommy, why are you mean to Dana?" Ella asks, her lips stained strawberry-red from the fruit she's sucking on.

I exchange a loaded glance with Will before focusing my attention back on my daughter. "What are you talking about, honey?"

"Dana says you hate her. You won't give her any food, and you won't let her sleep in Nana's room."

"And she's scared of the bad guy with a knife," Sam adds, stabbing at his neck in dramatic fashion.

Ella juts out a quivering bottom lip. "I'm scared of the bad guy too."

My hand begins to shake, the filling from my sandwich spilling onto my plate. *How dare she frighten my kids like that!* "When were you talking to Dana?"

"Just now. In the treehouse," Ella says. "She climbed up there because she was scared in the studio all by herself."

I force myself to smile as I attempt to reassemble my sandwich. "She doesn't have to be scared anymore. Daddy's going to install a security system for her so she can sleep in the studio and be safe."

Seemingly satisfied with my answer, the twins finish up their sandwiches and then retreat to the playroom to watch a movie.

"You're going to have to follow through and install that security system now," I say to Will, as I gather up the plates. "Otherwise, I'm going to be a liar as well as a mean mommy."

"I'll pick one up tomorrow," he promises.

"While you're at it, why don't you buy a couple of Nest cameras for the house too? I'd be a lot more comfortable knowing Dana wasn't sneaking in here when we're not home."

"Why would she do that?"

"She's done it before. She helped herself to Mom's dress, remember? I don't want her raiding our refrigerator during the night. Things have been disappearing."

Will drains his glass of water and gets to his feet. "Sounds like overkill to me, but if it makes you more comfortable, I will."

* * *

Dressed in an off-the-shoulder cerise top and dark skinny jeans, Dana hovers annoyingly over Will the entire time he's installing the cameras on the exterior of the studio. I can't tell from the kitchen window what she's talking to him about, but she manages to keep up a steady stream of conversation. By the time he's finished with the project, the twins are itching for him to take them to the park.

"Why don't you come with us, Morgan?" Will suggests. "I have to leave at 4 a.m. to catch an early flight, so this is our last chance for some family time this weekend."

We spend a couple of hours at the playground and arrive back at the house exhausted. After a quick dinner of pepperoni pizza, we put the kids to bed and retire for an early night.

"Sorry I never got those cameras installed at the house," he mumbles into his pillow.

I lean over to give him a goodnight kiss. "Don't worry about it. It was more important to spend time with the kids."

* * *

I wake with a start, gripped by a sense of panic that I've slept in. It's pitch black — too soon to get up. I'm about to reach for my phone to check the time when I sense heavy breathing in the room.

CHAPTER 17

"Will," I whisper, my fingers spidering their way across the covers to find him in the darkness. But his side of the bed is cold to the touch. Did he leave for the airport already? "Will, is that you?" I call out. I hold my breath, trembling beneath the sheets, waiting for an invisible entity to announce their presence. Did I just imagine I heard breathing? Was I dreaming?

A shadow twitches in the doorway, then vanishes from sight. I scream, shrinking back against the headboard. Keeping my eyes firmly fixed on the doorway, I reach out and fumble around until I find the switch on my bedside lamp. Soft light illuminates one side of the bed. My eyes flick haphazardly over every nook and cranny, but there's no one here. I slide out from underneath the comforter, my bare feet sinking into the soft carpet, grounding me in the familiar. Is Dana creeping around inside the house? Cautiously, I pad over to the door and peer down the dark hallway. My hand flies to my chest when I spot a tiny figure standing in the shadows. "Ella! What are you doing out of bed?"

Her fingers rub the bunny tucked under her left arm, while she sucks steadily on her thumb.

The fear thrumming through me gradually begins to dissipate. "Did you have a bad dream, honey?"

She considers this for a moment, then nods. "It waked me up."

"I'm sorry. Come here. Mommy will tuck you back into bed." I swoop her into my arms and carry her back to her room. She nestles beneath the covers and closes her eyes, falling asleep almost instantly. I envy her trust in the goodness of the world she inhabits. I wish I shared it.

Back in my own bed, I stare up at the ceiling, eyes sprung wide. My brain is firing on all cylinders, sifting through the last few minutes for answers. Was it really a nightmare that woke Ella, or did she hear me scream? The shadow I saw in my doorway looked taller than my daughter, but now I'm questioning everything. Perhaps it was just Will leaving for the airport. Did I even see a shadow? And what about the heavy breathing? Maybe I'm the one who had a bad dream.

* * *

The following morning, Dana shows up at the house while I'm skimming through the installation instructions for the Nest cameras.

"I see you've come to the realization that security's not such a bad idea, after all," she says, a mocking grin dancing on her lips. She reaches over my shoulder for the diagram on the table in front of me, her breath hot on my cheek. I flinch, hairs prickling on the back of my neck as the unsettling memory of someone breathing in my room last night comes rushing back.

"You look overwhelmed." Dana picks up the instructions and peers at them. "I can help you with this."

I snatch the leaflet back out of her hands, tearing it in the process. "No thanks. I'll handle it myself. What are you doing here anyway? You're not allowed in the house unless I invite you." I make a mental note to change the locks on the back door as soon as possible. I could ask for the key back but, knowing Dana, she's made a copy.

"No need to be so prickly. You're always harping on about my need to perform or leave, so I'm here to offer my services." She studies her nails. "After all, you're still paying me a salary, if you could call minimum wage a salary."

"With room and board thrown in. And a host of other benefits too."

Dana's mouth puckers. "I was exploited and overworked the entire time I was employed as your mother's caregiver."

My gut tightens. I'm vaguely aware that she's goading me, and a small voice inside me is warning me to send her packing before this turns physical, but the justice warrior in me rises to the occasion instead.

"Don't be ridiculous! You had every evening and week-end off. We treated you like one of the family — took you out to eat, brought you to the movies with us, gave you free rein of the house."

Dana rolls her eyes. "I was on call whenever you needed me. I can't begin to count the number of times you asked me to step in on my day off to save you from a meltdown."

The sound of my labored breathing fills the silence between us as I fight to control the rage roiling inside me. The only time she helped us out on her day off was the day she almost drowned my son. I could argue back-and-forth over her endless stream of lies, but it's pointless. She'll stand by her version of events because she wants what it gets her in the end. "As you were so overworked, I suggest you go back to the studio and take a break. You're wasting my time."

She throws me a long-suffering look. "Fine. Have it your way. But we both know you can't cope with the kids on your own, Morgan. You're a hot mess, just like your mother. You need me."

She slams the back door behind her with a loud thunk, and I flinch, adrenaline seeping from my pores. How dare Dana insult my mother's memory — twisting a sword in my wounds!

Shaking, I sink down into a kitchen chair and rub my cheek furiously, as if to erase Dana's hot, dragon breath from my skin. I'm trying to remember exactly what that heavy breathing sounded like last night. Could it have been her?

But what was she doing in the house? My eyes dart around the kitchen, instinctively settling on the refrigerator. I haul myself to my feet and march over to it. Staring at the contents, my suspicions are confirmed. I'm missing a package of cheese and some sandwich meat I picked up yesterday. She was here last night, helping herself to my food. It's not the first time things have gone missing. I slam the refrigerator door shut and begin pacing across the floor. Two can play at this game.

After peeking in on the twins in the playroom, I head out to the garage and rummage through a tub of miscellaneous ropes and chains next to Will's tool cabinet. I find the length of chain I'm looking for, grab a padlock from one of the drawers, and head back inside the house.

When I'm done with my project, I stand back from the refrigerator to admire my handiwork.

"What's that, Mommy?" Sam asks, bounding into the room.

My lips curl into a satisfied smile. "It's a lock to keep our food safe."

Sam's face falls. "But how is me and Ella s'posed to get our strawberry Gogurts?"

"Easy." I wink at him. "You ask me, and I'll get them for you."

He huffs loudly, his shoulders dragging downward at this setback on the road to independence.

It pains me to disappoint him, but I have to put an end to Dana's nocturnal food raids. I won't let her win even the smallest victory until she's out of my house and my life for good. And now that I'm on a roll, I'll do something about the laundry room too. I google a couple of local handymen and make an appointment with one who promises to be there within the hour for a premium charge.

A short time later, the doorbell rings.

"I'm Chuck. You called earlier," the balding man standing outside says. "Are you Morgan Klein?"

"Yes. Thanks for squeezing me in. I really appreciate it."

"So, what are we doing?" he breezes, as I lead him down the hallway to the laundry room.

"I need the lock on the back door replaced, and a lock installed on the laundry room door."

He raises his brows. "Dog chewing up your socks?"

I give a guarded smile. "Something like that. I have four-year-old twins. You can't be too careful. I don't want them choking on a laundry pod."

"Gotcha." He drops his tool bag on the floor with a thud and opens and closes the laundry room door. "A stainless-steel chain lock would be the easiest solution. The kids wouldn't be able to reach it, and you wouldn't have to worry about losing the key—"

"No! That won't work. I mean, I'd prefer a key. I . . . need to keep their teenage cousins out too. Can't have them getting high on cleaning products." I let out a high-pitched laugh. I probably sound as if I'm the one who's been sniffing furniture wax. There are no cousins, teenage or otherwise, but my answer seems to satisfy Chuck, who launches into a long-winded story about a neighbor's kid who overdosed on his father's motorcycle degreaser.

With my house fortified against any further night invasions by Dana, I set my mind to dreaming up other ways to turn up the heat on the painstakingly slow legal process of getting rid of my squatter. I'm almost giddy at the thought of conducting my very own form of eviction by a thousand cuts. I could try disabling the Wi-Fi. It wouldn't go over well with the twins, but it's not a bad idea. I could also flip the power switch on the condenser unit and kill the AC in the studio. It would serve Dana right to sweat in that box for a bit — she's forever going out and leaving the AC running full blast. It's on a separate system from the main house, so it won't leave us sweltering along with her.

My phone buzzes and I reluctantly break from my gratifying plotting session to take Will's call. He won't approve of what I'm doing, but he'll find out soon enough when he comes home this weekend. Until then, I'll relish conjuring up ever more creative ways to make Dana's life as miserable as she's making mine. It's petty, I know. Ordinarily, I wouldn't resort to such nasty tactics, but I'm at the end of my rope. I feel like I'm losing my mind, and I'm desperate to get back to the life I had before Dana came on the scene.

I force myself to smile into the phone. "Hey, babe! How was your flight?"

"Uneventful. Just landed. I'm waiting on an Uber. I'm calling because I got a voicemail from our lawyer. Turns out the paperwork for the eviction was filed incorrectly. I have to resubmit it."

Blood roars in my ears. "Are you kidding me? How on earth did that happen?"

"Clerical error. The point is, it will delay the eviction hearing by another week."

"*Noooo!* I can't do this, Will. She's driving me crazy. She—"

"I know! But it doesn't do any good to rant about it. If she's set on having her day in court, we have to go along with it. Maybe we'll get lucky, and she'll decide to move out before the court date rolls around."

I end the call more determined than ever to make that happen.

CHAPTER 18

The following morning, I text Andrea and invite her over for coffee. I'm eager to tell her about my guerrilla tactics campaign to expedite Dana's removal. I need a cheering section in my corner, and I can't count on Will — he would shut me down in a heartbeat if he knew what I was up to.

"Any updates on your squatting dilemma?" Andrea asks, when I hand her a latte.

I kick off my shoes and settle into the chair opposite her. "Not the kind I'm happy about. There was some sort of mix-up with the eviction paperwork and now Will has to resubmit everything. It's going to end up delaying the process by at least a week."

Andrea lets out a humph. "Pity. The sooner that freeloader vacates the neighborhood, the better for all of us. If you ask me, she's angling for a sugar daddy, and she doesn't care if he's married."

I grimace. "You might be right. She never misses an opportunity to manhandle Will. It makes him uncomfortable, but not half as uncomfortable as it makes me. Maybe that's the part she gets a kick out of — which is why I'm planning to send a little discomfort her way in return."

Andrea peers at me dubiously over her coffee mug. "What exactly do you have in mind? Nothing illegal, I hope."

"Tempting, but no. I'm just denying her access to the facilities she's enjoyed up until now. I put a lock on the refrigerator and the laundry room door."

"You didn't!" Andrea throws her head back and laughs. "That's classic! Good for you!"

"The less incentive she has to come into my house, the better. So if she comes knocking on your front door, be warned. She's probably looking for shelf space in your fridge."

"Not going to happen. She gives me the creeps." Andrea takes a sip of her latte. "How did Ella's dental appointment go?"

"Great. Dr. Patel is amazing. He extracted her broken tooth in no time at all — she didn't feel a thing."

"Poor baby. How did it happen anyway?"

"She tripped on a paver by the back door. I'm not sure how it got loose. Probably another one of Sam's digging projects."

Andrea's eyebrows shoot up. Her gaze flickers to the window, then back to me. "Funny thing is, I saw Dana hunched over your pavers a week or so ago. I didn't think anything of it at the time. Figured she'd dropped something on her way to the studio. You had already left to take the kids to preschool."

My grip tightens on my coffee mug. "I wouldn't put it past her to do something like that."

Andrea twists her lips. "Based on the stunts she's pulled so far, she might have been planning an injury lawsuit."

"But instead she injured my child. Thank goodness it was only a baby tooth Ella lost."

Andrea uncrosses her legs. "You need to be careful, Morgan. That woman is dangerous. Don't forget Sam almost drowned in her care." She drains her coffee and gets to her feet. "Thanks for the caffeine hit. I have to get back to work. Give me a shout if you need anything."

"Thanks," I say, hugging her goodbye. "Do me a favor and don't mention what I'm doing to Tom. If it gets back to Will, he'll think I'm taking things too far and try to talk me out of it. Believe me, I'm only getting started."

"Your secret's safe with me." Andrea winks as she heads to the front door.

I can't help but chuckle when I spot Dana walking up to the back door with her drawstring laundry bag only minutes later. I could lock her out, or intercept her and remind her she's not welcome in my house anymore, but I'm looking forward to seeing the expression on her face when she discovers the lock on the laundry room door. When she breezes into the kitchen, I arch a contemptuous brow and peer at her over the rim of my mug. "What part of the you're-not-welcome-in-my-home memo did you not get?"

She snorts. "What part of the I'm-entitled-to-my-day-in-court memo did *you* not get?" She flounces past me into the hallway leading to the garage. Seconds later, there's a loud thump that sounds like she's kicked the laundry room door. I brace myself when she reappears, her brows angled into a sharp V.

"I'm not going to play petty games with you," she barks. "Open the laundry room door, now, or I'll get my lawyer on the phone." Her gaze lands on the chain and padlock securing the handles on the refrigerator doors, and her frown deepens. "You're pathetic! Do you really think you can get me to leave by locking the refrigerator? I'm entitled to access as long as I live here."

I paste an annoying smile on my face. "The only thing you're entitled to is a roof over your head until the eviction process is signed off on in court. Your days are numbered. So why don't you beat it and take your dirty laundry to the laundromat like every other loser?"

The drawstring bag slips through Dana's fingers and she takes a step toward me.

I tense, my fingers curling tightly around the mug in front of me. What's left of my coffee isn't hot enough to do any real damage, but if I throw it in her face, it might be enough to distract her momentarily. Our eyes lock for a long moment, the unspoken threat taut between us. Then, something shifts in her expression. The muscles in her neck slowly relax, and she picks up her laundry bag. A part of me wishes she had lunged at me so I could have had her arrested. That would be one way to end this. But she's far too clever for that.

"I suppose you found a way to turn off the AC in the studio too," she spits out. "It's plenty cool in here."

I shrug. "The thermostat's been acting up. I'll have someone look at it."

"If my AC's not restored today, I'm calling the police. You can't legally cut power or water. Read the fine print!"

She turns on her heel and stomps out of the house. I stare down into my lukewarm coffee, my shoulders shaking with laughter. She has no one to blame but herself for the misery she's putting herself through. And there's lots more to come.

I give it until mid-afternoon before turning the AC back on. Dana's got to be suffocating in there by now. I play the same trick with the switch on the condenser unit several times over the next couple of days. I also unscrew the out-door lightbulb over the entry door to the studio when Dana is gone. Let her stumble around in the darkness and see how she likes it. When VV arrives on Wednesday, I give her strict instructions that she's no longer to clean the studio. "Dana's got nothing else to do until she moves out," I explain. "The least she can do is take care of her own space."

VV purses her lips, her duster already flicking into action. "She's not clean person, Mrs. Morgan."

"I know. Don't worry about the mess. I'll deal with it once I get her out of there — fumigate, repaint, whatever needs to be done."

"Is Dana leaving 'cause she's dirty, Mommy?" Ella asks, prancing about the room dressed for ballet. She hands me her scrunchie. "I can help her clean her room."

"That's very sweet of you," I say, spinning her around to braid her hair. "But Dana needs to learn to take care of her own room — just like you do."

Fifteen minutes later, I bundle the kids into the car and leave VV to work her magic. As I zip out onto the road, Sam spots a coyote that's been hit by a car. "Look, Mommy! It's bleeding!"

"It's dead, sweetie."

"Yuck!" Ella says, her nose glued to the glass to get a better look. "That's gross!"

"Yes, it is. Maybe I'll put it in Dana's bed."

Sam laughs, kicking the back of my seat.

Ella pouts at me in the rearview mirror. "You're mean, Mommy."

I grimace, wishing I hadn't spontaneously voiced the stomach-churning threat.

"I was just kidding." I plaster on a smile, searching for a quick fix. "Who wants to sing *If You're Happy and You Know It?*"

I breathe out a sigh of relief when the twins begin belting out the lyrics. I have to learn to zip my lips and not let my frustration with Dana spill out in front of them. The last thing I need is for Ella to tell her what I'm up to.

CHAPTER 19

I haven't seen Dana in two days. Come to think of it, her car hasn't moved either — which is odd, considering the fact that I've been turning off her AC for extended periods of time. I thought for sure my antics would have driven her out of the studio to seek respite from the heat, but apparently she's found some other way to stay cool. At least she hasn't attempted to come back into my house to use the facilities she feels she's entitled to. She's finally got the message that *mi casa* is off limits.

It's almost time to pick the twins up from preschool, so I grab a few snacks and head out to the car. Andrea waves at me from her driveway. "Doing okay?"

I force myself to smile. "Hanging in there."

She gestures with her chin in the direction of the studio. "I haven't seen your squatter in a few days. No progress in that department, I take it."

I twist my lips. "No. It's a waiting game."

"It's just plain wrong that the police can't throw her out," Andrea says. "It's screwed up — catering to the criminals. At least they caught a break in that serial killer case."

"They did?"

"Didn't you see the news this morning? They've identified him through DNA." She jangles her keys in the air. "Google it! I gotta run or I'll be late for my appointment."

When I pull up outside the preschool, I open a news app on my phone while I'm waiting for the kids to be released. I scroll through the headlines until I find what I'm looking for.

MAJOR BREAK IN SERIAL KILLER CASE.
DNA evidence on the body of the West Coast Killer's latest victim has led to the identification of a suspect. A warrant for capital murder was issued for Robert Rattler, forty-three, of Oakland, CA. An intensive manhunt is underway as of Monday evening. The U.S. Marshal Service, the FBI, and the California Bureau of Investigation, are working closely with local law enforcement agencies in the area to process leads and field calls from the public on possible sightings. Officials describe Rattler as "a six foot two white male with brown hair, weighing 210 pounds, with a gold-capped front tooth and a scar running down his right cheek." He is considered armed and dangerous. A reward is being offered for tips leading to Rattler's arrest.

I sink back in my seat and stare out the window. Identifying a suspect is one thing, neutralizing them is another. He's still a threat as long as he remains at large. My thoughts circle back to my own situation. I'm relieved the police have identified the West Coast Killer, but Robert Rattler is not impacting my life to any great degree, unlike Dana Becker. I'm still ticked off about the clerical error that has pushed her eviction out another week, but my fear is, that won't be the end of it. Dana is determined to milk us for everything she can, and I suspect she has a few more tricks up her sleeve. If she's anything like those serial squatters on TV, she could drag this out for years. I might have to up my game. But how? Unlike Dana, I don't have a criminal mind. I don't know what to turn to. The dark web? Should I hire someone to scare her into packing up and leaving town? Too bad the West Coast Killer isn't available.

The door to the preschool opens. I slip my phone into my purse and exit the car to join the other parents filing inside to pick up their kids. I can't allow myself to dwell on the worst-case scenario. Maybe the eviction hearing will put an end to this nightmare — *maybe*. I wish I had a little more faith in the system.

After running a couple of errands, I treat the kids to lunch out before heading back to the house. They take off to build a fort in the playroom and I pour myself a glass of water and sit down on the couch with my laptop. I fiddle around on Amazon for a bit, stocking up on a few items before tackling my emails. After spending a few minutes deleting and unsubscribing from junk, I groan when I spot an email from Dana. What does she want now? I've had my fill of her griping. I poked the bear by installing the locks on the fridge and laundry room. I expect she's come up with another slew of demands and threats in response. I'm tempted to delete the email without opening it, but it might be something I need to show our lawyer — additional evidence for our court date.

My jaw drops when I begin to read.

Morgan,

I can't take the abuse and threats anymore. You have reneged on every term we agreed on when I came to work for you, which I only did in the first place to help you out as you were so desperate and unable to cope with your mother's deteriorating dementia. In your hateful bid to illegally turn me out on the street, you have played every dirty trick in the book. You are literally trying to kill me by starving me, denying me access to basic essentials such as refrigeration and laundry, cutting off my AC, and spreading hateful rumors about me to your neighbors, and to your own children, who I have cared for as lovingly as I cared for your mother. I don't understand why you hate me so much, or why you say and do

such cruel and immoral things, but you have pushed me to my breaking point. I can't take it anymore. You win!
Sincerely,
Dana Becker

My eyes fly back and forth across the screen as I reread the email, my brain scrambling to make sense of it. Is she finally leaving? Is that what she's been doing for the past two days — cleaning out the studio and packing up her stuff? I need to speak with her. Maybe I did go a bit overboard with my questionable efforts to oust her. I can't let her leave on these terms. I slam my laptop closed and dump the contents of my glass into the sink. Despite a gnawing sense of guilt, a mixture of excitement and hope swirls in the pit of my stomach at the thought of Dana finally being out of our lives for good. I hurry down the hall to the playroom. "Kids, Mommy's going down to the studio to speak with Dana. Stay here until I get back."

"Can I go with you?" Ella asks, popping up from beneath a plaid blanket.

"No, honey. I'll only be gone a few minutes."

"Not fair!" Ella's curls retreat back beneath the blanket.

I hurry through the garden to the studio and bang on the door a couple of times. When there's no response, I walk around the side of the unit and try to peer through the bedroom window. The blinds are down, and the curtains are tightly drawn, but the small transom window up above is open — no doubt in a bid to keep the place cool. I go back around to the front door and hammer on it once more for good measure, before retrieving a stepladder from the garage. Leaning it against the wall beneath the transom window, I begin to climb.

I'm halfway up when a putrefying stench reaches my nostrils.

CHAPTER 20

Fear gives wings to my legs as I beat a hasty retreat back down to the ground, the ladder wobbling precariously beneath my weight. I sink down in the dirt, trembling violently as I try to process my racing thoughts. That sickening stench can mean only one thing. I plunge my hands despairingly through my hair. What has Dana done? I need to calm down and get a grip. I'm jumping to conclusions — being overly dramatic. The smell could be coming from rotting meat that she's left out — maybe deliberately, a parting shot to me for denying her access to the refrigerator and turning off her AC.

The other half of my brain is wrestling with the darkest possible scenario — that Dana is lying dead inside the studio. It's not a conclusion I want to entertain, but all the dots connect. She hasn't been seen in days, her car hasn't moved, and she sent me a very disturbing email that could be construed as a suicide note. I only just received it, but she could have written it earlier and scheduled it to be sent today. Maybe she wanted to make sure her body wouldn't be discovered until it had already begun to stink, figuring I deserved as much. A shiver ripples across my shoulders. This is so messed up. Did I drive her to this? I pat around in my pockets until I locate my phone, tapping with a shaky finger on Will's name. *Please, pick up! Please!*

Just when I've resigned myself to the call going to voice-mail, I hear Will's voice. "Hey, babe. I just got out of a meeting. What's up?"

I barely manage to drum up enough saliva to force the words out. "I . . . I think Dana's dead."

"What did you say? Hang on a minute. It's noisy in here. Let me get out of this conference room."

Scuffling sounds ensue before Will comes back on the line. "Okay, come again."

"She's dead — Dana's dead. At least I think she is."

"What do you mean you *think* she's dead?" Will's tone is laced with skepticism. "Is she breathing?"

"I . . . I don't know."

"Then check! For goodness' sake, Morgan, pull yourself together. Are the kids there? Did she fall or something? Did you call an ambulance?"

"No! She's locked herself in the studio. I don't know what to do. The twins are in the playroom."

Will is silent for a moment, processing this information. "Okay, so what makes you think she's dead?"

"She hasn't come out of the studio in two days, and her car hasn't moved."

"So maybe she's binge-watching Netflix." An edge of irritation has crept into Will's voice, almost as though he's decided I'm coming apart at the seams again.

"There's a terrible smell," I add. "I climbed up on a ladder to try and peek in the transom window. I only got halfway up before the stench about knocked me out."

"The smell could be coming from anything — old food, most likely." Now Will's tone is verging into the overly patient realm. I'm tracking each subtle change, silently begging him to believe me, but fearing he's losing faith in my sanity. "You banned her from using our refrigerator, remember?"

"She sent me an email ranting about how she couldn't take my abuse and threats anymore. It sounded like a suicide note. I'm afraid, Will."

I press the phone to my ear as his breathing grows ragged. I've got his attention at last. He's afraid now, too. "Morgan, listen to me. This is important. You need to hang up and call 911 right away. Tell them you need a welfare check on your tenant."

I begin to cry. "But what if they arrest me? Kumar already suspects us of poisoning Dana."

Will lets out an exasperated sigh. "No one's going to arrest you. You haven't done anything wrong. Dana's probably holed up in there ignoring you. And if anything has happened, that's on her. It's not your fault, or mine, or anyone else's. I'm going to hang up now. Call me back once the police get there."

I end the call and hug my phone to my chest. I can't do this. I can't call the police until I know for sure what's going on. What if Dana has left a suicide note in the studio blaming me for everything? Or maybe the smell is just a slab of meat gone bad that was left out on the counter, and I'll look like a fool in front of the police.

Heart pounding, I get to my feet and stumble back to the house to retrieve a spare key to the studio. I peek in on the twins lying on their bellies in front of the TV, engrossed in a movie. They'll be fine for a few more minutes — they know where to find me if they need me.

On my way back through the kitchen, I grab a tea towel to hold over my mouth. My legs feel like jelly as I trudge down the garden path to the studio. I'm quaking so much it takes several attempts before I manage to unlock the front door. Pressing the tea towel firmly over my nose and mouth, I gingerly push the door open. The stench of death fills the space.

My eyes land on the double bed in the far corner of the room where a bulky comforter hugs a motionless figure like a shroud.

CHAPTER 21

The breath vacates my lungs at the ghastly sight. She's done it — Dana's actually killed herself. And I'm to blame for pushing her over the edge. Her last words to me in that pitiful email ring through my head like a death knell of condemnation. Sweat needles the back of my neck. What have I done? I had no idea she was so fragile. I thought she was reveling in her power to manipulate the situation. I've totally misjudged everything. I take a faltering step backward and turn to flee back to the house, only to find myself face-to-face with the last person I expected to see.

"D-Dana!" I splutter.

She fastens an icy glare on me. "What are you doing here?"

"I thought . . . your car . . . where have you been?"

Ignoring my question, she elbows past me, coming to an abrupt halt inside the door. "Ugh! What is that awful smell?" She staggers back outside and takes a few hearty gulps of air. "It stinks like rotting meat in there."

Or rotting flesh. A sense of wooziness envelops me. If it's not Dana in the bed, then who is it? My mind implodes, disjointed thoughts scattering in myriad directions.

"What have you done?" Dana snarls. "Is this another one of your perverted attempts to get rid of me?" She pulls out her phone and jabs at the keypad. "I've had enough of your sick schemes. First you try to poison me, now you're trying to make the studio uninhabitable. I'm calling Detective Kumar."

"Wait! I . . . there's a body in there."

She eyes me suspiciously. "I don't know what game you're playing, but I'm not going back inside until the police get here. And neither are you."

I turn and jog back to the house, propelled by a sudden urgency to check on my children. Was the email designed to lure me to the studio? What if she's done something to Ella and Sam?

To my immense relief, I find them still happily occupied with their blanket fort. When the first officer shows up at my front door, I accompany him back down the garden to the studio. Dana climbs out of her car where she's been hunkered down in the air-conditioning, and tilts her head to the sallow-skinned, thinly mustached police officer. "I'm Dana Becker. I'm the one who called." She motions to me. "This is my landlord, Morgan Klein. I've been gone for a couple of days, and I came back to find her breaking into the studio where I live. There's a ghastly smell coming from in there. She's been waging a campaign of harassment against me, turning off the power and AC, denying me refrigeration — who knows what else she's been up to in my absence. I've no idea what you're going to find in there. Is Detective Kumar with you? She's well aware of what's been happening."

"She's en route." The officer turns to me. "Do you know where the smell's coming from?"

"I . . . I think there's a body in the bed," I croak out.

His expression darkens. "Wait here." He dons some gloves and a mask and heads inside the studio.

I fix a stony gaze on Dana. "I don't know what you're up to, but whatever you're trying to pin on me, it won't work."

She opens her mouth to respond just as a second squad car pulls up. Kumar climbs out and strides down the side of the house to where we're standing. "Why am I not surprised it's you two again? This better be worth my time." She throws us a scathing look and disappears inside the studio.

When she returns with the male officer a few minutes later, her shrewd gaze travels slowly over us. "The good news is that it's not a body. The bad news is that someone's playing a sick prank. There's a dead coyote in the bed."

Dana spins around, skewering me with an accusatory gaze. "I bet *you'd* know something about that."

I blink, reeling from shock. My mind goes straight to the dead coyote on the road. The twins must have told Dana what I said. She's setting me up. "Don't be ridiculous!" I say. "I thought you were in there this whole time. Your car hasn't moved in two days."

Kumar clears her throat. "You'll need to call for a bio-hazard cleaning service. It's not a pretty sight."

Dana jabs a finger in my direction. "You did this! You're doing every twisted thing you can to get me to leave." She presses a hand to her chest. "You told the twins you were going to put roadkill in the studio." Without waiting for my response, she wheels around to Kumar. "I want to file a complaint. She's been conducting an illegal campaign to get rid of me. She put locks on the refrigerator and the laundry room door, and she turned off my AC and Wi-Fi. That's why I've been gone — I've been staying with a friend. The conditions here are unlivable. This is just her latest disgusting attempt to drive me out before I have my day in court."

I fist my hands at my sides. Dana's a lot cleverer than I gave her credit for. I can see where she's going with this, and it doesn't look good for me. I need to get a grip and set the record straight. "I didn't put a dead animal in your bed, if that's what you're suggesting," I say, fighting to appear calm.

"Ask her kids!" Dana says, allowing her bottom lip to tremble ever so effectively. "They'll tell you all about it."

I shoot her an indignant glare. "Leave my kids out of this!"

Dana edges closer to Kumar, her tone a perfect mix of wheedling and plaintive. "See what I mean? She's been threatening me like this for days. She's deranged. She can't cope — that's why I was hired to help with her elderly mother. Morgan's been even more of a basket case since she passed away. Her husband's at his wits' end. I'm the one left caring for the twins while he sends her off to the spa to try and unwind — anything to keep her sane."

Something explodes inside me at the barefaced lies pouring from her lips. I lunge at her, grasping for purchase, my fingers briefly grazing her cascading hair. She screams in my ear, flailing in exaggerated fashion. Kumar grabs me from behind and holds me back as I thrash around trying to break free.

"She's crazy," Dana whimpers. "I've had enough. I want to press charges." She graces me with the smallest of triumphant smirks before falling into the young officer's arms, shaking — no doubt with laughter as she buries her face in his chest.

* * *

It's only after I've been cited and released that I remember to call Will.

"Is Dana okay?" he blurts out before I get a word in.

"Fine." I stare morosely at the suitcase lying open on my bed. "She was staying at a friend's place for a couple of days and didn't bother telling me."

"Good. I told you it was nothing to worry about." Will hesitates. "Did you ask her what the smell was? You didn't go into the studio, did you?"

I break down in tears as the whole sorry story spills out. "She's pressing charges — assault and trespassing. I didn't even touch her. Kumar grabbed me before I could get ahold of her. You need to catch a flight home. She's taken out a temporary restraining order. I'm banned from the house."

CHAPTER 22

Will

I try to curb my anger as I pull up outside the Airbnb where Morgan is living temporarily — at least, I hope that's the case. I can't believe she was foolish enough to assault Dana in front of a police officer. I have no idea, yet, what the repercussions are going to be from the charges, but the last thing the kids need to see is their parents continue to fight over this wretched situation. They've had enough upheaval in their lives lately — losing their nana, the relationship with Dana souring, Sam almost drowning, Ella knocking her tooth out, and now being shuffled between their house and an Airbnb.

Morgan tried to talk me into moving in here with her, but I balked at the idea. I convinced her it would be better for me to stay in the house, and not leave Dana with free rein to trespass in our absence. The truth is, I think Morgan could use some down time to cool her jets and reflect on the damage she's done. If I stay here, we'll spend the whole time bickering. I'm furious with her for not taking my advice to call the police to conduct a welfare check on Dana. Taking it upon herself to break the law and enter the studio makes me wonder if she did put that dead coyote in there after all.

When I asked the twins about it, they backed up Dana's version of events. It's possible it was Morgan's doing, but not likely. I don't think she has the stomach for such a sick, twisted prank. Still, she's paying the price for being a hot-head now — we all are. I'm not in a good place as it is. I'm struggling to process losing JT and Tommy so suddenly. It's brought back memories I've taught myself to forget over the years — memories too dangerous to be allowed to resurface, but which keep trying to poke their way through to the light, regardless. I can't have the police digging around in my past — which is why I've taken steps to avoid that possibility.

I turn my thoughts back to the present as I reach into the back seat for my jacket. If Dana refuses to drop the assault and trespassing charges, we're going to rack up a small fortune in legal fees fighting them. The cost of evicting her pales in comparison. I grimace as I unplug my phone from the car. What if these new charges delay the eviction process even further? I climb out and lock my BMW, casting a wary glance around the unfamiliar neighborhood as I make my way to the front door. I'm not sure how well I'm going to be able to mask my anger at Morgan for the situation she's got us into. I didn't want her to hire Dana to begin with. Anyone with an ounce of sense would have gone through an agency. I paste a strained smile on my face when the door opens and the twins latch themselves onto my legs, jumping up and down with excitement.

"Daddy, do you want to see our new bedroom?" Sam squeals.

"Sure thing, buddy. Let me talk to Mommy for a few minutes and then I'll come upstairs and find you."

The twins scamper off, and I turn to Morgan. She stares back at me, arms crossed, not a hint of remorse in her expression.

It's far from a warm welcome, but I expected as much after chewing her out on the phone earlier about what happened. "Shall we talk in the kitchen?"

"I thought you might enjoy a tour of my downsized quarters first," she says, arching a condescending brow.

"Please don't, Morgan. It's not my fault you're stuck here."

She follows me into the kitchen and leans back against the counter, arms still folded in front of her. "She set me up, Will. The whiny email, the roadkill Ella told her about, pretending she was staying at a friend's house while she spied on me, waiting for me to go into the studio, taunting me in front of a police officer."

I brush a hand wearily across my brow. After talking to Kumar earlier, it's clear that Morgan was the unhinged one. "The law's the law. Bottom line is you assaulted her. What did you think was going to happen?"

"I wasn't thinking! That's the whole point! She goaded me into it!" She throws her hands up in the air and groans.

"I warned you not to go into the studio. I told you to call the police. How hard would it have been to do what I asked, for once?"

She gives a disgruntled snort. "A lot of good the police were when they got there."

I squeeze my brow between my thumb and forefinger. This isn't getting us anywhere. I need to find some common ground. "Have you heard back from your lawyer yet?"

She gives a tight nod. "I could be facing up to six months in jail and a one-thousand-dollar fine. It's so lame. I barely grazed her hair."

I sink down on a bar stool. "There may be another way out of this. I talked with Dana last night."

Morgan's lips morph into a disgusted scowl. "How touching! Did you share a bottle of wine while you recounted your respective grievances about my volatile nature?"

I curl my hand into a fist, muzzling my rage. "We spoke on the phone. She was very reasonable. She might be willing to drop the charges under certain conditions."

Morgan rolls her eyes. "And what would those conditions be?"

"An apology, for one."

"That's not going to happen. What else does she want?"

I blow out a breath. If the idea of simply apologizing falls flat, the rest of the conditions aren't going to go over well, either. "Reinstatement of the previous terms of your verbal agreement. Meals provided Monday through Friday, full access to the kitchen and laundry room, studio cleaned by VV, and so on. In return, Dana promises to perform her agreed-upon duties — childcare and light housework."

"Absolutely not. I don't want her in my home ever again."

I rest my forearms on my knees and lean toward her in a gesture of appeal. "Morgan, do you want to come back to the house, or do you intend to live here until the court cases are heard?"

She looks away and glowers out of the window. She's cornered, but that doesn't mean she'll cave to reason. Her propensity for making irrational decisions knows no bounds, as she has clearly demonstrated. I press on. "We can't afford to rent an Airbnb for months on end, in addition to paying legal fees for two separate lawsuits. Not to mention the fact that I could end up losing my job if my boss gets wind of any of this. I've already taken a couple of days off this week. How am I supposed to care for the kids and work?"

"They can stay here during the week."

"That's impractical. We'll have to move all their stuff back and forth — ballet gear, swim gear, toys, bikes, clothes, medicine. What if they need something from the house while I'm gone? You don't have access, thanks to the restraining order. If you'd just apologize, it would save us so much grief. Take the stupid locks off the fridge and the laundry room door, let Dana help out around the place for the next few weeks, and this will all be over before you know it."

"I feel like you're trying to pressure me into doing something I don't want to do."

"I'm not pressuring you. I'm trying to persuade you to come to the right decision. Our family's in danger of falling apart, Morgan. We need you home. You've been fraying at the edges ever since your mom passed away — fretting over

100

that note, imagining someone's watching you — and this situation with Dana is threatening to push you over the edge."

"So that's what this is really about. You're afraid I'm going to have another breakdown and you'll be left picking up the pieces."

I tent my fingers together and soften my expression. "Morgan, you're my wife, and I care about you. Of course I'm worried about you. Look at me, please. Can you just apologize so we can be together again as a family? Isn't that what's most important?"

She chews on her bottom lip, refusing to meet my gaze. "I'll think about it."

I nod, only partly appeased, but clinging to the hope that I might have gotten through to her. "I'd appreciate an answer before I fly out on Monday."

"What time are you leaving?"

"After I drop the kids off at preschool. I have a 10.30 a.m. flight."

* * *

Shortly after nine o'clock on Sunday night, I get a call from my boss's personal assistant.

"Jeremy's had a heart attack," she says, struggling not to cry. "He had a stent put in, he's going to be fine, but he needs you in Denver to do the presentation tomorrow. I've got you on the five-thirty flight out of here in the morning."

I hang up and check the details in the email she sent. It's too late now to take the twins to the Airbnb. But I can't let Jeremy down in his hour of need or I'll definitely be out of a job.

Reluctantly, I make the decision to enlist Dana to help. She can sleep in the guest room tonight and drive the kids to preschool in the morning. I won't text Morgan about the change of plan until I land. I can't risk her violating the restraining order by coming to the house.

I'm afraid of what she might do.

CHAPTER 23

Morgan

I'm milling around in my pajamas enjoying my coffee in the early morning sun on the back deck of the Airbnb, when I get a call from the twins' preschool teacher.

"Hi Morgan, it's Priscilla. You know we have the field trip to the apple farm this morning—"

"Oh, I'm so sorry! Did Will forget the permission slips when he dropped the twins off? I can drive over there right now and sign them for you. We've had a lot of upheaval lately and things have been falling through the cracks. If I leave right away, I can be there in twenty minutes."

"No need. We have the permission slips on file," Priscilla answers. "The reason I'm calling is because the twins aren't here. Is Will running late, perhaps?"

An uneasy feeling flutters in the pit of my stomach. "He was supposed to drop them off on his way to the airport. Are you sure they're not there?"

"I checked right before I called you. They haven't arrived yet. We're not leaving until ten so there's still time. I'm just trying to get a head count for the bus."

"I understand. Let me try calling Will and I'll get right back to you."

When I hang up, I check my messages and notice I have an unread text from him.

Jeremy had a heart attack. I have to fly to Denver this morning to do his presentation. Dana will take the kids to preschool.

The coffee mug falls from my hand and smashes on the deck, ceramic shooting in all directions. I dash back into the house, dialing and redialing Dana's number. Fear thrums like static in my brain when she doesn't pick up. She doesn't respond to any of my panicked texts either. All I can think of is VV's warning to be careful. My stomach is a seething mass of white-capped terror. I try Will's number again, but he ignores me. He's probably put his phone on silent. I pace back and forth across the kitchen floor, gripped by an indescribable panic as I wrestle with what to do. If Dana has abducted my kids, every minute counts. I can't take any chances. I'll never forgive myself if something happens to them. I grit my teeth and dial 911.

"So let me get this straight," the officer who shows up at the Airbnb repeats. "You moved in here three days ago, after you were slapped with a restraining order by your nanny. Your husband and the nanny remained at your house, and the nanny was responsible for dropping the kids off at school this morning."

"No! Well, yes, sort of. My husband was supposed to take the kids to school, but he had an emergency at work, so he asked Dana to take them instead. But she never showed up. I'm afraid for their safety — she might have abducted them. She tried to drown my son once. She's been threatening us with lawsuits and such. Like I told you already, we're going through a legal eviction process with her. Please! You have to help me. Call Detective Kumar — she knows what's been going on. My kids are only four years old. You need to do something!"

The officer raises a placating hand. "Okay, let's take this one step at a time. I've dispatched a patrol to the house to see if your nanny and the kids are there. Once we establish that they've left the residence, we'll issue a BOLO alert."

He has barely finished speaking before his radio crackles and a voice comes over the line. "We've located Dana Becker and the Klein twins. They're in transit to Sunshine Montessori."

The room spins around me. I sink back down in my chair, exhaling a relieved breath at the welcome news.

The officer nods in my direction, then steps outside to continue the conversation. When he returns a few minutes later, his expression has a surly tinge to it. "Your nanny explained she had a flat tire when she got up this morning. She would have let you know, but her phone battery died. She claims you've been turning her power on and off."

My cheeks grow warm. "What? No! That's not true! I might have turned the AC off a couple of times, that's all."

The officer throws me a skeptical look. "Kumar filled me in on a little background information. I understand there's been some friction between you and Miss Becker. I need to advise you that wasting police time with a misleading or false statement is a crime."

"It wasn't false or misleading," I say, clenching my jaw. "My four-year-old twins were missing. They didn't show up for school and Dana wasn't responding to texts or phone calls. My husband left our children in the hands of a maniac."

The officer hitches a brow, speaking volumes.

I grimace inwardly. Admittedly, *maniac* was a poor choice of words, considering the fact that I'm the one in coffee-splattered pajamas, bed hair on full display, who's been banished from my house.

The officer pockets his notebook. "It sounds like you've been through a lot lately, losing your mother and all, so I'm going to give you a break." He hesitates, before adding, "My experience with tenants who dig in their heels is that a carrot usually works better than a stick. If I were you, I'd thank your nanny for bailing your husband out, rather than berating her for not getting the kids to school on time. Sounds like it wasn't intentional."

The minute the squad car pulls away from the curb, I call the preschool to make sure Sam and Ella have arrived. Priscilla is nice enough to let me speak with them, but they don't have much to say. They're too excited to be going on a field trip with their friends. When I hang up, I begin calling all the tire shops in town to find out if Dana Becker contacted any of them this morning. I explain that she's my younger sister and has a learning disability and can't remember who she ordered a tire from. Most people are sympathetic, but no one has heard from her. It confirms my suspicions that she made the whole thing up to freak me out — another notch on her belt. She's an expert at pushing my buttons, and masterful at getting the authorities on her side. As far as they're concerned, I'm the crazy one.

When I pick the kids up from school at noon, I quiz them about what happened. "I heard Dana had a flat tire this morning."

"A man came and fixed it for her," Sam says, sounding pleased with himself at being the source of such valuable information.

I frown at him in the rearview mirror, my fraught nerves jangling. "What man?"

Sam shrugs. "I don't know. He had kind of curly hair."

I'm shaking so hard I can barely drive the rest of the way home. Did Dana have a strange man at the house? He could have been a pedophile for all I know. Or another freeloader staking out our house. I rake through my frenzied brain, trying to recall the description they gave of the serial killer on the news. Did they mention curly hair? I rub a hand over the back of my neck, my skin prickling. I know I'm being ridiculous, but I can't help tying myself up in paranoid knots.

By the time I reach the house, I've managed to get my emotions halfway under control. I make the kids a snack, then try Will's number again. It's almost an hour later before he calls me back.

"Quit blowing up my phone with messages," he fumes. "You know I had an important presentation today. And I had to take the managers out to lunch afterward. There's a lot riding on this. What do you want?"

"Why didn't you bring the kids to me on Sunday night instead of enlisting Dana's help? I only found out about it when the school called me to say the kids were running late. Dana claims she couldn't contact me because her phone battery was dead."

Will sighs. "Sam and Ella were already fast asleep in their beds when I found out about Jeremy."

"I don't care. I made it clear I don't want her in our house or anywhere near our kids."

"It was an emergency."

"Did you know she had some strange guy at our house? Sam saw him. Neither of us were there to vet this person. It could have been anyone — a criminal. That's unacceptable."

"It wasn't a stranger. Dana texted me to let me know a friend of hers was going to stop by and change her tire for her."

"And how did this *friend* know she had a flat if her phone battery was dead?"

"I don't know. Maybe it died after she texted him. Why are you being so difficult, Morgan?"

"Oh, so now I'm being difficult because I'm concerned about my kids being in the clutches of a madwoman?"

"You need to calm down. You're the one who sounds deranged. At this point, I honestly don't know who my kids are safer with — you or Dana!"

CHAPTER 24

I toss my phone on the couch and bury my face in a cushion. I can't believe this is happening. Will hung up on me. He's actually siding with that sick woman. Can't he see what's going on right in front of his nose? She's deliberately doing this, trying to come between us — just like she tried to do with Sam and Ella, playing favorites. I chew on a fingernail as I contemplate what her endgame could possibly be. Does she have her sights set on Will? My mind flashes back to the negligee she showed up to our house in. I'm convinced it was a calculated move on her part. She's upped her game ever since, abandoning her humdrum appearance for a decidedly sexier look. Come to think of it, I haven't seen her wearing those ugly glasses of hers in weeks — I'm guessing they were only a prop.

Does she really think she can seduce Will and replace me as his wife and the twins' mother? A jolt of fear goes through me at the thought. She's already wheedled her way into Ella's heart. And Sam seems to have forgotten his earlier grievances, thanks to some slick bribery on her part — sugary treats and gifts go a long way to securing a four-year-old's allegiance. Still, I'm their mother and there's no question that they love me. Nothing Dana can do will take that away.

The more pressing danger is that she'll manage to drive a permanent wedge between Will and me. It's remarkable how much she's accomplished in such a short space of time. She's had me kicked out of my own house, slapped me with a restraining order, convinced the police I'm the crazy one, and even persuaded my husband that I'm becoming unhinged. I've underestimated her manipulative powers. The problem is that the more I try to warn Will about what she's up to, the more he thinks I'm being unreasonable and overreacting — which only seems to prove Dana's claims about me. I need to strategize, take my time for once, and make a calculated plan to defeat her.

The thought of apologizing turns my stomach, but the longer I'm banished from my home, the more leeway I'm giving that witch, and the more I'm exposing my husband and my kids to her toxic ways. As long as I'm stuck in this Airbnb, she has the upper hand. It's beyond nauseating to picture her rejoining us for family meals and puttering about in my kitchen, helping herself to whatever she wants, but if I'm honest with myself, I'm not going to survive alone here for much longer. I need to be with my family.

After agonizing over my options, I resolve to do what needs to be done to get back home. I shower, dress in straight-leg jeans and a white T-shirt, and apply a full face of makeup. I may be going to grovel at my enemy's feet, but I don't want to look like the deranged, ousted, older woman while I'm at it. I sit down on the edge of the bed and pull out my phone. I'm not doing this for Dana. I'm doing it to win my husband back and protect my kids, and to regain control of the situation. I'll arrange to meet her in a public place so she can't claim I assaulted her again or make some other insane move. But we can't meet in a noisy restaurant either to have this conversation. I'm weighing my options when my phone beeps with a message from VV.

I need to speak with you.

I groan. What now? Dana better not have upset VV. The last thing I need is for her to quit on me in the midst of this predicament. I quickly tap out a response.

Sure! You can call me now. :)

I squirm impatiently, waiting for the phone to ring. Instead, VV messages me back.

No. I need to meet you.

The knot in my stomach tightens. Now I'm really afraid she's going to quit. Dana must have done something outrageous. What other reason could there be for VV wanting to leave? We love her like family. I need to fix this right away. I message her back and arrange to meet for lunch at a nearby park after she finishes cleaning our house. I pocket my phone and get to my feet. There's no point in texting Dana until I find out what's going on with VV. One fire at a time.

I distract myself by fixing some sandwiches — PB&J for the kids, and turkey and cheese for the adults. The remainder of the morning drags on until it's finally time to pick up the twins from preschool.

"Guess what, kiddos, we're going to the park for lunch today, and VV's going to meet us there."

"Yay! The park!" Sam sings, thrashing his head side to side as I buckle him into his car seat.

Ella blinks solemnly up at me. "Why's VV coming?"

"So she can visit with me. I haven't got to see her in a few days."

"Because you don't live with us anymore, right, Mommy?"

I bristle as though she's pronouncing a life sentence. I dread to think what she's telling the other kids at school. "I'm going to be moving back in very soon, sweetie, I promise you that."

She gives an approving nod before jamming her thumb in her mouth.

I grimace as I start up the engine. I can't break that promise. I need my kids to know they can trust me. I have no choice now but to suck it up, apologize to Dana, and accept her terms.

When we arrive at the park, we make our way to the playground area and seat ourselves at a nearby picnic table. The kids make short work of their sandwiches before hightailing it over to the slides and swings. Moments later, VV trudges into view. She greets the kids first with hugs and cuddles, then joins me at the picnic table still dressed in her colorful housekeeping tunic. "Hello, Mrs. Morgan." She sets her oversized purse on the bench next to her. Her smile is hesitant, communicating unease about our impending conversation.

I reach a hand across the table and place it on hers. "What's wrong, VV? Did Dana say something to upset you?"

She purses her lips, her eyes flitting briefly in the direction of the twins. "She is bad lady, Mrs. Morgan."

"I'm so sorry. Whatever she said, you can tell me. I'll speak to her about it. She'll be gone in a few more weeks and then you won't have to deal with her anymore. Please don't tell me you're considering quitting because of her. You know how much—"

"She no say anything to me." VV sighs and reaches for her purse. "I find something in your bed."

I stare at her open-mouthed.

"So sorry, Mrs. Morgan." She throws a discreet glance around her, then pulls something from her purse and drops it on the picnic table in front of me.

CHAPTER 25

Bile creeps its way up my throat as I stare, dumbstruck, at the silky black camisole lying on the picnic table in front of me.

"Is not yours, Mrs. Morgan," VV says, her pained tone telling me she wishes with all her heart it was.

"No. It's not mine," I confirm, a tremor creeping into my voice. "Where exactly did you find it?"

"I change the sheets and then I see it fall on the carpet."

I press my fingers into my eye sockets to stem the tears threatening to erupt. My heart is banging against my ribs so forcefully it feels like it's trying to break free. How in the world can it be beating this hard when I feel like I just died inside? No wonder Will's been defending Dana, trying to placate her at every turn. She's already seduced him. It's the old cliché — the husband and the nanny. Andrea suspected Dana was after a sugar daddy, and she was right all along. Too late now to swallow my pride and apologize in a bid to save my marriage. The verdict is in. Dana has won.

I pull a tissue from my purse and dab at my eyes, a knot of resolve hardening in my belly. She only wins if I let her. She's counting on me being weak, but she doesn't know me as well as she thinks she does. I'll keep on fighting as long as

I have something left to fight with. "VV, I need you to keep this to yourself for now. Do you understand?"

She nods mutely. "Sorry, Mrs. Morgan."

"You did the right thing," I reassure her. "I'm upset, but I needed to know about this."

VV gestures to the camisole lying on the table between us. "Maybe Dana put in bed to make you mad, Mrs. Morgan."

"Perhaps." I take a quick picture of it, then hook my finger through the spaghetti strap and toss the offending garment into the trashcan next to the picnic table. It could be another one of Dana's guerrilla tactics, but it's also possible my husband has been deceiving me about how he really feels about our squatter. That's what I need to figure out. And I can't do that until I move back home.

VV sniffs and dabs at her nose with a tissue. "I have work now." She zips up her purse and gets to her feet.

"VV, wait! I need your help with something."

"Yes, Mrs. Morgan. What is it?"

"Can you loan me your cleaning kit and uniform on Friday?"

Her eyes widen. "I no understand."

"I need to get into the studio after I drop the kids at school. But I can't risk being seen by anyone. If I violate the restraining order, I could go to jail. I have to go incognito — as Veronica Valdez. Will you help me?"

She stares at me dubiously for a long moment. Just when I think she's going to refuse my request, she nods. "Okay, I do it."

* * *

I manage to find a black wig in a party store that's adequate for my purposes. It won't pass muster up close, but at a distance, I could easily be mistaken for VV, dressed in her distinctive housekeeping tunic. I'll keep my shades on and hope that if any of the neighbors see me entering the studio, they'll assume it's VV arriving to clean. Andrea has promised to attest to it if I run into any issues.

After parking one street over from my house, I pull out my phone to turn off the camera on the gable of the studio, and make sure Dana's car is gone. I'm decked out in VV's colorful cleaning scrubs and rubber gloves, her tote slung over one arm, but I still keep my head ducked to avoid eye contact with anyone I might run into. I can't risk being drawn into conversation or my cover will be blown.

When I reach the studio door, I swivel slowly around to make sure I'm not being observed by a passerby. My hand shakes as I place the key in the lock and turn the deadbolt. I brace myself for a lingering stench, but I can't detect even the faintest odor from the coyote carcass. The exorbitant fee we paid the biohazard cleaning service was worth every penny. Although the smell is gone, the studio is a complete mess, as usual. I don't know how VV ever managed to clean the place without tripping over something and breaking her neck. Maybe that's what Dana was hoping would happen. I push the door shut behind me and set the plastic cleaning tote on the floor. I'm estimating she'll be gone for a couple of hours at least, but I want to get out of here as quickly as I can. Just the thought of her and Will possibly in here together too creeps me out.

I pick my way carefully through the sea of belongings strewn around the room, and over to the bed in the far corner. When I open the bedside cabinet door, an assortment of items tumbles out — books, and clothing, for the most part. I take a couple of quick, calming breaths, before hastily sorting through the pile, searching for anything of note — any evidence that she's been with Will. Photos, perhaps? A cardboard accordion file organizer stashed at the back of the cabinet catches my eye. I fish it out and thumb through the compartments. It contains mostly receipts, some tax returns, and a photocopy of a birth certificate. I pull the document out, curious to see where Dana was born, but it's the name that grabs my attention — *Patty Merkler*. What is Dana doing with Patty Merkler's birth certificate? My brain fires off in several directions at once. Is she pretending to be someone else? I take a quick photo of the document and return it to the organizer.

When I've satisfied myself that there's nothing else of interest, I shove everything back inside the cabinet and slam the door, hoping it stays put. Next, I open the drawer and begin sifting through the miscellaneous items it contains: coins, wrappers, charging cables, and crumpled tissues.

At the back of the drawer, I discover a folded sheet of newspaper. I throw a quick glance over my shoulder to make sure the coast is clear, before smoothing it out and examining the black and white photo inside. It looks like a high school graduation picture. I skim over the faces of the girls, but I don't recognize Dana. I have no idea of the photo's significance, but she must have saved it for some reason or another.

Shock ricochets down my spine when the studio door suddenly bursts open.

"*You again*! How dare you break in here!"

CHAPTER 26

"I'm calling the police," Dana snarls, pulling out her phone.

I hold up a gloved hand. "No! Wait! I can explain."

"I don't need an explanation. I can see perfectly well what's going on here. It's called breaking and entering and you just added another charge to your growing rap sheet."

"I'm . . . helping VV out." I point to the cleaning tote on the floor. "She can't make it today — family emergency. If you don't want the studio cleaned, that's fine. I'll leave you to do it yourself." I attempt to slip past her, but she grabs hold of me and squeezes, her grip like a tentacle around my wrist. "Oh no you don't! You're not walking away from this!"

She stabs at the screen of her phone and presses it to her ear. "This is Dana Becker. I'm calling from—"

Seizing my chance, I rip free of her grasp and take off running.

She yells after me, but to my relief, she stays on the phone and doesn't pursue me — no doubt hoping the police will.

When I make it back to my car, I immediately lock the doors, half-expecting to see her running toward me swinging a sledgehammer, like in some B-rated horror flick. I dial VV's number as I peel out of my subdivision. I have no idea where

I'm going. I only know I have to keep driving and get out of here before the police show up and arrest me.

"VV!" I blurt out the minute she answers. "Dana came back early and caught me in the studio. She called the police. They're probably going to show up at the Airbnb to question me. What should I do with your stuff? I need to get rid of it."

"Come to my house," VV replies. "I take it."

When I pull up minutes later, she ushers me inside, her motherly face a reassuring mask of calm.

"I don't know what I was thinking." My breathing comes in panicked gasps as I rip off the wig and rubber gloves and toss them on the table. "I could be jailed for this. She caught me red-handed."

"Listen to me, Mrs. Morgan," VV says in a stern voice. "I know what we do. We say it was me cleaning the studio."

I stare at her for a long moment, processing the idea. "You'd be willing to lie to the police for me?"

Something shifts in her expression. "Dana always make trouble. I no like that woman."

I scrub my hands over my face, trying to think it through. It could work. It's Dana's word against ours. No one else saw me. But is it fair to ask VV to put everything on the line for me? I'm the one who took the risk and entered the studio knowing I was breaking the law.

"Are you sure you want to do this?"

VV gives a resolved nod. "Tell me everything what happened, Mrs. Morgan."

I'm quiet for a moment as I picture how it went down. "I let myself into the studio and set down your cleaning tote — it's still in there somewhere. I forgot to grab it when I bolted."

VV shrugs. "Is okay. What you do next?"

"I made my way over to the bed and searched through the bedside cabinet. I was looking at a photograph when Dana walked in. She was livid. She threatened to call the police and have me arrested for breaking and entering. I begged her not to. I told her you had a family emergency, and I was helping you out. But she didn't buy it. When she got on the phone with

116

the police, I made a break for it. She grabbed my wrist — she's surprisingly strong — but I managed to get away."

VV cocks her head to one side. "Which wrist she grab?"

"The left one." I frown at her. "Why?"

"Show me."

I pull up my sleeve and show her the marks from Dana's iron grip.

VV promptly holds out her left wrist to me. "Squeeze hard, Mrs. Morgan, very hard."

I let out a nervous bark of laughter. "No, VV! I don't want to hurt you."

"You want go to prison?"

"No, of course not! Do you? I'm pretty sure it's a felony to lie to the police — it's illegal, at any rate."

"Who is bad person, Mrs. Morgan? You, me, or her?" She holds her wrist out once more. "Do it!"

Reluctantly, I take hold of it and squeeze until she shrieks.

"Good," she says, shaking out her arm. "Now, go!"

I swallow hard. "Thank you. I'll call you once the police arrive. Don't forget they'll be listening to everything we say."

* * *

When Kumar and another officer come knocking, I answer the door with a picture-perfect perturbed expression on my face. "I didn't expect to see you again before the court date."

"May we come in?" Kumar asks.

"Of course." I step aside and usher them through to the tiny open plan kitchen and family room. "What's this about?"

"Dana Becker called to report that you broke into her studio again." Kumar taps her fingers on the table and eyes me questioningly.

Her studio. I frown, quickly correcting my face to neutral. "I have no idea what she's talking about. I haven't been near my house since she slapped me with that restraining order."

Kumar's molten gaze bores into me. "She said she caught you in the act. According to her, she walked in on you going through her stuff."

I paste a look of outrage on my face. "She's lying! That woman will say and do anything to make my life miserable. She can't get past the fact that she's being evicted."

"So you weren't wearing a wig and pretending to be VV, the woman who cleans for you?"

I give a disconcerted laugh. "Of course not. But this is VV's day to clean the studio. Have you talked to her yet? Maybe Dana's confused."

An exasperated scowl crosses Kumar's ordinarily imperturbable face. It's clear she's tired of the ongoing feud between my squatter and me. "Go ahead and call your housekeeper. Let's hear what she has to say about it."

The minute VV answers the phone, she bursts into tears and starts rattling away in Spanish.

"VV, calm down." I raise my voice to make myself heard. "I can't understand you. What's wrong?"

"I tell you she bad lady, Mrs. Morgan. I clean studio today and she come back early and attack me. She say I steal her things. I no steal. I never steal."

"Of course not. I know that." I throw a quick glance in Kumar's direction. "VV, the police are here with me. Dana told them it was me who was cleaning her studio today."

There's a long pause, then VV sniffles. "I no understand."

Kumar waves her hand to get my attention. "Ask her if she'd be willing to accompany us to the studio to talk to Dana so we can figure this out."

I trace my fingers over my brow. "What about the restraining order?"

"You can wait in the squad car. I'll bring Dana out to talk to you."

I run the proposal past VV, and she does a convincing job of reluctantly allowing herself to be talked into agreeing to Kumar's proposal.

* * *

My stomach flutters with nerves when we pull up at the curb outside my house. VV and I wait in the squad car with

Kumar's partner while she walks down to the studio. Minutes later, she comes back into view with a sour-looking Dana in tow. Kumar's partner opens the squad car door, and VV and I climb out and stand next to it.

Dana's scorching gaze rakes over me. "Is this the best you could come up with — strong-arming your help to lie for you so you could break in and go through my stuff?"

I paint on a pleasant smile. "I don't know where you came up with that story, Dana, but you and I both know it's not true. No one *broke* into the studio. VV used her key. She was here to clean, as promised."

Dana shifts her focus to VV, staring her down. "What did she do — threaten to deport you, or fire you, if you didn't lie for her?"

VV raises her chin defiantly. "I no lie for Mrs. Morgan."

"Do you think I'm stupid?" Dana yells. "I can tell you apart. I was standing right next to Morgan — close enough to grab her to try to stop her from fleeing."

"You lie." VV rolls up her left sleeve and holds her bruised wrist out to Kumar. "She say I steal her things. She hurt me. I want to press charges."

CHAPTER 27

"She's the one who's lying! I didn't touch her!" Dana protests. "I swear it was Morgan in the studio."

Kumar raises a hand to placate her. "Okay, let's all calm down and take a deep breath. As I understand it, nothing was taken, nothing was broken, and no one was harmed. For my part, I'd like to be able to write this whole incident off as a misunderstanding. My recommendation is that both sides agree not to press charges and walk away. Of course, it's entirely up to you if you want to hire lawyers and drag this out in court."

Dana crosses her arms and heaves out a disgusted breath. "Fine! I'll drop the breaking and entering charges if VV drops the bogus assault charge. But the charges I already filed against Morgan stand." She narrows her eyes, her gaze darting from me to VV. "And I don't want to see either of you in the studio again. I'll clean it myself."

Kumar turns to VV. "Are you in agreement?"

She gives a demure shrug. "Yes, is okay for me."

"Then my work here is done." Kumar nods in my direction. "I'll take you and VV home."

* * *

When I pick the kids up from preschool later that day, they're bouncing off the walls, high on sugar from cupcakes one of the moms brought in to celebrate a birthday. I need them to burn off some of that energy before we retire to the tiny Airbnb with its thin walls and noisy floors. "Who wants to go to the park?" I say, as I escort them out to the car, dragging their backpacks.

"Me!" they shout in unison, hands shooting up in the air.

I grin back at them. "The park it is."

The minute they run off to play, I sink down on a bench, my mind replaying everything that happened this morning. How can I ever repay VV for what she did? I owe her big time. I need to think of some tangible way to thank her for sticking her neck out like that for me. If it hadn't been for her, I'd be sitting in a jail cell right now. She played her part perfectly — without overdramatizing a thing. Kumar swallowed it, hook, line, and sinker. At least, I think she did. She might still have some lingering suspicions about my integrity after the alleged poisoning incident.

I'm lost in thought when the twins come running over hand-in-hand with two familiar faces.

"Mommy, can Patrick and Esther come see our new house?" Ella asks, bouncing up and down with excitement.

My mouth drops open. "I . . . thought you guys moved to Florida?"

Patrick gives a confused shake of his head. "We live here."

"Please, Mommy!" Ella repeats.

"Um, some other day, sweetie." I rub my arms, thrown for a loop by Patrick's response. Did Dana lie about her sister moving to Florida? Maybe I misunderstood her, and they were only going there on vacation.

Ella juts out her lip. "Not fair!"

"Your Auntie Dana's not allowed in our house anymore," Sam announces.

Patrick gives an embarrassed laugh and kicks at the turf beneath his feet. "She's not our auntie. She was our sitter while our mom was in the hospital."

I plaster on a frozen smile as I digest the information. So she wasn't working for her sister at all — another fabrication. Everything I thought I knew about Dana Becker is turning out to be a dried-out husk of a lie, if that's even her real name. She could be Patty Merkler for all I know. But why is she using an alias? I need to do some serious digging, something I should have done before I hired her. I can start by having a conversation with Patrick's mother.

"Is your mom here, honey?"

He shakes his head. "She's back in the hospital. She has cancer. We have a new sitter now, but she's really old so she doesn't play with us."

I flash him a sympathetic smile. That's one dead end, but it won't deter me.

When the twins get hungry, we load up in the car and drive back to the Airbnb. I set them up with some PB&J sandwiches and fruit, then pull out my laptop. After locating the picture I took of the birth certificate, I type the name into Google. A slew of results bombards me. I begin scrolling through the various images of all the Patty Merklers and Patricia Merklers in the world — accomplished women with impressive careers ranging from pediatric dentist to information technology manager. None of the photos look anything like my squatter. Next, I check Instagram, Facebook, and LinkedIn, but nothing even remotely matches the woman I know as Dana Becker.

The next logical step is to sign up to one of those background check websites. I'm reluctant to waste another penny on Dana, but it's cheaper than hiring a PI to get the information I'm after. With a resigned sigh, I retrieve my credit card from my purse and purchase access to the most highly rated background check website Google presents me with. I punch in the details from the birth certificate, then wait with mounting frustration as the slow-moving green bar on the screen searches for information, all the while reassuring me that it's accessing billions of records to fulfill my request. I've ordered everything — social media, personal details, criminal records, properties, cars, contact info. Whatever Dana's hiding, I intend to find it.

The results finally flicker onto the screen, and I begin scanning through them with an air of desperation. I was hoping to confirm my suspicions that Dana has a criminal record, but to my disappointment, Patty Merkler doesn't even have a speeding ticket. Then again, it might not be Dana's birth certificate. I already know she's a con artist — milking us for free rent. Maybe she's committed identity theft using multiple aliases. The remainder of the results prove just as disappointing. It appears Patty Merkler is an uninteresting human being who owns no property and has undergone long periods of unemployment. Her father and her older brother, Cooper, are both deceased, and her mother is a retired insurance broker who resides in Anaheim.

I slam my laptop closed, wishing I could get my money back. I've learned nothing that will help me get rid of Dana, and nothing I can use against her. As I slide my credit card back into my wallet, my fingers brush up against the scrunched-up newspaper photo at the bottom of my purse. I'd forgotten all about it, until now. I'd crumpled it in my fist to hide it when the studio door burst open. When I bolted, it was still in my hand.

I flatten it on the table and study the faces of the high school students. This time I skip over the girls and focus on the boys. My jaw slackens with shock when I find myself looking into familiar eyes curtained by dark, shoulder-length hair. It can't be — can it? I pick up the photo and peer at it more closely. It's definitely him. I check the names listed below to make sure: *William Klein, back row, third from left.*

My eyes flick distractedly through the remaining names, one of them jumping out at me: *Cooper Merkler.*

CHAPTER 28

My fingers shake as I compare the spelling of Cooper's last name with the birth certificate: *M-E-R-K-L-E-R.* It's a match. Same last name. It can't be a coincidence. Cooper Merkler was in my husband's high school class. Why does Dana have Patty Merkler's birth certificate? My head is spinning trying to figure out what's going on. Could Dana be Cooper's sister? But surely Will would have recognized her. Nothing about this is making any sense. I need to confront him. If he's sleeping with Dana, it's time he came clean about it. He'll be furious when he finds out I broke into the studio again, but there's no way around it. If I tell him it was VV who discovered the birth certificate, he'll know I orchestrated it anyway.

I set my laptop aside to mull it over, and check on the twins, who are happily occupied playing on their iPads. I feel like a bad mother giving them so much screen time this week, but most of their toys are still at the house and there's not a lot to do in the Airbnb — no play equipment in the backyard. I'll ask Will to bring over some of their favorite toys when he drops them back on Sunday night. I can't have them ogling screens the whole time they're here. I haven't given Will an answer yet, about apologizing to Dana, but I'm not sure it matters anymore. Things have taken a dramatic turn. She has made it clear she's unwilling to drop the original charges against me. But I'm fearful that won't be enough to satisfy her now that I've made her out to be a liar in front of the police. She's not going to let that go without inflicting some kind of punishment in return. I just don't know what to expect, or when to expect it.

By mid-afternoon, the twins are bored and pestering me about when their dad is coming to pick them up. It breaks my heart to know I won't see them again until Sunday evening. We're living like a broken family, behaving as though we're divorced. And it doesn't have to be this way. Will could choose to stay here with me and the kids. So why is he so insistent on sleeping at our house? Is it really because he's afraid Dana might trespass in our absence? Or is he only too eager to welcome her in once the kids have gone to bed? My thoughts drift to the black camisole. It's possible Dana planted it in our bed to taunt me, knowing VV would run straight to me when she found it, but I can't rule out the alternative — that my husband has been taking full advantage of my mandated absence. Has he been carrying on with Dana behind my back all along? I have to know what I'm dealing with, however much the truth hurts. As I ponder my options, an idea comes to mind.

With the promise of ice cream as a distraction, I buckle the kids into the car and drive to the nearest big-box electronics store to find a simple tracking device I can attach to Will's vehicle. I could check his location on my phone, but he's no fool. If he has something to hide, he might leave his phone behind, and I'd be none the wiser. I need to be able to follow him and make sure he's not meeting Dana somewhere outside of the range of Andrea's eagle eye. Maybe I'm being paranoid, but I'd rather be paranoid than a fool.

The retail assistant in the electronics store is a pimply-faced teenager with a snarky attitude, and between him and the twins, who are tugging on my sleeve begging for ice cream, I feel myself begin to unravel. "Here, play on my phone for a few minutes," I say, handing it to them to distract them.

"What type of tracker are you looking for?" the assistant asks, with a cavernous yawn, suggesting he's been up half the night playing video games. I make a mental note to do a better job of monitoring the twins' screen time. I can't risk them morphing into some version of this sorry attempt at adulting.

"The kind that tracks," I snap back.

He scratches at his nonexistent stubble. "Hardwired, portable or OBD plug-in?"

I answer him with a blank stare.

"The plug-ins communicate well with various vehicle subsystems, and they provide better overall car security," he fires off. "If a thief manages to remove the OBD tracker, you'll get an alert right away."

"Nothing that plugs in. I need a portable tracker. Something magnetic, perhaps?"

His eyes glitter with the first indication of interest in our conversation. "Gotcha. You need a hidden device to keep tabs on someone."

I throw a nervous glance at the twins, but they're not paying any attention to our conversation. "Yes. A teenager." I let out an uncomfortable laugh.

He gives me a withering look and proceeds to show me my options. I settle for a small, highly rated device that comes in a waterproof magnetic case guaranteed to attach easily to any vehicle.

"You won't have a problem with this one," he assures me, as he rings it up. "Comes with a ninety-day warranty."

"Perfect!" I tap my credit card on the reader. It won't take me that long to find out if my husband is cheating on me.

With the kids safely buckled in their car seats, I blaze a trail to the ice cream store. I need to get back to the Airbnb before Will shows up.

"Okay, kids, hurry up and pick a flavor," I say, checking the time. "Daddy will be home soon."

Sam selects chocolate after pretending to agonize over the decision like he always does. Ella goes back-and-forth between strawberry and vanilla, then settles on rainbow sherbet. I manage to find an empty booth and set the kids up with an ample supply of napkins. I've just sat down opposite them when my phone rings. VV's daughter's name pops up on the screen. I frown as I reach for my phone. She only ever calls if VV's sick and can't make it to work.

I press the phone to my ear, trying to ignore the niggling feeling of worry in the pit of my stomach. "Hey, Julia, how's it going?"

"Not good." Her voice cracks.

My gut starts to churn. If VV's had a heart attack or something, I'll never forgive myself for dragging her into this mess and causing her so much stress. "What's wrong?"

Julia begins to sob. "Mom's been abducted."

CHAPTER 29

A chill wafts over me. "What do you mean, *abducted*?"

"Some little kid riding his bike saw her being shoved into a van." Julia's voice cracks. "Mom was on her way home from work. The police haven't confirmed it, but they think it might be the West Coast Killer."

Blood roars in my ears. The other patrons in the ice cream shop blur together like a paper chain of figures as my head begins to spin. "How do they know it was VV? Does the kid even know what he's talking about?"

"He described Mom's floral scrubs. He thinks the van was gray, but he couldn't give them a license plate, or any other details." Pain permeates Julia's voice, like she's trying to talk with a razor blade in her throat. I want to comfort her, but my vocal cords are frozen. My body jerks with silent tears.

"His last kill was only fifty miles north of here," she goes on. "The police think he might be heading for the southern border."

I drag in a ragged breath. "Did the kid get a good look at VV's abductor?"

"Not really. He said he had on a hoodie and something hiding his face — it could have been a balaclava."

My mind is fraying, drugged by a mixture of anger and helplessness. I can't believe this is happening — a horror that far and away eclipses my own crisis. "Do you want me to come over?"

Julia lets out another shuddering sob. "No. The house is full of people, and there are news crews on the street. Just pray they find Mom, please. The police will want to talk to you. They asked me for the names of everyone Mom's been in contact with over the last couple of days. I have to go, Morgan. The feds need to speak with me."

She hangs up and I sink back into the couch, my own problems paling into insignificance in comparison to what she's going through. The situation is serious if the FBI are involved. It's terrifying to think VV might be in the hands of the West Coast Killer. I can't help the first horrible thought that comes to mind. *Why couldn't it have been Dana?* Why did this have to happen to the kindest woman on the planet — a mother and a grandmother? She has people in her life who love and need her. As far as I'm concerned, Dana is disposable. I drop my head into my hands and groan. Does that make me an evil person too?

* * *

I deflate even further when Will shows up at the Airbnb. I had planned on launching straight into everything I found out about Dana, and confronting him about the class photograph, but instead, I burst into ugly sobs. He follows me into the kitchen and pulls me into an awkward hug. I cry even harder when his familiar arms encircle me.

"Morgan, please don't. I know this isn't ideal, us living apart and shuffling the kids back and forth like this, but I'm not the one who got us into this mess."

"It's not that," I blubber. "I mean, it is, but something else has happened. Something much worse."

Will raises his brows in alarm. "What is it? Is it the twins?" His eyes dart around the space and then back to me. "Where are they?"

"They're fine. They're watching TV in my bedroom. It's VV. She's . . . she's been abducted."

A look of utter incomprehension envelops Will's face. He studies me intently, as though trying to assess my mental state. "What do you mean she's been abducted?"

"Abducted — as in taken. A witness saw her being shoved into a van. The police are working on the assumption that the West Coast Killer has struck again. The FBI are at her house, and news crews. It's awful. Julia's a mess."

Will takes a step back from me and sinks into a chair. "When did this happen?"

"Late this afternoon. VV was walking to the bus stop after a cleaning job. A kid on a bike saw it all go down."

A look of horror flickers over Will's face. I know what's going through his mind. The thought of anyone harming VV is too much for any of us to bear. What kind of monster abducts a defenseless grandmother?

"Do the police have any leads?" Will asks.

"No. The kid thinks the van was gray, but he didn't know the make or model, and he didn't get a license plate." My voice cracks and I swallow a sob. "The police speculate the West Coast Killer's heading for the border."

Will drags his hands through his hair. "What are they doing to find VV?"

I give a listless shrug. "I don't honestly know."

The doorbell rings and I grip the arms of the chair I'm sitting in. "That might be the police."

Will throws me a panicked look. "The police? Why are they here?"

"They're talking to all of VV's friends and acquaintances as part of the investigation."

Will gets to his feet, a flinty expression on his face. "I'll handle this. Just answer their questions as briefly as possible. Whatever you do, don't start spouting off about unrelated issues, and keep Dana out of it."

I bristle at his condescending tone. Does he really think I'm going to sit here and babble on about our squatter when

VV's been abducted? He acts like he doesn't want to talk to the police, when we should be doing everything we can to help them find VV. I don't know why he's so worried about shielding Dana.

I inch up in my chair when Will reappears alongside Kumar and her partner. Will gives me a loaded look, before crossing his arms and sitting down in a chair as far away from me as possible. I notice the almost imperceptible tilt of Kumar's brows as she observes our unspoken interaction. She's probably wondering why we aren't huddled together on the couch, arms wrapped around each other for support. But our relationship is adrift in uncharted waters after everything that's happened, and VV's abduction might be enough to push it over the edge. I bite my tongue to keep the questions I'm wrestling with from tumbling indiscriminately from my mouth. I'm not sure how much Kumar will be able to divulge in an ongoing investigation anyway.

"VV's daughter said she spoke to you earlier on the phone," she begins. "I take it you're both aware of the situation."

She looks between me and Will, inviting a response.

I give a shaky nod. "Yes. We're devastated. VV's like family to us." Tears sting my eyes. "Do you know anything at all? Have you got any leads on her whereabouts?"

"We're working with the witness to extract as much infor-mation as possible." Kumar consults her notebook. "Did VV mention anything to you about being stalked or threatened? Was she scared of anyone?"

"Not that I know of."

"Have you seen any strangers lurking in the neighborhood?"

"No." I hesitate, suddenly remembering the feeling of being watched. But that was just me being paranoid, wasn't it? I never actually saw anyone. "What are you doing to find her?" A tear trickles down my cheek and I dab at it with the back of my hand.

"We're allocating all the resources at our disposal," Kumar assures me. "And the FBI is assisting."

"Time is not on her side," Will interjects. "The other women were all killed and their bodies dumped within forty-eight hours."

"As I said, we're doing everything we can to locate her." Kumar holds his gaze. "Which brings me to my next question. Will, where were you this afternoon between three-thirty and five?"

CHAPTER 30

Will sits still as a statue, a thin crease in his brow the only indication of the rage he's fighting to contain at Kumar's question. "I've been out of state all week on business. I just got back into town this afternoon."

Kumar's expression remains deadpan. "Where did you fly in from?"

"Denver."

"And your flight arrived at what time?" Kumar's pen hovers over her notebook, her eyes never leaving Will's face.

"I couldn't tell you exactly what time we landed." He gives a strained laugh. "These airlines are seldom on time anymore. If it's not weather, or mechanical issues, it's some unruly passenger holding things up. I've run into a few of those lately."

Kumar's lips stretch into a thin smile. "I'm going to need you to be more specific than that."

I twist my sweating hands in my lap, trying to ignore the knot of unease throbbing in my throat. Why is Will doing precisely what he told me not to do — babbling needlessly? My ordinarily unflappable husband looks nervous, for once. To be fair, it's a stressful situation, but Kumar's just doing her job.

"Show her your boarding pass," I interject. "You have it on your phone, right?"

His stare burrows into me like a drill bit. I toss my head indignantly. I know he doesn't want the police looking at his phone, but this is hardly the time to be worried about privacy. If he has nothing to hide, why is he acting so jittery?

Kumar gives an approving nod. "A boarding pass will suffice."

After a beat of hesitation, Will fishes his phone from his pocket and taps on it, working his jaw side-to-side, something he only does when he's irritated. I count to three, feeling my patience ebb away. All he has to do is pull up his boarding pass so Kumar can verify his arrival time.

I breathe out a sigh of relief when he finally passes her the phone. She studies it for a moment, takes a picture of the screen, then hands it back.

"So you landed in LAX at 1.55 p.m. and arrived at the Airbnb at what time exactly?" She turns to me, a staged frown of puzzlement on her brow.

"I . . . I think it was around five-thirty, right?" I reply, flicking a questioning look Will's way. My pulse drums a dull beat in my ears. I didn't know he had gotten an earlier flight. Even if traffic was heavy, it couldn't have taken him more than an hour to get to the Airbnb. He always travels carry-on, so he wouldn't have had to wait around for luggage. What took him so long to get here?

Kumar poses the question for me. "Where were you between the hours of two and five-thirty?"

Will scowls. "What's this got to do with the investigation into VV's abduction?"

Kumar sets down her pen and appraises him. "Does the question make you uncomfortable?"

The edge in her tone tells me she thinks Will's hiding something. Are my worst fears about to be confirmed? Was he with Dana?

He shifts in his seat. "I managed to catch an earlier flight. I stopped at a friend's place on the way here."

Kumar swoops up her pen again with a long-suffering air. "Name and address?"

Will clamps his lips together in a thin line. "Fine. I went by our house before I came here. I wanted to make sure our squatter hadn't been trespassing in my absence, or vandalized anything."

My heart slugs erratically in my chest. More lies. Why did he try to hide where he was? Did he stop by the house for another kind of rendezvous?

Kumar's eyes brighten with a curious gleam at the admission. "And what did you find at the house?"

Will shrugs. "Everything seemed to be in order."

"Did you speak with Dana Becker?"

He clears his throat and glances away. "Briefly. She was on her way out."

Kumar makes a note of the information, then signals to her partner and gets to her feet. "Thanks for your cooperation. We'll be in touch if we have any further questions."

The minute the front door closes behind them, I round on Will. "Why didn't you tell me you went to the house? Are you having an affair with Dana?"

"What? Are you insane?" He shakes his head in disgust. "How can you even think such a thing?"

"I have my reasons." I cross my arms and glare at him. "What did you two talk about?"

"Exactly what I told the detective," he growls. "Nothing! I greeted Dana in passing — that was the height of it. Now back off and let me think for a minute."

"About what?"

"VV, us, the lawsuits — all of it! I'm spinning my wheels trying to hold everything together, keep a roof over our heads, and now the police are questioning me about our missing housekeeper. I can't afford to hire another lawyer, especially not a criminal defense attorney."

I wrinkle my forehead in confusion. "Why would you need one? You didn't do anything."

"That's not the point. We're already on the police's radar with assault charges, and accusations of poisoning flying back-and-forth, now this. Obviously I'm going to fall under suspicion."

"Well maybe you shouldn't lie to the police! Kumar was only doing her job. She's racing against the clock to save VV from a serial killer. We're assisting with the investigation. We're not suspects."

"I don't know if the police are convinced of that." Will flops down on the couch and drops his head into his hands. "This is a lot to come home to."

I wet my lips, my stomach churning. I can't put it off any longer. I need to confront him. "There's more."

He blinks up at me, twitching like a startled bird. "What do you mean?"

I sink down on the couch next to him. "Dana Becker's not who she claims to be. I think she knows you from years ago." I pull out my phone and scroll to the photo I took of the birth certificate. "I found this in the studio."

His eyes narrow to slits. "Please, tell me you didn't go in there again."

"I had to find out who she is. That woman is destroying our lives. You can't expect me to sit back and take it. It's *our* studio. She's occupying it illegally. I have every right to go in there if I want to."

Will presses his hands to his head. "You don't get it, Morgan! You could go to jail for this. Does Dana know you were in there?"

"What does it matter?"

"Does . . . she . . . know?" he repeats forcefully.

"Of course not," I lie. "Do you want to see this or not?"

He takes the phone from me and enlarges the picture of the birth certificate.

I catch a subtle shift in his expression. I lean closer. "Do you recognize that name?"

He scratches his forehead, acting as though he's mulling it over. "*Merkler.* No. I don't know anyone with that name."

I can feel the lie wedged between us — in the tremor of his hand, and the harried glance he shoots my way. But he's not going to come clean unless I back him into a corner.

I slide the high school photo out of my pocket and lay it down in front of him. "Oddly enough, one of your class-mates was called *Cooper Merkler*."

CHAPTER 31

Will stares at the photo, fear flashing across his face before he quickly composes his features.

"Tell me the truth. Is Dana Becker really Patty Merkler?" I ask. "What's her connection to Cooper?"

Will closes his eyes briefly and takes a long breath. "Patty and Cooper were brother and sister. And no, Dana is not Patty — she looks nothing like her. I don't know who she is, and I don't know what she's doing with Patty's birth certificate. But I will tell you this — you'd better keep your mouth shut about it. You shouldn't have gone poking your nose into Dana's stuff. You could go to jail for violating the restraining order."

"I don't care! She got me kicked out of my own house. I'm going to do whatever I have to do to find out who she is and what she's up to. Why are you so protective of her? What does she have over you?"

He gives a perturbed shake of his head, not meeting my eyes. "Nothing. But some things are best left alone. She'll be out of our lives in a couple more weeks."

I snap my fingers to get his attention. "Look at me, Will! Why all the lies? *Are* you having an affair with Dana?"

"No! Of course not. Why do you keep asking me the same thing over and over?"

"It's a fair question. She paws all over you every chance she gets. And you two have the place to yourselves, now. You have to admit she's a very attractive woman."

"You're the one who wanted to hire her!" Will fumes. "And you have no one to blame but yourself for the fact that you've been banished from the house. Meanwhile, I'm stuck justifying myself to you! This is all your doing, Morgan, so don't put it on me!"

His answer provokes so many more questions, I hardly know where to begin. I consider showing him the picture of the black camisole, but it proves nothing, and will only get him more incensed, and he might clam up entirely. Right now, I need to keep him talking. More than anything, I want answers about his past. "Okay, forget Dana for a minute. Why did you lie to me about not knowing anyone named Merkler?"

Will flinches, as though he's in pain. "I didn't want to tell you about it. It's a sad story, that's all. It happened a long time ago, it's not something I enjoy talking about."

I quirk an eyebrow. "Better start at the beginning, then. I deserve an explanation."

He interlaces his hands and rests them in front of him, still averting his eyes. "There's not much to tell. It's a lesson in stupidity. When I was in high school, Coop and I, and a couple of other friends, went camping down by the river near West Mountain Ranch one night. We took some tequila and my dad's truck — he was locked up for a few months for a DUI at the time. The irony, huh?" He frowns, staring down at a spot on the laminate wood floor. "We were sixteen, drinking and carrying on — just being kids. At some point during the night, Coop wandered out of his tent and fell into the river. We found him the next morning."

I let out a gasp. "Drowned?"

"Yes." Will's voice comes out thick. "It was awful. His younger sister, Patty, was only ten at the time. There was an investigation, of course. It was ruled an accident, but our parents still grounded us for the rest of the semester. It was the worst time of my life. Even now, I hate thinking about it."

"I can understand why. That's horrible!" I lose myself in thought for a moment, trying to imagine a sixteen-year-old Will sobering up and discovering his friend had drowned during the night. No wonder losing two of his high school friends recently had hit him so hard. Not to mention VV being abducted.

"So now you know the whole sorry story. And why I swore off drink. My dad almost killed someone driving drunk, and one of my friends drowned while I was sleeping off a hangover."

"I'm sorry you lost your friend," I say, gathering my thoughts. "But it still doesn't explain why Dana has a copy of Patty Merkler's birth certificate. If it's a case of stolen identity, that's a crime. What if she's planning to blackmail you? We need to call our lawyer and get some advice. If there's fraud involved, we might be able to fast track the eviction."

"No!" Will blurts out. "There could be a perfectly legitimate reason why she has Patty's birth certificate. She might be a friend of hers."

I squeeze the cushion I'm holding in my lap, trying to contain my mounting frustration. He's still dancing around the issue, as though he has something else to hide. "So why is she making our lives miserable? It can't be a coincidence that she found us. If she and Patty are friends, maybe they blame you for letting Cooper drink so much that night. This could be some kind of twisted campaign of revenge Dana is waging on Patty's behalf." I pin a determined gaze on Will. "I don't care what you say. We need to pass this information on to the police. Dana's not up to any good, whatever her end game is."

Will leaps up and grips me by the shoulders. A shiver goes through me at the frenzied look in his eyes. "Do not call the police, do you hear me? I could lose my job with all these investigations and rumors swirling around me. The last thing I need is for the cops to drag up some old story from high school that's already been investigated. It's horrible that Cooper died, but it was no one's fault other than his own."

"So what are you suggesting — that we sit back and wait to see what Dana does next to destroy our lives?"

Will strokes his chin, a strange glint in his eyes. "Leave it to me. I'll handle her."

CHAPTER 32

Will refuses to discuss the situation any further. Despite his assertion that he'll handle Dana, I'm not sure there's much he can do — or wants to. My efforts to get rid of her have only worked in her favor, which is why I'm stuck here in the Airbnb for the foreseeable future.

It's late, and the kids are hungry, so we end up ordering pizza, which they chow down on with glee, oblivious to the strained atmosphere between us. It's a far cry from the mood we usually start the weekends on. Will and I pick apathetically at the pepperoni on our pizza. The thought of swallowing even the smallest bite turns my stomach. On top of my own woes, I'm worried about VV. I check my phone incessantly for a message from Julia. I don't want to keep bugging her. If there's good news, she'll let me know right away. In this case, no news is bad news.

My thoughts drift to Cooper Merkler. What happened to him was undeniably tragic — another regrettable under-age drinking statistic — but teenagers die all the time after getting drunk and doing stupid things. It doesn't make sense that, thirty years later, Cooper's sister would enlist Dana to punish Will for something that wasn't even his fault. The revenge angle doesn't add up. Is there some other reason

Dana targeted us? Or is there more to the story that Will's not telling me? After all his lies to date, I don't trust him. He practically broke out in a sweat when I suggested sharing our concerns about Dana having Patty Merkler's birth certificate with Kumar. If Cooper's death was ruled an accident, what is Will so afraid the police will uncover?

While he takes the kids upstairs to pack their overnight bags, I clear away the pizza boxes and paper plates. When I'm done tidying up the kitchen, I pull out my laptop and open up my browser. I do a few searches for drownings in the Claremont area in 2003, and it doesn't take me long to find an article that sounds a lot like the story Will told me.

ALCOHOL WAS A FACTOR IN
CLAREMONT TEEN'S DROWNING.

Police say the sixteen-year-old was camping at West Mountain Ranch with friends when he left his tent during the night and entered the river alone. Fire crews responded to the campsite around 9.30 a.m. Sunday after the teen's friends called 911.

I spend a few more minutes searching for additional information, but the articles all mirror one another, and none of them name the minor who drowned. When I hear the sound of Sam and Ella thudding down the stairs, I slam my laptop closed and put on the kettle to make hot chocolate. I don't want to let them go just yet. I may have been ejected from my home, but some weekend rituals can continue.

By the time they're halfway through their hot chocolate, Ella has fallen asleep in Will's lap and Sam's eyes are drooping.

"They're wiped out. I'll put them to bed here," Will says. "I'll pick them up in the morning instead."

While he takes the kids upstairs, I curl up on the couch and turn the TV on, hoping for an update on VV. After a few minutes, Will reappears and leans against the doorframe, listening in to the local news channel with me.

142

Police are searching for a kidnapped woman and they're asking for the public's help. Veronica Valdez is described as a Hispanic female in her mid-fifties, about 5'1" tall, and weighing approximately 160 pounds. An eyewitness reported seeing a woman being forced into a gray mini-van by an assailant in a ski mask shortly before 5 p.m. on Hertfordshire Avenue south of Baldwin Park. The suspected victim was walking to the bus stop after finishing work for the day when she was snatched. Officers have looked at residential surveillance video in the area, but it does not show the abduction. If you can help, call Crime Stoppers at 800-222-8477.

"The whole thing makes me sick to my stomach," I say, rubbing the gooseflesh on my arms. "What if they don't find her in time?"

Will stares at the TV, his face set like stone. "Then our lives are going to be turned upside down, in more ways than one." He reaches for his coat lying on the couch. "I should go. It's getting late."

"Don't go." I tug on his sleeve. "Stay here tonight, please. You can sleep in the guest room if you're still mad at me. I don't feel safe alone with the kids. This whole thing with VV has me freaked out. The West Coast Killer could be anywhere."

Will's expression softens. "Fine. Just for tonight. I'll fetch my bag from the car."

I can't deny I'm shocked when he takes his bag straight to the guest room. It only ramps up my paranoia about what he's doing behind my back. When I'm sure he's sound asleep, I creep back downstairs and retrieve the tracker from my purse.

Today will be the last time he lies to me about where he's going and who he's been with.

CHAPTER 33

Despite knowing the tracker is installed on Will's BMW and synced with my phone, I can't fall asleep when I crawl back into bed. The combination of my unfamiliar surroundings and the turmoil in my head works like a triple shot of caffeine. I while away the hours sifting through everything I've found out about my squatter to date, and trying to figure out what the connection between Dana Becker and Patty Merkler could be. My mind goes back to the very first time I met Dana in the park. My life became a rollercoaster after that not-so-chance encounter, beginning with the strange note I found in Mom's pocket, then her sudden death, my son's near drowning, getting kicked out of my house, criminal charges, and a host of other indignities. In the midst of my obsessive musing, I remember that VV has been abducted, and I'm struck with a fresh punch of guilt that I've been so caught up in my own dilemma that I've forgotten her desperate plight. I pray they find her before it's too late.

I wake from a troubled sleep the following morning to the high-pitched squeals of the twins as Will wrestles with them in bed — comforting sounds that herald the start of an ordinary weekend. Evidently, they've discovered him in the guest room. I get dressed quickly and head downstairs to start breakfast.

I'm rummaging around in the cabinets looking for a mixing bowl when Will strides into the kitchen. "No need for that. I'm taking the kids out for pancakes on our way back to the house."

I arch a defensive brow. "Was that an invitation?"

He tightens his lips. "You're welcome to come, but you'll have to drive yourself. I'm not coming back here afterward."

"First, you and I need to have a conversation. I'm not about to sit in some restaurant playing happy families and pretending nothing's wrong when I feel as if our marriage has been torpedoed."

Will folds his arms in front of him. "Then let's talk now. The twins are busy playing with the stuffed animals I picked up for them at the airport."

I reach for two mugs from the rack on the counter. "Coffee?"

He shakes his head. "No, thanks. I'll wait for breakfast."

I slip a pod into the Keurig and carry my mug over to the table, gesturing for him to join me. He slumps down in the chair opposite me like a chastised schoolboy. I study his expression as though he's a stranger. Every feature on his face is so familiar, but I don't trust what lurks beneath. The lies about his past have brought me to this in-between place of not knowing where I stand with him, or where he stands with Dana. At first, I was worried she was trying to seduce him, but maybe she's trying to destroy him. What if the note in my mother's pocket was intended for Will — a warning of sorts that Cooper Merkler's family is out for revenge? Maybe we're all targets, even the kids. I wrote the loose paver and the incident at the pool off as unhappy accidents, but what if they were anything but?

"I know you're mad at me for asking if you were having an affair with Dana," I begin, "but I have good reason. VV found something disturbing when she was changing the sheets on our bed." I pull up the offending photo on my phone and show it to him.

He glances at it, then gives a disgruntled shrug. "What's that?"

"What does it look like? Don't play dumb with me, Will. It's a black camisole and it's not mine."

His brows shoot halfway up his forehead. Is he faking surprise? Or does he honestly not know how it ended up in our bed?

"Any idea who it belongs to?" I ask, pocketing my phone.

"How would I know?" He stares at me, a series of emotions flashing in his eyes like carriages behind a train: shock, horror, panic, guilt. I can't get a read on what's going on inside his head, and I can't be sure of anything that comes out of his mouth.

"If you'd installed those cameras in our house like you promised, we wouldn't be having this argument. I'm beginning to think it was a deliberate omission on your part." I glare at him. "Either our squatter planted that underwear in our bed, or she was there by invitation."

His expression darkens. "Or maybe you and VV dreamt this up between you to get back at Dana for slapping you with a restraining order."

I huff out an indignant breath. "Don't be ridiculous! VV would never do something like that."

Will narrows his eyes at me. "We both know that's not true. She can't stand Dana. And she would lie through her teeth for you. You've been waging a petty campaign of revenge against Dana ever since she refused to move out — turning off the AC and what not behind my back."

My cheeks flush with indignation. "I didn't plant the camisole. Is that your best defense when you're caught? I can't trust you, Will. You've been lying to me, hiding things. And why are you so afraid to talk to the police? You say you're worried about them bringing up an accident from thirty years ago. Why does it matter? You weren't responsible."

"That's irrelevant. These kinds of things can jeopardize a career if they get out. People talk. Neighbors talk — which is why I've told you before not to go gabbing about everything to Andrea. You think people are on your side, but that's only true until there's something to be gained by betraying you — like selling a story to the media."

I press my hands to the side of my head. "You're not making any sense. We're not the criminals here. Andrea's no fonder of Dana than I am — she's not going to turn on us. You obviously have some connection with our squatter, past or present — maybe both. As your wife, I have every right to ask if there's something going on between you."

Will stands abruptly, his chair screeching across the floor. "I said I'd handle Dana, and I will." He pulls out his car keys and calls down the hallway. "Are there any hungry little people here who like pancakes?"

Delighted shrieks accompany the pitter-patter of tiny feet racing to be the first to the front door. Will turns to me. "Are you coming?"

His words hit me like an icy front. I pretend to consider the grudging invitation for a moment, then shake my head. "No. Go ahead. I have some things I need to take care of. I'll see you tomorrow."

He gives a curt nod. "I'll bring the kids back around five. I need to get some work done tomorrow night. I have an important client presentation in New York on Monday."

I kiss the twins goodbye, then sit back down at the table to finish my coffee, an uneasy feeling in my gut. Something is going on. Will never misses an opportunity to spend every last minute of every weekend with the kids. Is he planning to meet up with Dana? I pick up my phone and dial Andrea. I'll enlist her services for a Sunday night surveillance mission.

CHAPTER 34

I throw in a load of laundry, then check my phone again for any messages from Julia. I'll give her another hour or so before calling. I'm desperate to know what's happening in the search for VV. I take a quick shower, then turn on the local news, but they're only repeating the same information from last night and asking for the public's help again. The newscaster gives a vague description of the gray van that was spotted, as recent photos of both VV and Robert Rattler flash across the screen. I swallow the lump in my throat as I study the closeup of VV's abductor. He looks like the kind of brute who's chiseled his conscience away to nothing — ugly inside and out, with a serpent-like facial scar and a gold-capped front tooth. Not to mention the fact that he's built like a refrigerator. At six foot two, he's over a foot taller than VV. She wouldn't stand a chance against him. And he doesn't look the type to show his victims any mercy.

When I can't take it any longer, I reach for my phone. "Hey, Julia. Did you get any sleep last night?"

"Not much. I kept waking up with a start, thinking it was all a bad dream, then remembering it really happened. It's the worst feeling in the world."

"I can only imagine. I feel sick every time I think about your mom. I just turned on the news. They don't have anything new to report. Do the police have any leads on Rattler's whereabouts?"

"Not yet. They're confident they're going to get him now that they've identified him, but that doesn't help Mom. They may not reach her in time."

"At least they know he's driving a gray van. There's only so long he can hide from such an extensive manhunt."

Julia sighs. "I don't know if I totally trust what the kid said. The way he described it, there would have to have been two people involved in the abduction. He said someone shoved Mom into the back of the van and climbed in after her, and then the van took off right away. That makes no sense. All the DNA evidence indicates Rattler works alone. Some profiler with specialist training flew in today to talk to the kid to try to figure out if he's telling the truth or making stuff up."

I grip the phone tighter in my fist. "Are you saying there's a chance she hasn't been abducted?"

"A slim one. It's probably just wishful thinking on my part. Where else could she be?"

"I don't know, but we need to hold on to hope. I hear a lot of voices in the background. I'd better let you go, but I'm here if you need me."

"Thanks, Morgan. I'll let you know the minute I hear anything."

I hang up and dial Andrea's number next.

"I was just about to call you," she says. "I saw Will pull up a little while ago with the kids. Do you want to go into town and do some shopping or something? I hate the thought of you hanging out at the Airbnb all weekend by yourself."

"That's sweet of you, but I think I'll sit tight. I want to do some more digging around online and see what else I can find out about our squatter."

"That reminds me, Officer Kumar stopped by to ask if I'd seen you at the house on Friday — the day of your covert cleaning operation. I said I hadn't, but that I'd spoken to VV."

"You're a lifesaver. I can't thank you enough for having my back through all of this."

Andrea tinkles a laugh. "That's what good neighbors are for. Did you find out anything?"

"Not what I expected. It turns out Dana might have some connection to Will from the past." I fill Andrea in on the birth certificate and the high school graduation photo, and Will's account of Cooper Merkler's demise.

She lets out a soft whistle. "Weird he never told you that story about his friend drowning before."

"He says it was too traumatizing. He doesn't like talking about it."

"Hmm . . . I can understand why he doesn't want to talk about it with other people, but not even with his own wife?"

I cringe at her words. Will's secretive nature is extreme, but I've been making excuses for him for so long. "You know how he is — he keeps his cards close to his chest. I wish he wasn't so paranoid. I'm sure it's not healthy for the kids, but that's just how he is."

"Speaking of secrets," Andrea says, "he went down to the studio Friday afternoon when he got back into town. Did you know that?"

I bristle at the revelation. Not an outright lie, but the truth is always diluted. "Are you sure? He told me he only spoke to Dana briefly in passing."

I detect a slight hesitation before Andrea responds. "That's not what I saw. He knocked on the studio door, and she let him in. They were together for at least thirty minutes. I left to go to the store after that, so it could have been longer. I don't know what time he arrived at the Airbnb to pick up the kids."

"Five-thirty. He lied about where he was yesterday afternoon until the police pressed him on it."

"I'm sorry, Morgan. It might have been completely innocent. Maybe he went down there to fix something. You know how Dana is, always complaining about one thing or another, wanting something installed or replaced. I'm sure it's nothing to worry about."

I squeeze my eyes shut. "Except that VV found some black underwear in our bed when she was cleaning the other day."

"What?" Andrea gasps. "Did you confront Will about it?"

"He denies knowing anything about it. I suppose he could be telling the truth. Dana might have planted it just to stir things up. She never misses an opportunity to cause friction."

After a lengthy pause, Andrea asks, "What does your heart tell you?"

"It tells me what I want it to tell me, so it's not a good gauge. I need facts. I put a tracker on Will's car last night, so he won't be able to lie to me any more about where he is. At the risk of becoming a bit of a pain, I have another favor to ask."

"Of course, anything. I'm here for you. You know that."

"Will wants to drop the kids back at five tomorrow. He says he needs to work on a presentation — which I suspect is totally bogus. I was going to ask if you'd be available to watch Sam and Ella here at the Airbnb. He's up to something. He says he's going to handle Dana. I need to find out what that means."

CHAPTER 35

Will

Much as I adore spending time with the twins, my mind is distracted this weekend. I haven't been able to drum up enough enthusiasm to play catch with them in the backyard like they wanted to, so I've stuck them in front of the TV to compensate — something I rarely do. I'm sick to my stomach about what's happened to VV. I can't even talk freely about it to Morgan because it will freak her out, but the odds are that VV's dead already.

Rattler's standard operating practice is to kill his victims and dump them within twenty-four hours of abducting them. It could be days before someone discovers her body. He usually leaves them in some location where he knows they'll be found, but not right away — at the side of a hiking trail, or near a river, or in some off-the-beaten-path RV park. Some unsuspecting hiker or fisherman — occasionally a camper — stumbles across the jarring sight of a woman's decomposing body and alerts the authorities.

I massage my throbbing temples as I turn my attention to the more immediate problem of what to do about Dana. I was floored when Morgan told me she had found Patty

152

Merkler's birth certificate in the studio — but not for the reasons Morgan thinks. It changes everything. All this time, I blamed her for inviting Dana into our home and putting us in the unenviable position of having to evict her. Now, I realize Dana targeted Morgan as an entry point — but it was me she was aiming for. Something about her always made me feel uncomfortable. At times, I thought she was trying to seduce me. At other times, I'd catch her looking at me like she wanted nothing more than to drive a stake through my heart. I know now those are the occasions when the mask slipped. I'm very familiar with masks.

Some sleepless nights, I can still hear Cooper's strangled sixteen-year-old cries as we wove donuts around him, tires catapulting dirt and pebbles into his face. I had laughed like a lunatic, floored the gas pedal, and sped off in a cloud of dust, leaving an inebriated Cooper doubled over at the side of the logging road, a deserted silhouette in the setting sun, never to be seen alive again.

Tommy had thought it was hilarious. "Did you . . . see . . . the look on his face?" he choked out, jubilantly slapping the cracked dashboard on the passenger side of the Toyota Tundra as we clanked our way deeper into the forest.

A ripple of pleasure had coursed through my veins at the raw, panicked plea in Cooper's eyes. It made me feel powerful, but not as powerful as watching someone die.

Jay was the only one who had reservations that night. He was in the back seat, swigging from a bottle of tequila as we fishtailed around the hairpin bends on the winding road that led to the river. He couldn't believe I was going to make Coop walk the rest of the way to our camp. I sneered at him and made some lame joke about Coop needing a chance to sober up.

I could have gone back and picked him up, but I was sick of him tagging along, bumming cigarettes off us, thinking we were buddies. I thought that would be the end of it. I never dreamt he would morph into a nightmare that would haunt me all these years later.

I told Morgan I would handle this, and I will. I texted Dana earlier today and arranged to meet with her at the park under the guise of offering her money to drop the assault charge she's pursuing against Morgan. I suggested meeting at five-thirty, but she texted back that she can't be there until eight. Maybe it's better this way. By then, the park will be emptying out — fewer people around to overhear our conversation. I can't talk to her at the house with that hawk-eyed Andrea next door — she reports everything back to Morgan. I caught her watching me from her kitchen window on Friday when I risked going down to the studio to try to talk Dana into dropping the charge. I suspect Andrea dislikes me because I keep turning down her dinner invitations. I'm not interested in becoming buddies with Tom, and I don't like Morgan socializing with Andrea either — neighbors are in your business before you know it.

"Daddy, I'm hungry," Ella calls out, running into the office where I'm parked in front of my laptop, staring mindlessly at the blank screen.

Sam comes tearing in after her, clutching a plastic truck in his hand. "Can me and Ella have a snack?"

"No, kids. It's time to go." I get to my feet. "Pack up your things. You're going to eat dinner with Mommy tonight. Daddy has work to do."

"Not fair! Can we stay with Dana?" Ella asks.

"Not tonight, sweetie."

Ella blinks up at me. "Is she going to be our new mommy?"

"What? No! Of course not! Why would you think that?"

"Because Mommy doesn't live here anymore."

I hunker down to her level and place my hands on her shoulders. "Your mom does live here. She's just staying at the Airbnb for a couple of weeks until Dana leaves."

Sam stomps his foot. "I don't want to go there no more. I don't like that house. It doesn't have swings or any fun stuff to do."

"I know, son. But it won't be for much longer." I ruffle his hair, wondering if I'm fooling myself. If things start to unravel, my marriage will be the first casualty. Morgan doesn't trust me anymore, and for good reason. I've been lying to her — cutting and pasting my past into an acceptable scrapbook of memories. It would devastate her to know the truth. I can live with what I've done, but she wouldn't be able to. Tommy Hodgson couldn't either. He drank himself to death. How fitting that he drowned in his pool. I wouldn't be surprised if a guilty conscience brought on Jay's cancer, too. After they passed away, I thought I was the only one left who really knew what happened that night.

Now, I'm not so sure.

CHAPTER 36

Morgan

The minute Will takes off after dropping the twins back, I text Andrea, who's parked out of sight around the corner.

"Mommy has to run a couple of errands," I tell the kids. "If you're good, I'll pick up some candy at the store for you. You can watch a movie with Andrea while I'm gone."

"Yay!" Sam jumps up and down on the spot. "Can we have popcorn too?"

"Absolutely. I'll make sure to tell Andrea you're allowed an extra big bowl tonight for being good while Mommy's gone."

I curve my lips into a smile that's at odds with the apprehension swirling around in my gut. What if I'm wrong, and all Will is doing is working on his presentation? But then I remember all his other lies. What if I'm right and he's got something going on with Dana — something unresolved from the past, or the present, or both? I'm not sure I want to find out what it is, but the uncertainty is killing me.

"Thanks for loaning me your car," I say to Andrea on my way out the door. "The kids' car seats are in my Suburban, just in case there's an emergency and you need to go somewhere. I'll try and be as quick as I can."

She waves me off. "Take your time. Tom's not expecting me back any time soon."

I plug in the seatbelt in Andrea's Hyundai and check the tracker app on my phone. So far, so good. Will appears to be heading home, just like he said. Next, I check the studio cameras. Dana's car is gone from its usual spot. A flurry of relief goes through me. I might be worrying unnecessarily about our squatter seducing my husband.

On the way to my house, I take a quick detour through a drive-through coffee shop and order a large latte with an extra shot. Probably not the best idea, given the fact that I'll need the bathroom before too long. I should have done some online research on how to properly surveil someone. This is my first attempt, so I haven't thought things through, and I'm ill-prepared. I haven't eaten dinner and the only snacks I've brought with me are some gum and a small packet of trail mix sprinkled with M&Ms. Hopefully, the sugar will keep me awake. At least I had the good sense to bring a baseball cap to hide my face, and I'm dressed in black workout gear — which more or less guarantees me anonymity. It helps that I'm driving Andrea's car, which makes me less conspicuous.

As I drive in the direction of home, I track Will's arrival on my phone. A short time later, I crawl slowly past our house and glance down the driveway to the studio. Dana's car is still gone. She might be staying at her friend's house again. I park at the end of the street behind a camper van, turn off the engine, and settle in to wait. As the minutes tick by, my optimism increases that Will isn't up to anything nefarious, after all. The tracker hasn't moved, and Dana hasn't returned. How long should I give this before I call it a night? An hour? Two?

By seven-thirty I'm starting to feel foolish and in dire need of the bathroom. After hemming and hawing, I drive to a nearby park to use the public restrooms. I'll know if Will leaves the house, but I might miss Dana returning. It's frustrating, but a risk I'll have to take. I check my phone again after I come out of the restroom, relieved to see that Will's car hasn't moved. I climb back into the Hyundai and switch on the engine just as a familiar blue Honda Civic pulls into the entrance at the other end of the parking lot. My eyes bulge. Dana! What are the odds?

Shrinking down in my seat, I pull down my visor, even though I know she can't possibly see me from that far away. My heart thuds as I turn off the ignition again. What is she doing here so late in the day? It's not the best time for a woman to go walking alone, with the light already beginning to fade. I wait for what seems like forever, but she doesn't get out of her car. She must be on her phone.

A steady trickle of worn-out kids and spent parents are loading up in their cars, abandoning the park to the evening dog walkers and hardcore joggers. There are enough other vehicles dotted around the parking lot to make me inconspicuous, but I'm not sure how long that will last. I'm debating whether or not to call it a night when the tracker app on my phone sends me an alert that Will is on the move. A strange needling sensation creeps steadily over my skin as I watch his car travel across the screen in the direction of the park. Moments later, his black BMW enters the far end of the parking lot and wheels into the spot next to Dana's.

I suck in a sharp breath, my throat strangely dry. My instincts were right, after all. Why else would they be meeting in the shadows, behind my back? It's the ultimate betrayal. Will lied to me — *again*. I was hoping we might have been on the same page when it came to our litigation-happy squatter. Apparently, I've been duped.

Somehow, I need to make my way over there undetected. It's not as if I'll be able to hear what they're saying, but at least I'll know if this is a romantic tryst, or something else. I curl my hands into fists. Part of me wants to brazenly march over there and confront them. I'm about to do just that when I notice them exiting their cars. They walk briskly toward one of the paths that winds through the park. My heart begins to pound. I can't lose them now. I hurriedly stick my headphones in, then clamber out and lock the car.

Dressed in black jogging gear, with my cap pulled down, they won't recognize me at a distance. If I'm careful, I might be able to get close. I jog over to the path they disappeared down and trail them, making sure to stay behind a young couple walking a large golden retriever. I try to quell the panic threatening to assail me, and focus instead on the task at hand by pretending it's two strangers I'm surveilling, and not my husband and our squatter.

Anything to distance myself from the truth about to unfold.

CHAPTER 37

As I walk, I keep my head down, pretending to be listening to music, only occasionally glancing in front of me to make sure Will and Dana are still in sight. The couple with the dog suddenly veer off into an open area of the park. I drop back a few paces, but Will and Dana have already turned a corner and disappeared from view. After a minute or two, I proceed along the pathway. It's not long before I catch sight of them again, sitting on a bench on the other side of the hedge that separates the path from a sloping, grassy bank leading down to a duck pond. They have their backs to me, and they're deep in conversation. I hesitate, debating what to do. They'll hear the crunch of my footsteps approaching, and they'll know if I suddenly stop. But it's the perfect opportunity to try and overhear what they're saying from behind the cover of the hedge. I glance over my shoulder at two men jogging along the path in my direction. This could be my chance to get closer, undetected. I wait until the joggers pass me, then fall in behind them, matching their stride. As soon as I'm level with the bench where Will and Dana are sitting, I drop to my haunches behind the hedge. I squeeze my eyes shut and hold my breath for a moment to make sure I've pulled it off. Silently, I untie a shoelace. If anyone comes by, I'll pretend to be retying it.

The evening air is still, and Will's voice carries clearly over to me. "I'll make it worth your while financially."

Gingerly, I push back the foliage and peer through the hedge. Will and Dana are sitting at either end of the bench, staring straight ahead like they're undercover agents exchanging information in a spy movie. I can't help but feel some measure of relief that their clandestine meeting appears to be strictly business. But I'm also shocked to discover that Will's idea of handling Dana is to buy her off — no wonder he didn't want to involve me. I'm pretty sure that's illegal. Maybe he was afraid the police would get wind of it.

"I'm not dropping the charges," Dana says. "Morgan deserves everything she has coming to her. She's out of control. She violated the restraining order and broke into the studio again. Did she tell you that?"

"I didn't come here to discuss my wife. What do you want, Dana?" Will's voice drops to a menacing growl. "If that's even your name. How do you know Patty Merkler?"

Dana's head swivels in Will's direction. "Morgan found the birth certificate, didn't she?"

Will stuffs his hands into his pockets. "If you're living in our home under an assumed identity, I have the right to know. Or is Patty Merkler a friend of yours?"

Dana snorts. "Patty's an addict. I think we both know why she went down that path. I found her online. I told her I'd tracked down her brother's killer, thinking she might want to know where you were so she could finally get justice for Cooper, but she was too far gone. All she cares about is her next high. She could be dead in a gutter by now, for all I know."

Will rubs a hand behind his neck. "I don't know what she told you, but what happened to Cooper was a tragic accident."

Dana slides closer to him on the bench. "It wasn't an accident. I know what you did. I know everything."

"We didn't mean for anything to happen to Coop. He wandered out of his tent and fell into the river. No one heard him. We were out cold."

161

Dana curls her lip in disgust. "Except that's not really how it went down, is it?"

Will jerks his head toward her. "What do you mean?"

"Don't play games with me. Like I told you, I know everything."

"You can't believe anything Patty says. She doesn't know—"

"Forget Patty! Patty can't remember what happened yesterday, let alone thirty years ago. But there were others who knew the truth about what went down that night."

Will rubs his brow in an agitated fashion. "The other guys I was camping with are dead too. Jay Taft passed away from cancer recently, and Tommy Hodgson drank himself to death."

My left leg is almost numb, so I cautiously shift position, taking care not to disturb the foliage.

"It's true Tommy was a raging alcoholic," Dana goes on, "but the exact cause of his death was drowning. Appropriate, don't you think? I didn't find him very remorseful when I caught up with him, but I guess he had a guilty conscience after all. He drowned himself in his pool later that night."

"You . . . you met with Tommy? How did you know him?" Will asks.

"I didn't. I tracked him down and introduced myself."

My blood chills. Something about her tone tells me it wasn't a cordial introduction. Could Dana have had something to do with Tommy's accidental drowning? The ball of fear in my throat is almost choking me. Is she on a mission to avenge what they did to Cooper on Patty's behalf? *I know where you live.* Is Will next?

"What did you want with Tommy?" Will asks.

Dana lets out a mirthless laugh. "I take it Jay didn't tell you?"

"Tell me what? You're talking in riddles."

"He reached out to me on his deathbed."

There's a beat of silence before Will speaks again. "Why?"

Dana stares off into the distance. "He wanted to come clean about everything. He told me the real story about what went down that night. Not the version you all agreed to swear to the next day. He gave me a signed confession."

"I . . . I don't know what you're talking about."

"How about the fact that you left Cooper Merkler on the side of a logging road near the river in the dead of night, drunk out of his face? And then you drove off. You were the driver, Will — the ringleader."

He groans and leans forward, elbows on knees, his head dropping into his hands. After a few minutes he straightens up. "Look, I'm not proud of it, but I never meant for anything to happen to Coop. That was a long time ago. I can't undo it, and I've made my peace with it. Why do you care so much about Cooper Merkler, anyway?"

Dana slides right up next to him on the bench. "I don't. I care about the other man you murdered that night."

CHAPTER 38

"I don't know what you're talking about," Will growls.

"I think you do. Jay Taft gave me a written confession. Shame Morgan didn't find it in the studio when she was going through my stuff. It would have been most enlightening for her to learn that you've been living a lie all these years. Your wife deserves to know the truth about what a lowlife, murdering scumbag you are. It was all your idea that night, wasn't it? Jay said he tried to talk you out of it, but you weren't having any part of it. You thought you'd have a little fun on your way to the campsite — playing Russian roulette with other people's lives."

"You can't trust what Jay told you," Will says. "People always spout nonsense when they're dying. He was probably drugged up on morphine."

"How would you know if he was of sound mind or not? You cut off contact with him after high school. He told me he tried to reach out to you several times. He wanted to go to the police and confess. But you flat out refused. You insisted on burying the truth about what a sick, twisted monster you are — getting off on other people's fear. You destroyed two families that night. And here you are now, living your best life, driving your fancy BMW, with your bubbly little wife

164

and your two perfect kids, instead of rotting in a prison cell like you deserve. Well, that's about to change."

A jogger goes by and there's a momentary lull in the conversation. I busy myself with my shoelace, still peering through the hedge. Will glances over his shoulder to make sure the jogger has disappeared before turning back to glare at Dana. "Who do you think you are — some kind of vigilante for justice?"

"In a manner of speaking."

"I'm done with your games. What do you want? Are you trying to blackmail me? Is that why you tried to seduce me?"

Dana lets out a grating laugh. "Don't flatter yourself. I wanted you, all right — but not in the way you thought. I wanted access to your life so I could destroy everything you had. Let's just say I'm an interested party and I'm about to become your worst nightmare. The time has come to pay the piper."

Will's shoulders stiffen. I can almost feel the animal instinct mustering in him before he springs. Shock reverberates through me as he lunges toward Dana and locks his hands around her throat.

I clap a hand to my mouth, but not in time to trap the muffled choking sound that escapes me.

Will's head swivels in the direction of the hedge, his eyes roving left and right, searching for the source. I freeze in place, wishing I could melt into the shrubbery. My heart thunders in my ears. Seizing on the distraction, Dana breaks free from Will's grasp and takes off running down the grassy embankment. Will lets out a growl of rage and flies off in pursuit. I jump to my feet, bolt into the darkness, and sprint back to the parking lot. I'm completely winded by the time I reach Andrea's car, but I don't take a second to catch my breath. I scramble inside and speed out of the park, almost colliding with a dog walker in reflective gear. He raises a fist at me, the angry scowl on his face only making me tremble more violently.

I step on the gas, desperate to get back to my children. I can't believe what I've just witnessed. I didn't think Will had a violent bone in his body. I suddenly feel like my husband is a stranger. My heartbeat is becoming more erratic by the minute, and I'm increasingly disoriented. I lost my baseball cap in my frantic sprint back to the car, and my hair is falling over my face, partially obscuring my view. Instead of slowing down, I throw caution to the wind and accelerate.

My mind sifts back through the conversation I over-heard. I can't imagine what horrendous thing Will has done that could be any worse than leaving a drunk friend alone in the dead of night. He lied to the police about what really happened, and he got away with it. But where does Dana fit into the picture? Everything is flashing before my eyes as I drive: the sadistic sneer on her lips, the rage in Will's voice, the myriad headlights coming at me from oncoming vehicles, the disconcerting sequence of traffic lights, and then the jar-ring explosion of sound as metal collides with metal, and my airbag erupts.

* * *

I wake up in the hospital to the murmuring of a nurse repeat-ing my name. "Morgan, *Morgan*, can you hear me?"

I blink, as she slowly comes into focus. I give a small nod, wincing at the pain in my neck. "What . . . what happened?"

"You had a car accident."

I look up at the ceiling, straining to recall the details. "I remember driving somewhere, but I don't recall what happened."

The nurse rubs my arm gently. "You were very lucky. No concussion or broken bones. Just some whiplash and bruising. We're keeping you in overnight for observation, just to be sure. I put your phone on the bedside cabinet. We're still trying to get ahold of your husband, but there is someone here who would like a word with you, now that you're awake."

I stare at her in horror, my skin prickling when it all comes back to me like a dagger to the heart. *Will killed a man* — two, if you count Cooper Merkler.

CHAPTER 39

My head feels like it's exploding. Bits and pieces of the conversation I overheard between Will and Dana flit back to mind. *Jay wanted to come clean about everything. I know what you did. I know everything.* According to Dana, Will is a murderer — responsible for the deaths of two men. Does that make him a serial killer? My skin crawls at the thought. Will is nothing like Robert Rattler. There has to be an explanation. He may have left Cooper alone that fateful night, but he didn't mean for him to die. Whatever other death Dana is alluding to, it must be in the same vein — some kind of unwitting mishap. Kids do stupid things when they're drinking.

And yet, there's a nagging disquiet in my gut. I'm still in a state of shock after watching Will grab Dana by the throat — lunging at her like an enraged animal.

It's not the man I know and love. But do I really know him at all? I've always put his secretive ways down to his introverted nature — have I been played for a fool?

An unwelcome voice startles me out of my reverie. "Hello, Morgan. How are you feeling?"

My breathing slows when Kumar strolls into the room and sits down next to my bed. I wilt inside at the thought of conversing with her. I can't face her right now — not when

I'm still trying to process witnessing my husband commit a crime and hearing him accused of others. My pulse drums in my ears, doubling in pace with every second that ticks by. I'm half hoping I'll set off the machine I'm hooked up to, and the nurse will come running back in and spare me from being interrogated by Kumar. Why is she here anyway? Has Will been arrested? Did Dana report him to the police? This won't help the case against me. My stomach knots with a new fear. If Will and I both end up in prison, what will happen to our children? I still don't know who Dana is, and why she's doing this to us. She must have some connection to the other man she accused Will of killing. Is her endgame blackmail, or does she want Will behind bars?

Kumar coughs politely, prompting me to respond.

"Sorry, Detective. My mind's all over the place. I'm fine, thanks — a bit shook up, but I came out of it relatively unscathed."

"Glad to hear that. I was trying to reach you to follow up on the assault charge when I found out you'd been in an accident."

My eyes spring wide. "My kids! I need to text Andrea and let her know. She's with the twins at the Airbnb. She'll be wondering why I'm not back by now."

Kumar reaches for her radio. "I'll send an officer to inform her."

I wait until she's finished rattling off instructions, before posing the question that's worrying me most. "Was anyone else hurt in the accident?"

"Thankfully, no. The driver of the other vehicle walked away. He claims you swerved right into his path."

I squeeze my eyes shut. "It was my fault. I was distracted."

Kumar cocks her head to one side. "Any particular reason why?"

My eyes slide away from her penetrating gaze. "I have a lot on my mind right now. The situation with our squatter is stressful. And I'm worried sick about VV."

"Where were you coming from when the accident happened?"

"I went for a jog at the park to clear my head. Andrea offered to stay with the kids to give me a break."

Kumar frowns. "Didn't your husband have the kids all weekend?"

My cheeks redden. "Yes, but he needed to get some work done tonight."

"Strange time to go jogging — alone, in the dark." Kumar studies me appraisingly, her gaze like acid, dissolving my lies. "I want to caution you, Morgan. Whatever you do, don't violate the restraining order. You're on thin ice as it is. The worst thing you can do is try to take matters into your own hands. Is there anything you want to tell me?"

I give an awkward shrug. "There's nothing to tell."

She slaps her thighs and gets to her feet. "Okay, I'll let you get some rest. We can go over your statement pertaining to the assault once you're discharged."

"Wait! What happened to the car I was driving? It's my neighbor's. I need to let her know."

"It was towed to a body shop. I'll text you the address."

I mumble my thanks. "Are there any updates on VV?"

Kumar's expression remains neutral. "We're pursuing several reported sightings. So far, they haven't amounted to anything." She walks over to the door, then turns back to me. "Take my advice and don't go jogging at night again. There's a killer at large. You can't be too careful."

CHAPTER 40

When Kumar leaves, I sink back on my pillows, the adrenaline leaking from my body. I lie beneath the sheets, shivering like a wet dishrag. *Is there anything you want to tell me?* Why didn't I just come clean with her when I had the chance? Now I'm a party to multiple crimes — accessory to murder, for all I know — in addition to the mess I've already got myself into. Not to mention the fact that my husband is a dangerous man. I should alert the police before someone else gets hurt. Surely he wouldn't lay a hand on me or the kids, would he?

My phone buzzes and Andrea's name flashes across the screen. "I'm so sorry about your car!" I blurt out.

"Forget the car. It can be fixed. More importantly, are you okay?"

"Mainly just bruised and a bit shook up. They're keeping me here tonight for observation."

"Don't worry about the twins. They're fast asleep in bed. I can stay here with them tonight. Let me know if you need me to pick you up from the hospital tomorrow."

I sigh with relief. "That would be great. Will's flying to New York early in the morning, and the hospital hasn't been able to get ahold of him. I really don't know what I'd do without you. What will you tell Tom?"

"I just got off the phone with him. I said you ran out to pick up some pizza and had a fender bender. He's not concerned about the car. He just wanted to know that you were okay. Did you find out anything?"

A shadow fills the doorway. I glance over to see Will standing there clutching a bunch of flowers. Blistering fear prickles over my skin. "I've . . . got to go, Andrea. I'll call you when I'm discharged."

* * *

Will walks over to the bed and kisses me before sitting down in the chair next to me. He sets the flowers aside and takes my hand in his. "What happened, babe?"

I swallow the jagged lump in my throat. Inhaling slowly in and out, I remind myself that he doesn't know I overheard his conversation with Dana. My heart pitter patters beneath the sheet. Am I holding hands with a murderer? I wet my lips and repeat the lie I fed Kumar. "I was distracted, worrying about Dana. Next thing I know I'd swerved into oncoming traffic. I'm just thankful no one was seriously injured. I feel terrible about Andrea's car."

Will frowns. "Why were you driving her car?"

I shrug. "I went out to pick up pizza. She was parked at the curb, so it was easier to take her Hyundai."

"You never mentioned Andrea was coming over when I dropped the kids off." His eyes pierce me with a scrutiny I've never felt from him before.

I flap my hand dismissively. "It was a last-minute thing. She's offered to stay with the kids tonight, too. The nurse said they've been trying to reach you. Why didn't you pick up?"

Will's face closes over. "I had my phone on silent. I told you I was working on my presentation."

I chew on the inside of my cheek, disturbed at how easily the lies flow from his lips. We're good at lying to each other, but my lies are hardly consequential in comparison

171

to what I'm finding out about Will. "Did you go anywhere this evening?"

He narrows his eyes. "Why do you ask?"

"No reason. You must have gone out to get something to eat at some point. There's no food in the house."

"Late lunch. I wasn't hungry." He folds his arms in front of him. "Any news about VV?"

"Kumar left a few minutes before you arrived. She says there were a couple of reports of sightings, but they didn't pan out."

"You need to be careful with that serial killer on the loose," Will warns, reaching inside his jacket. "You never know who might be following you."

The breath leaves my lungs when he sets my black baseball cap on the table next to me.

CHAPTER 41

"How much of my conversation with Dana did you hear?" Will asks, tenting his fingers and tapping them together. I count the beat inside my head, trying to keep myself from screaming. I fight to keep my expression neutral, but it feels as if my eyeballs are bulging, betraying the fear gripping me. I'm scared of my own husband — maybe I always have been. I can't let him see. "I don't know what you're talking about."

Will sighs, his gaze sweeping around the small room.

I throw a quick glance at the door, trying to summon my courage by reminding myself that I'm safe here. There are people walking up and down the hospital corridor. It's not as if he could put a pillow over me and smother me without anyone noticing. I can't believe I'm even having these thoughts, but my mind is splintering under the weight of everything that's happened.

"Someone was on the other side of the hedge, listening to us." Will's delivery is slow and deliberate, almost reflecting to himself. He picks up my baseball cap and runs the tip of his finger around the rim. A shiver shoots down my spine. He's always so methodical and in control of his emotions. Is this really the man I saw throttling Dana? Would he have killed her if I hadn't disturbed him?

"I discovered the tracker on my car. I know it was you at the park, Morgan. I saw a figure running away, and I found the black cap you bought at Big Bear last year."

My fingers curl around the bedsheet, squishing it in my fist like a stress reliever. "You said you would handle Dana. You were about to strangle her," I whisper. "Are you crazy? You could go to prison for attempted murder. I can't believe she hasn't had you arrested already."

"Give me a break, Morgan. I wasn't squeezing her neck. I was only trying to scare her."

"Well you did a good job of that, although I doubt it's the last we'll see of her. Is it true what Dana said — that you deliberately left Cooper stranded that night?"

Will drops his gaze and pinches the bridge of his nose. He remains still as a statue for a moment or two before looking up at me. "None of us wanted that kid to come camping with us to begin with, but he insisted on tagging along. We thought it would be funny to make him walk the rest of the way. Don't you think I regret it every day of my life?"

I shake my head. "No, I don't. If you did, you would have owned up to what you did a long time ago. I think you regret Jay Taft's deathbed confession that exposed your lies. Who was the other man you killed that night?"

The crease between his brows deepens. "Some guy crashed his car and died earlier that evening. I don't know why Dana thinks I was responsible. I didn't even know him."

I curl my lip in disgust. "You must know something. There has to be a reason she blames you for his death. Were you racing him? Was it some kind of road rage incident? Who is Dana Becker anyway?"

"I don't know!" Will thunders, jumping to his feet and striding over to the door. "You know as much as I do. I've had my fill of this inquisition."

"You'd better find out what she wants before the police come knocking!" I yell after him. "You can bet she'll be filing assault charges against you. I'm sure she has the bruises to prove it."

"I've already told you I'd handle her, and I will." He stomps out of the room without as much as a goodbye.

I press my hands to my cheeks, trembling all over. If assaulting Dana is his idea of handling things, I need to put a stop to this insanity before it goes any further. Will is a danger to himself as well as others. I should call Kumar and tell her what I witnessed, but there's a lot at stake. Will could go to jail. He might never speak to me again. His kids might never see him again. But if I keep silent, I dread to think what he might do to Dana — if he hasn't already. I want her out of the studio more than anything. But I don't want her to get hurt at his hands. I wish I knew what her agenda was. She said she's an *interested party*, but she has no relationship to Cooper Merkler, other than trying to get his sister on board her campaign for revenge. Her connection must be with the other man who died that night. I need to find out who he was.

I close my eyes, suddenly overcome by weariness. I'll work on it tomorrow. Will is off to New York in the early hours — provided he's not arrested — which will give me time to figure things out.

* * *

The following morning, Andrea arrives at the hospital to drive me home. The twins hover around my bed, wide-eyed, as I gather up my things.

"Any news on VV?" I mutter discreetly to Andrea.

She shakes her head. "Nothing."

"Did you sleep here last night, Mommy?" Ella asks.

"Yes, sweetie. I had a sore head, but I'm all better now."

She slips her small hand into mine. "We can get some ice cream on the way home to make you feel better."

"Please, Mommy," Sam adds, pulling on my sleeve.

I chuckle. "Maybe later. We need to drop Andrea home first."

"Are you sure you're going to be all right by yourself?" she asks, her brow wrinkling in concern when we pull up at the end of our street. I offered to take her all the way to her house, but she doesn't want Dana spotting my Suburban and reporting me. I'm tempted to tell Andrea what happened last night, but how do I tell her she's living next door to a murderer?

"I'll be fine," I reassure her. "Thanks for everything. And I'm so sorry again about your car."

"Tom has already sorted out a rental for me. By the way, I left the fridge at the Airbnb stocked, so try and take it easy this week. Call me when you get a chance to talk."

She climbs out and waves before walking off down the street. I wait to make sure she reaches her driveway safely. Will may be out of town, but as long as Rattler's still out there, none of us are safe.

CHAPTER 42

True to her word, Andrea has filled every shelf in the refrigerator with staples — fresh fruit and vegetables, treats, and everything in between. I give a wry grin as I tear open a package of cheese sticks for the twins, who are clamoring for a snack. This place may not be home, but at least I don't have to unlock the refrigerator every time I want to take something out. I suspect Will has already removed the locks at our house. He wasn't a fan to begin with, and it's not as if there's anything much in the fridge to steal, with him being gone all week and me stuck here for the foreseeable future.

I set the twins up with their snacks and coloring books, then pull out my laptop and do a search for car accidents near the West Mountain Ranch camping area on the date Cooper Merkler drowned. I stumble across some data sites that aggregate monthly accidents by city, in addition to a few miscellaneous articles — *LOCAL MAN IDENTIFIED IN FATAL CRASH FOLLOWING POLICE PURSUIT; MAN KILLED IN ROLLOVER CRASH* — but none of them match the exact date in question. I need more information to drill down on the results. Maybe Will remembers the name of the man who died. I reach for my phone and shoot him a quick text. I can see by the bubbles that he's typing a reply, but the minutes go by and he doesn't respond. I turn my attention back to my laptop until my phone finally chimes.

I don't remember his name. You need to drop this.

I let out an exasperated sigh as I message him back. *Don't tell me what I need to do. It's your fault we're in this mess.*

I'll take care of it. I've got everything under control.

What's that supposed to mean?

He doesn't answer. I wait for several infuriating minutes before firing off another text. *Don't do anything stupid.*

When he still doesn't respond, I send one final message. *Call me. We need to discuss this.*

I get to my feet and slide my phone into the back pocket of my jeans. He'll probably make me wait until he calls to wish Sam and Ella good night. While the kids are happily occupied with their coloring projects, I set about pulling out ingredients to prep for dinner. My stomach is heaving so much I doubt I'll be able to eat, but cooking is a distraction, if nothing else. I want to call Julia and ask about VV, but it's too distressing when there's never anything new to report. And then there's the unspoken fear that it's already too late. It's been more than forty-eight hours since VV was abducted — more than enough time for Rattler to have killed her and disposed of her body. It's getting harder to keep hope alive as time trickles away.

I've just sat down to dinner with the twins when the doorbell rings. The sound shoots through every last nerve ending like a lightning bolt. There are only a handful of people who know I'm here. Kumar's warning flashes into my head. *There's a killer at large. You can't be too careful.* For some reason, the first face that comes to mind is Rattler's mugshot. For once, I wish I had a gun in the house.

"Someone's at the door, Mommy," my ever-helpful son pipes up, his mouth full of macaroni.

I give him a tight smile as I get to my feet and walk to the door like I'm on the way to the electric chair. My heart is doing double time as I peer through the peephole. I sink back against the wall, weak with relief when I see Kumar standing outside. I shouldn't be happy to see her, but she's the lesser of two evils in my present reality. I suck in a quick breath as I open the door.

"Detective, you're just in time for dinner," I say, a tad too cheerily.

She gives me a bemused smile before following me inside.

Sam stares at her. "Why is the policeman here, Mommy?"

"Police*woman*, silly," Ella corrects him.

Kumar winks at the twins. "That looks yummy. Macaroni and cheese was my favorite when I was a kid."

"You can have some if you want," Ella says.

"Thanks, kiddo, maybe next time." She turns to me. "Perhaps we could have a word in private."

I carry my plate over to the sink and dump it on top of the dirty pots, unable to still the shake in my hands. "Let's go out on the deck."

I open the sliding door, and we take a seat at the small table on the patio. It's a balmy evening, but I can't help shivering as I wait for the next bombshell to drop. Kumar clears her throat. "Dana had an appointment with me at the station today regarding the assault charge she filed, but she never showed up. She's not answering her phone either. I went by the studio and her car is gone. I was wondering if she'd moved out, perhaps." She pins a keen gaze on me.

I give a nervous shake of my head. "No. I wouldn't still be here if she had."

"What about your husband? Has he seen her?"

My chest tightens. Does Kumar know about the assault in the park? Is she testing me — probing to see if I'm an accessory to the crime? Do I really want to add *lying to the police* to my rap sheet? "He's in New York." I glance at my watch. "He'll be calling soon to wish the kids good night if you want to speak with him."

Kumar flashes me a practiced smile. "I need to get back to the station. When you talk to him, ask him if he's seen or heard from Dana." She gets to her feet, then pivots toward me. "If you change your mind about getting anything off your chest, you know where to find me. I'll see myself out."

My legs are too weak to stand for several minutes after she leaves. It's only when my macaroni-encrusted kids start chasing each other around the kitchen that I force myself into action and run them a bath. While they splash around in the bubbles with their plastic zoo animals, I sit on the toilet lid and scroll through my phone, looking for articles about car accidents. There has to be more to Dana's story. I know Will's hiding something.

After drying the twins off with a towel, I bundle them up in their pajamas and read them a bedtime story.

"When's Daddy going to call?" Ella asks in a plaintive voice when I close the book.

I check the time again. It's past seven o'clock. He should have called by now. I dial his number, but he doesn't pick up. "I'll try texting him, sweetie. Maybe he had to work late."

The kids are waiting for you to call.

A moment later, I watch the gray bubbles bounce on the screen.

Wish them good night for me. I'm handling our problem.

CHAPTER 43

A chill snakes over my shoulders. How can Will be handling our problem when he's in New York? My mind jumps to every catastrophic scenario imaginable. *He's hired a hitman. Laced Dana's food with arsenic. Published her address to the dark web and left a spare key to the studio under the mat.* Of course I'm being ridiculous. He probably means he's negotiating with her — offering her even more money to quietly exit our lives.

I tuck the kids in and turn on their nightlight. "I'll come back in as soon as Daddy calls," I promise them.

He *will* call, I'll make sure of it. Nothing's important enough to prevent him from taking a couple of minutes to say goodnight to his children. Back in the kitchen, I grab a water from the fridge and try his number again. When he doesn't pick up, I message him. *I need to talk to you. Call me!* He doesn't respond so I dial his number repeatedly over the next twenty minutes, intermittently texting him irate messages. *Pick up! I'm serious, Will. Don't ignore me!* It's almost nine o'clock before he finally responds.

Got things under control. You have nothing to worry about anymore. Off to bed now. xoxo

I grit my teeth and groan. How can he leave me hanging like this? Of course I'm worried — I'm worried sick. I'm afraid of what he might have done in his zeal to eliminate our squatter problem. All I want is a little reassurance that he managed to talk Dana out of pressing charges and into getting on the road and out of our lives. I'm about to dial his number again when I see he has his phone on *do not disturb*. It's midnight in New York. He's not going to pick up now. I toss my phone on the couch and get up to brew a cup of tea. My thoughts turn to VV and how terrified she must be, if she's still alive. I haven't heard anything from Julia all day. But I already know there's nothing to relay. Kumar said none of their leads have panned out, and it didn't sound like they were any closer to finding Rattler or VV.

Tea in hand, I return to my laptop at the kitchen table. I'm no further forward in my quest to find out the name of the man who died in the car accident. Will claims he doesn't remember. But that seems unlikely if he killed the man. Whatever Dana knew, Will was desperate to stop her from talking. Why didn't she report him for assaulting her? Did he manage to pay her off? I tap on our banking app and click into our savings account. The first thing I see is the most recent transaction — a withdrawal of five thousand dollars. I inhale a sharp breath, a flutter of excitement rising up from my gut. It's a lot of money to lose, but a small price for peace of mind.

My phone starts ringing and I jump to my feet. *Finally!* I snatch it up from the couch and see Andrea's name on the screen. My heart sinks a little. I'm not in the mood for neighborly gossip, especially not about what I uncovered on my surveillance mission. It's getting harder and harder to pretend I'm okay when my world is imploding. "Hey, Andrea," I say, trying to sound upbeat.

"Sorry to call you so late, Morgan. How are you doing?"

"Fine." I let out a heavy sigh. "As fine as can be expected considering the fact that I have a squatter living in the home I'm banned from."

"Speaking of Dana, that's why I'm calling. When Tom was taking the trash out a few minutes ago, he noticed the studio door was lying open. Dana's car's been parked there all day, but neither of us have seen her since yesterday. We're a little on edge after what happened to VV, so Tom walked down there to check it out, but there was no sign of your squatter. He closed the door to keep the rodents out. Hope that was okay."

Acid carves a pathway up my throat. I force my parched lips to move. "Yes, of course. Thanks, Andrea."

"Is everything all right? Did Dana move out?"

"Not that I know of. I wish." My eyelid twitches erratically, dark thoughts flapping around inside my head. If she did leave, I suspect it wasn't voluntarily. *What have you done, Will?*

"Do you want me to call the police and have them check to make sure nothing's been stolen?" Andrea goes on.

"No!" I say, a little too forcefully. "I don't want to aggravate the situation. Dana's probably just gone to stay with her friend again and forgotten to close the door properly. I've been at Will to take a look at that latch. We might need to replace the door. It's old and . . ." I trail off, suddenly aware that I'm blathering on about nothing to hide the fact that I can't have Andrea calling the police. Not until I know for sure what Will has done. He might have bribed Dana to leave, or run her out of town with threats. But what if it's worse? Sweat prickles along my hairline. I've seen firsthand the violent streak he's kept leashed beneath his veneer of composure and self-control.

There's a long pause before Andrea asks, "Morgan, they're not having an affair, are they?"

I give an overwrought laugh. "No! Nothing like that. I was mistaken."

"Oh good. Glad to hear it. Let me know if you hear from Dana. My nerves are shot with the manhunt for Robert Rattler so close to home now."

I hang up and bury my face in my hands. It feels like my whole world is crashing down around me. Best case scenario, Dana has accepted five grand from Will and disappeared. But what if the money was to pay someone to finish the job he started?

183

CHAPTER 44

I scurry back and forth across the kitchen floor like a demented mouse as I contemplate what could possibly have become of Dana. I know in my gut she didn't forget to lock the studio door. She's fastidious about keeping us out. Something must have happened to her. Why else would her car still be parked outside? It doesn't look good. It explains why Will didn't want to call me back — he's trying to figure out how to tell me what he's done. Did he pay someone to shake her down for Jay Taft's signed confession, and make her disappear before the court dates roll around? My head pounds as my thoughts turn darker. There's a lot riding on making sure Dana is adequately dealt with. This isn't only about the squatting situation. Or even the assault charge. It's about covering up a murder from thirty years ago. And what better way to do that than by killing the only living witness.

After a mostly sleepless night, I throw back a couple of shots of espresso and pour the kids some cereal.

"I want eggs," Sam whines.

"Not today. Mommy's tired." I give an exaggerated yawn.

"You should take a nap," Ella says.

"That's a good idea. Maybe I will, later." I rub my burning eyeballs and carry my mug back over to the coffeemaker. Last shot, or I'll be shaking like a wet dog all morning.

As I slide another pod into the coffeemaker, my phone lights up with an unknown number. I frown at the screen. It's early for a telemarketer. "Hello?" I press the phone tight to my ear to dampen the twins' high-pitched giggles as they toss Cheerios across the table at one another.

"Morgan, this is Cynthia Barker, Jeremy's PA. He would like a word with you, if you're available."

"Uh . . . yes, sure." I open the sliding door to the deck.

"Hold, please," Cynthia chirps.

My thoughts bolt in a thousand different directions as I sink down in one of the plastic chairs. Why does Jeremy want to speak with me? Will is one of the company's top performing managers. Perhaps they're planning to present him with some special award. Or maybe it's bad news. Beads of sweat form along my hairline as speculation swirls inside my head. Has Will siphoned money from the company to pay off Dana? What if the five thousand dollars was only a deposit? *No!* He wouldn't do something like that. If nothing else, Will's a company man. He would take out a second mortgage before he did anything to jeopardize his career. I straighten up when Jeremy's voice comes on the line. "Good morning, Morgan. Hope I didn't wake you."

"No, I was just getting the kids their breakfast." I fall silent, wanting him to get on with it and drop the chitchat.

"The reason I'm calling is that I've been unable to get ahold of Will."

I squeeze my eyes shut, silently berating my husband. It's one thing for him to disregard my calls, but does he really think he can ignore his boss? "I . . . think his phone's acting up. He's been texting, but he hasn't been able to call me either." A slow heat creeps up the back of my neck. I don't know why I'm lying to cover for him. Some part of me is still hoping this is all a horrible misunderstanding.

"I see." Jeremy's tone is laced with skepticism. "And where exactly is he texting you from?"

I trace my fingers lightly across my brow, thrown for a loop by the question. Shouldn't Jeremy know where Will is?

I know he's still recovering from his heart attack, but he has Cynthia to keep him informed. "New York. He had that big client presentation there yesterday."

After a loaded pause, Jeremy clears his throat. "He missed it, Morgan. He was a no-show. He hasn't checked in with the office today either. I'm doing everything I can to save the deal, but if I can't get ahold of Will today, we can kiss that contract goodbye."

I try to speak, but the words stick in my throat. If Will didn't go to New York, that means he didn't hire someone else to handle our problem — he handled it himself. Blood roars in my ears.

"I didn't know that. I mean . . . he didn't say anything to me. Maybe he's sick or something." I clamp my lips shut. I'm not making any sense. I don't even know what I'm trying to say. I'm torn between defending him and throwing him under the bus.

"Look, Morgan, this is awkward, but I understand you moved out of the house recently. If you and Will are having some kind of relationship issue, you have my full sympathy. However, I can't allow it to tarnish our company's reputation with potential clients. Please let Will know he needs to be there by noon today or he's fired."

After a steely goodbye, Jeremy ends the call. I pull my knees up to my chin, trembling from a mixture of cold and terror. Yesterday, I thought my world was imploding. Today, I'm sure it is. Nothing would induce Will to throw away his career like this — nothing other than doing whatever it took to avoid going to prison.

I can't help wondering if he knew all along who Dana was. I feel guilty now about all the psychological abuse I put her through. Maybe Will really did try to poison her the night she ended up in the hospital. As devious as she is, she's not the one racking up murders.

I dread to think what Will has done to her.

CHAPTER 45

I glance through the sliding glass door at the kids helping themselves to more Cheerios. If I were a better mother I'd go in there and give them a hand pouring the milk, but I don't think my legs will hold me. Shock is seeping through my veins, numbing me into a paralytic stupor. I'm sitting here in the rubble my life has become, trying to figure out exactly when the bomb went off. Was it when I first met Dana in the park? Or when I invited her into my home? Perhaps, when I caught Will in his first lie. Or when I witnessed him put his hands around Dana's neck?

My eyes are locked on the jug of milk balanced precariously in Sam's chubby hands and guided by Ella. The dull thump in my chest is the only lingering evidence that something more catastrophic than spilled milk has occurred in my ordinary world. I squeeze my phone in my fist, editing in my mind what I don't want to say to Will, but what has to be said. A sob sticks in my throat as I tap out a message summarizing the chaos in my head.

We can't come back from this.

My finger hovers over the send arrow, then moves to cancel. I can't sign the death warrant on our marriage by text. We need to have a real conversation. I have to find out exactly what Will has done — not just yesterday, but thirty years ago, too — before I make an irrevocable judgment call on ripping my family apart.

I force myself to my feet and head back inside the house to avert a milk mishap destined to leave Cheerios floating in a puddle like sodden lifebuoys. I dread the thought of what it will do to the kids if Will is arrested. They're too young to be told the truth, but they'll find out one day. I've seen those crime story specials where a teenager discovers that the loving dad who raised them was actually a monster — a mafia boss or a serial rapist. I can't imagine what that kind of pulverizing revelation does to a person's psyche — it can't be good.

I lift the jug from Sam's hands and add a splash of milk to the generous helping of Cheerios already surfing over the rim of his bowl. For once, I don't make a fuss. It's a distraction, which is precisely what I need, so I can try calling Will again and end this ordeal, one way or another.

I retreat to my bedroom and retrieve my phone from the pocket of my robe. That's when I remember the security cameras on the perimeter of the studio. When I pull up the images on my phone and check the dates, my heart sinks. The recording feature was turned off two days ago. A prickling sweat breaks out on the back of my neck. It confirms my worst fears — evidence of Will's meticulous planning.

I dial his number, enraged when he doesn't pick up. I was willing to give him the chance to explain himself, but I've reached my breaking point. In desperation, I send one last text. *I know what you've done. I'm calling the police.* I stare at the screen, willing him to respond, but my last-ditch telepathic command goes unanswered.

I dial Kumar's number next. "It's Morgan Klein. I need to report a crime."

"Okay, I'm listening," she answers, her voice unruffled, as though I'm calling to say *hello*.

"You told me you can't get ahold of Dana. I'm afraid my husband might have done something to her."

"What makes you think that?"

"I followed him the night of my accident. I put a tracker on his car. To be honest, I thought he was having an affair with Dana."

"Go on," Kumar prompts.

"He met up with her at a park near our house. They were sitting on a bench, talking. I hid on the other side of the hedge."

"Could you hear their conversation?"

"No," I lie. "I . . . I couldn't make it out. I think they were arguing."

"Did it turn physical?"

"Yes. Will assaulted Dana. He put his hands around her throat and tried to strangle her. I interrupted him and she managed to get away." I start to sob. "But now she's missing. I'm afraid he might have caught up with her and finished the job."

"I thought your husband was out of state on business?" Kumar says, a sharpened note in her voice.

"I thought so too. But his boss called me this morning. He said Will didn't show up for an important client presentation. He can't get ahold of him."

"Do you think your husband and Dana had some kind of lover's spat?"

My stomach clenches. Maybe I should go along with that theory, for now. I'm not ready to admit to Kumar what I overheard and throw my husband under the bus for a thirty-year-old murder I don't know for sure he committed. "It's possible. He lied to me about meeting her that night."

"Okay, text me Will's license plate number and a recent photo. I'm heading your way now."

She ends the call, and I collapse on the bed and weep. It was supposed to be Will and me against Dana, not me and Dana against Will. He keeps blaming me for causing this crisis, but he's wrong. I brought a squatter into our lives, but he brought a vigilante maniac. It all circles back to him and whatever awful thing he's covering up.

My phone starts to ring, and I dry my eyes and scrabble around on the bed to find it. My heart leaps when Will's familiar face flashes on the screen. *Finally!*

"Will! What took you so—"

"Help me, Morgan! We're heading to the Old Summit Bridge," Dana rasps. "He's going to kill—" Her voice cuts off abruptly.

I press the phone tighter to my ear, shaking with fear. I can hear someone breathing on the other end — slow, steady, contemplative breaths. "Will? Is that you?"

Several agonizing heartbeats later, he finally answers.

"I'm sorry, Morgan. It's the only way."

CHAPTER 46

"Will! Wait!"

Despite my impassioned plea, the line goes dead.

I stand there staring at the screen on my phone for several seconds before managing to unfreeze my mind and jump into gear. I yank open the bedroom door and run to the kitchen like the house is on fire. "Kids, get in the car! Quick! We're going to see Daddy!"

Sam's mouth drops open, soggy cereal on full display. "But I haven't finished my—"

"Later. We've got to go now."

"Can I bring my stuffed animals?" Ella asks.

"Not this time!" I say, swooping her into my arms. "We'll be back before you know it."

I snatch the car keys off the counter and jog to the front door. Sam trots along after us, protesting all the way. The thunder of my pulse fills my ears as I pull the front door closed behind us and dart across the asphalt to the carport. I fumble with the kids' car seats, my fingers vibrating with fear as I strap them in. I'm trying not to panic — trying to stay focused on getting to the bridge as quickly as possible without freaking the kids out. I know I can talk Will out of

191

this. He's not himself. The fear of facing up to what he's done is clouding his judgment.

The twins pepper me with questions as I back out of the carport: *Can we get pancakes with Daddy? Is this a school day? Are we going back to our house?* The questions blend into one incessant buzzing in my head as I tear out of the subdivision.

"Ssh. Mommy's got to make a phone call." I wish I'd thought to bring their iPads. Now they're going to be listening to every word I say. I'll have to speak in code. I plug in my phone and dial Kumar's number.

"He just called me," I blurt out.

"O-kay. Let's clarify. *Who* called you?" she asks.

"Will. He's going to . . . K . . . I . . . L . . . L . . . her. He's headed to the Old Summit Bridge."

After a loaded pause, Kumar asks, "Are the kids with you?"

"Uh-huh. Listening."

"Don't go anywhere. I'll be right there. I'm sending a unit to the bridge right now."

"I'm already on my way. I can talk him out of it."

"No! Think of your kids, Morgan. This is a volatile situation. You don't want to expose them to anything dangerous."

"He's their father. He won't hurt them." I end the call before Kumar can argue with me. She tries calling me back, but I let it go straight to voicemail.

"Who was that, Mommy?" Ella asks.

"A friend." The last thing I want is for my kids to know I'm turning their father in to the police.

"She said *think of your kids*. That's me and Ella." Sam giggles.

Ella scowls at him. "It's not funny. She said it's *dangerous*."

"Is it, Mommy?" Sam asks.

I try to laugh, but it sounds more like I'm choking. "Of course not. We're going to see Daddy, remember? Daddy's not dangerous, silly!" An image of Will lunging at Dana flashes to mind, and I swallow the hard knot in my throat.

"He's big and strong like me," Sam says, kicking the back of the passenger seat.

My stomach twists at the pride in his little voice. If only he knew what his father was capable of.

"Here, take my phone and play a game. Be nice and take turns." I stretch my arm back, dangling the phone from my fingertips.

"Yay! Thank you, Mommy," Sam says, snatching it right before Ella grabs it.

She promptly bursts into tears. I glance anxiously in the rearview mirror. I shouldn't have brought the kids with me, but what choice did I have? I have to reach Will before it's too late.

"Mommy, you have a message." Sam holds the phone up for me to see.

"I can't read it. Pass it to me, please!"

"But you said we could play a game."

"You can, after I read the text!"

Sam huffs loudly, before leaning forward in his car seat and handing me back my phone. I'm hesitant to take my eyes off the road to read the message. The crash is still fresh in my mind and we're coming up to a busy intersection. The minute the light turns red, my gaze flicks to the screen. It's from Julia.

They've found a woman's body.

I let out an anguished moan.

"What's wrong, Mommy?" Ella asks, her voice wavering in alarm.

"Nothing, sweetie," I mumble distractedly. My fingers shake as I type.

Is it her?

They haven't identified her yet. She was stabbed in the same way as Rattler's other victims. Badly decomposed.

Stay strong, Julia. It might not be her.

I doubt she believes that. I'm not sure I believe it myself. But I'm not going to be the one to shatter her hope. Even

193

though the logical part of my brain tells me VV's already dead, I'm fighting to keep believing against all odds.

Another message pops up on the screen.

Police are here. Got to go.

The light turns green and I hit the gas. It might be too late for VV, but not for Dana. I'm more determined than ever to reach Will before he does something stupid.

"Mommy, can we have your phone back now?" Sam asks.

I toss it in Ella's lap. "Remember what I said. Take turns."

To my relief, they finally agree on a game, and settle into it, passing the phone back and forth. I grip the steering wheel tightly, my chest aching with the soul-destroying news that another woman's body has been discovered. The odds that it isn't VV are slim, but there's still a chance — she's only been gone a few days, and Julia said the body was already badly decomposed.

I race along the remote, leafy, winding road that leads to the Old Summit Bridge in an isolated area roughly ten miles out of town. I'm the only car on the road, although I'm picking up on the faint wail of sirens. I navigate the bends with a newfound ferocity, the twins tilting in their car seats first one way and then the other. I have to reach Will before the police do.

At last, the bridge comes into view across the switchbacks in the road. My eyes widen as I catch sight of a large duffle bag toppling over the guardrail into the river.

CHAPTER 47

Out of the corner of my eye, I catch the glint of the sun reflecting off metal. Half a heartbeat later, Will's BMW lurches forward from beneath a leafy canopy at the side of the road and disappears across the bridge. Too shaken to keep driving, I slam on the brakes. My phone goes flying out of Sam's hands and I hear it skid under the passenger seat. I sit hunched over the wheel, my entire body frozen with shock. I can't believe what I just witnessed. I can only guess what was in that bag.

"Mommy! Why did you do that?" Sam cries, flailing his legs in frustration.

I grope around beneath the seat next to me until I retrieve the phone. I hesitate, my fingers hovering over the keypad, but there's no sense in calling the police — help is already on the way. The sirens are growing louder with every passing minute. I hand the phone back to Sam and put the car in gear. I can't just sit here and wait for the cavalry to arrive. I need to do something. I'm closer than the emergency vehicles. Maybe I can save Dana. There's a chance she's not dead yet. Perhaps the bag got caught in the weeds or overhanging branches. I veer around the last few bends in the road then screech to a halt right before the bridge. I pull over onto the shoulder and turn off the engine.

"Mommy will be right back," I tell the kids. "I need to check something real quick."

"Okay," Ella mumbles, not even glancing up from her game.

They're completely oblivious and, for once, I'm thankful for the magnetic power of the screen blinding them to the evil that has just unfolded before my eyes.

I jump out of the car and scramble down the bank through a patch of prickly weeds to the river. My gaze darts left and right among the rocks, eddies and fallen logs, searching for any sign of the bag. Did it sink already? It looked like it was made of canvas, or some similar fabric. I have no idea if a body in a bag would float. The river is far too deep and wide for me to wade into. But I can't give up. I can still hear her voice on the phone. *Help me, Morgan!* My heart is beating so rapidly it's taking my breath away. With every second that passes, the hope of finding Dana alive diminishes. It makes the horror of what happened to VV all the more poignant. I don't want to think about what her last minutes were like at Rattler's hands, or what was going through her head. I can't do anything for VV, but if I can reach Dana before it's too late, it might go some way to assuaging my guilt at how I mistreated her. I'm not an evil person. I did what I did in a misguided attempt at vigilante justice — which makes Dana and me more alike than I care to admit.

I glance up toward the bridge at the sound of sirens. Flashing beacons light up the embankment as emergency vehicles converge. From my vantage point, I can see two police cars and an ambulance already on the scene. I wave my arms frantically, then scramble back uphill, eager to reach my kids before all the chaos frightens them. Kumar exits the second squad car and strides over to me.

I jab a finger in the direction of the river. "I saw a duffle bag fall from the bridge. It looked like a . . . a body bag."

"When?" Kumar demands, her eyes flicking to the river and back.

"Just a few minutes ago — five, ten at the most. I tried searching along the bank in case it got wedged in the rocks, but I don't see any sign of it. It must have floated on down river."

"And your husband?"

I swallow down any lingering reservations I have about exposing Will for who he really is. "In his BMW — headed north."

Kumar gives a curt nod before relaying the information over her radio and requesting a dive team. "Stay with your kids. We'll take it from here."

A moment later, one of the squad cars wheels off around the corner in pursuit of Will.

Kumar and another officer clamber down to the water's edge and start making their way along the riverbank. I watch as she pulls out a pair of binoculars and slowly scans down-river. I turn away from the distressing sight and walk back with a heavy-footed tread to my car. The twins have long since lost interest in their game and are staring, noses pressed to the glass, at the ambulance parked behind my Suburban.

"Can we go see Daddy now?" Sam asks, heaving a sigh.

I flash him a watery smile as I unbuckle his seatbelt. "Soon. You two can play in the back for a few minutes."

Ella pulls her thumb out of her mouth and fixes a questioning gaze on me. "Why is that police lady here?"

At first, I think she's talking about Kumar, but then I notice another female police officer standing guard next to us, one hand on her gun. I assume she's stationed here in case Will comes back and poses a threat. But then another more chilling thought occurs to me. She might be keeping an eye on me to make sure I don't flee the scene.

Kumar knows there's no love lost between me and Dana. What if she thinks it was me who tossed her over the bridge?

CHAPTER 48

From somewhere inside the car, my phone trills with an incoming message. I suck in a sharp breath. The unwelcome thought that it could be Will eats at me like acid. What could he possibly say to justify what he's done? I need to persuade him to turn himself in.

"Where's Mommy's phone, kids?"

"It falled on the floor again," Sam answers.

"Whereabouts?" I demand, frantically patting the floor mats.

Sam shrugs. "I dunno. Can we go home now?"

At last, my fingers latch onto my phone, and I yank it out from underneath my seat. I tap the screen and a new message from Julia pops up. *It's not Mom! No new leads.*

Relief courses through my veins. Finally, some good news in the midst of the burgeoning nightmare that has become my life. I type out a euphoric response, then add a string of hearts. Sinking down in my seat, I close my eyes briefly. It's good news, but not great news. VV is still missing, presumed dead, and the police have no new leads. My brain is fried from the ups and downs of the adrenaline surges I've endured in the past forty-eight hours. I just want for this all to go away, for my life to be normal again. But I can never go back — normal was a lie.

When I open my eyes, Kumar is walking over to my car. The hair on the back of my neck prickles. Her stride conveys urgency, but her expression gives nothing away. I open the door and climb out, closing it firmly behind me. I don't want the kids overhearing anything she has to say.

"Did you find it? The . . . the bag?" I can't bring myself to say *body*. I know in my heart that's what I saw fall from the bridge. The size, the shape — even the way it fell indicated it contained something weighty, like a human body. I know he killed her. He practically admitted it. *I'm sorry, Morgan. It's the only way.* Acid seeps up the back of my throat. It takes a certain level of arrogance to think he can get away with it — just like he did thirty years ago. I guess he never changed.

"We didn't spot anything from the bank," Kumar says. "The dive team just arrived further downstream. If the bag's in the river, they'll find it."

I give a shaky nod. "I got a text from Julia. The body they discovered wasn't VV."

Kumar eyes me thoughtfully. "We got word this morning that Rattler struck again up north. A woman was abducted getting out of her car to check her mailbox."

My stomach knots as I digest the disturbing news. "That shoots holes in the theory that he's heading south to the border."

"Either that, or we're dealing with a copycat killer here."

Dread slithers through my veins as I contemplate the possibility.

Kumar's radio crackles and she steps aside to respond to it. I take the opportunity to peek in on the kids. It won't be long before one or the other of them will need the bathroom or want a snack. For now, they're content playing I Spy, so I leave them to it.

I flinch when Kumar places a firm hand on my shoulder. Her gaze drills into me. "I need you to come with me. Officer Rogers here will take care of the kids for a few minutes."

My eyes widen, confusion swirling up from my gut. Am I being arrested? "I . . . I don't understand. Where are we going?"

"I need you to identify a body in your husband's vehicle."

My legs almost buckle beneath me. "Will?"

"Not Will — a female. The patrol officer found his abandoned car. He crashed into a tree and must have taken off on foot. His passenger's dead. She has no ID on her, and no purse. It would be helpful if we could notify the next of kin."

She bundles me into the back of her patrol car and we take off, followed by the ambulance. Disoriented, I stare out the window. It must be Dana. My thoughts are fraying like string. None of it makes any sense. If she was in the car with Will, who was in the bag he threw into the river? And what was Dana doing riding in the car in the first place — a *passenger*, not a hostage? Were they running away together? Did they stage everything to deceive me? I shiver, hugging my arms around my body. Is it possible I misinterpreted what I saw at the park that night? I press my fingers into my temples, trying to work it out.

If Will knew I had put a tracker on his car, then he knew I would follow him. It might have all been a show to dupe me. Maybe *Help me, Morgan, he's going to kill me* was a well-delivered line designed to lure me here. They could have tossed a bag of rocks in the river for all I know.

And I played along — the crazy wife who's losing the plot.

CHAPTER 49

Dread kneads my insides like dough when I spot Will's BMW wrapped around a tree up ahead. The passenger side door is wide open, and a police officer is standing guard next to it.

Kumar opens the back door of the squad car and waits for me to climb out.

A wave of guilt hits me. I desperately wanted my squatter out of my house, but I never meant for her life to end like this.

Kumar directs a meaningful gaze at me. "Ready?"

"I . . . I'm not sure. I've never seen a body in a car wreck before."

"All you need to do is take a quick look and tell me if you recognize the victim."

A rivulet of sweat runs down my back as I follow Kumar over to Will's car and force myself to look inside. I let out a jagged breath. The dead woman's face is partially obscured by the airbag, but it's clearly not Dana Becker. This woman is considerably older — I'm guessing in her sixties — slightly overweight, bristly, gray hair clustered on her shoulders.

I step away from the car and heave a couple of deep breaths, fighting to understand through a cloud of confusion. Is Dana in the river after all?

"Do you know her?" Kumar prompts.

I shake my head, tears unexpectedly pricking my eyes. I don't know this stranger and yet I'm crying for her. Or maybe it's VV I'm crying for, or perhaps what's left of my life as I know it.

"Are you sure it's not a friend or a relative of your husband's?"

"I'm sure. I mean . . . as far as I know." I throw Kumar a helpless look. How can I be certain of anything after all Will's lies? He had a lot more secrets than he admitted to. I might never uncover them all.

"What about someone he works with?"

"It's not anyone I've ever met. But it's a big company." I press my fingertips to my temples. "That doesn't make sense either. Why would a woman from his company be with him when he's supposed to be in New York?"

Kumar throws me a circumspect look. "No idea. I was hoping you might be able to tell me that."

"What happens now?" I ask.

"I've radioed for backup and a K9 unit to pursue your husband. All indications are that he fled into the forest."

My gaze travels to the tree line and the thousands of acres of national forest beyond. "He's not the survivalist type. He won't last long out there."

Kumar flashes me a sympathetic smile. "We'll do our best to find him. Let's get you back to your kids."

Several squad cars with flashing lights race by us on our return trip. I hope they capture Will soon — for the kids' sake and for mine. I can't bear the thought of watching the news night after night as they update the public on the manhunt for Will Klein, wanted for murder. I'm not going to protect him from the consequences of his actions any longer. I'm ready to tell Kumar everything I know.

But there's still so much I don't understand. What was he doing with that older woman in his car? My mind misfires as I try to piece it all together. Was he planning to kill her? An icy chill ripples through me at the thought.

Was that what Kumar was hinting at when she mentioned a copycat killer?

CHAPTER 50

Back at the Airbnb, I call Andrea to break the news to her that Will is on the run. I'm a blubbering wreck and not making any sense whatsoever, but to her credit, she jumps in her rental and heads straight over. She insists on remaining on the phone with me the entire time she's driving, as though she's afraid I might do something stupid in the interim. When she arrives, she sets the kids up with popcorn and a movie in the master bedroom, then makes me a cup of peppermint tea and joins me and my box of tissues on the couch.

"I blame myself," I say, staring morosely into my mug. "I shouldn't have gone into the studio and searched through Dana's things. If I hadn't found that birth certificate and photo, none of this would have happened. We could have waited a couple more weeks and let the eviction process run its course. But I thought I knew better. I wanted to take control of the situation and force Dana's hand."

"No sense torturing yourself now," Andrea admonishes me. "Dana's connection to Will's past would have come out sooner or later. She had some kind of agenda in mind — blackmail, most likely."

I reach for a tissue and blow my nose. "But it wouldn't have driven Will to murder. That's on me. I kept at him to do something about her. And when he wouldn't, I started my own pathetic campaign to antagonize her into leaving. When he finally confronted her, he flew into a rage and tried to choke her. And now he's killed her."

"You don't know that. You don't know for sure what he threw in the river. It's possible Will and Dana were both in his car when it crashed. Maybe they did run off together and they dumped the bag in the river to throw you off the trail. It could have been weighted down. That's why you couldn't find it — it would have gone straight to the bottom."

I give a puzzled shake of my head. "No. It doesn't explain the other woman in the car. And why would Dana call me pleading for help if they were running away together? It would have been simpler to buy some plane tickets and leave without a word. I almost wish they had been having an affair. It would be an easier pill to swallow if Will turned out to be a cheater rather than a murderer."

"You can't think like that. We don't even know for sure if Dana's dead. They haven't found her body."

"It's only a matter of time." I rub my fingertips gently around my temples. "I'm worried Kumar thinks I'm involved."

"Why would she think that?"

"She knows Dana and I had a contentious relationship. She witnessed me assaulting her."

Andrea tosses her head. "It's ridiculous to think you would be involved in murdering Dana. Frankly, I'm not convinced Will killed her either. He's not the friendliest neighbor to have, but I can't picture him doing anything that egregious."

I try to take a sip of tea, but my lips are trembling too much to swallow anything. Andrea doesn't know about Dana's accusations from thirty years ago. Or my suspicion that Will might be a copycat killer. It's all going to come out at some point, but I'm so disgusted and embarrassed by everything he's done that I can't bring myself to tell her the full extent of it.

The doorbell chimes and I flinch, spilling hot tea over my fingers. My eyes lock with Andrea's.

"Stay here," she says. "I'll see who it is."

There's a muffled exchange and then Andrea reappears with Kumar at her side. My stomach tightens. The only news she can be bringing is on a scale of bad to worse.

I knot my hands in my lap, my gaze fastened on her face. I can't tell from her deadpan expression if they've captured Will or not. My brain floods with a thousand questions. What if he tried to resist arrest? Was he alone when they captured him, or was Dana with him? Is he dead or alive?

Kumar clears her throat. "I'm sure you're wondering about your husband. I'm afraid we haven't found him yet."

I sit still as a statue, waiting for her to continue — to drop whatever bombshell she came here to deliver. I know she didn't drive all the way to the Airbnb to tell me they haven't found Will. Have they discovered Dana's body? The room begins to spin around me, and I drop my head into my hands, half afraid I'll pass out.

Andrea places a hand on my shoulder. "Are you okay, Morgan? Do you need to lie down?"

I shake my head, beads of sweat clinging to the back of my neck. "No. I just want to get this over with." I look directly at Kumar. "Did you find the bag?"

"Not yet. The divers are still searching the river. The reason I'm here is because the coroner found something significant in the coat pocket of the deceased woman in your husband's car — an address scribbled on a piece of paper. I sent a couple of officers to check the place out."

She pauses, the rapt gleam in her eye catching me by surprise. "It turned out to be an abandoned farm thirty miles or so east of here. My officers conducted an extensive search of the property. They found a woman tied up in one of the outbuildings."

CHAPTER 51

Kumar clears her throat. "She was drugged, so it took a while for the officers to identify her, but I can confirm now that it's your missing housekeeper, Veronica Valdez."

I gasp, relief coursing through my veins like a powerful drug. *VV's alive!* My mind scrambles to try and figure out what this means. How was the dead woman involved in VV's abduction? Was she working with the West Coast Killer? My overloaded brain struggles to pull it all together. Unless VV was abducted by a copycat killer. Competing thoughts circle my head like sharks. I can't think straight anymore. Have I been married to a sleeping monster all these years? *My husband, the serial killer.*

"Mrs. Valdez was taken to the hospital to be evaluated," Kumar goes on. "My understanding is that she doesn't have any serious injuries and is expected to make a complete recovery."

"That's wonderful news!" Andrea slips an arm around my shoulder and squeezes it.

"Yes, it is," I add, in a breathless whisper, gripping the arms of the chair I'm sitting in. "It's the best possible news we could have gotten. Does Julia know?"

Kumar nods. "We notified the family first. Julia went straight to the hospital. As you might expect, she was blindsided by the connection to Will. She wants answers that we can't give her at this point in time. I've asked her not to speak to the press until we can complete our investigation and have identified the dead woman. We're in the process of combing through all our missing persons reports, with the assistance of the FBI. If there's any chance this is the West Coast Killer, or the work of a copycat killer, we're going to need their expertise." Her eyes meet mine, a beacon of compassion. "The kid who witnessed Veronica Valdez's abduction indicated that two perpetrators were involved. We can't rule out the possibility that your husband is working with Rattler."

Andrea gasps, her hand slipping from my shoulder as if she's just been informed that I'm contagious. I stare blankly at Kumar. I'm too numb inside to push back. It's not as if I haven't had the same thought myself. If Will murdered thirty years ago, what's to stop him doing it again now? Maybe he never stopped. A shiver ripples down my spine. The FBI needs to know about Dana's claims. But what if Will comes after me for betraying him?

"Is there anything else you can tell us that might be helpful?" Kumar asks.

I swallow the fear curdled in my throat. My silence will only endanger more lives. "Dana told me Will has killed before — thirty years ago. He was only sixteen at the time."

Andrea raises a brow. "Are you talking about when that kid got drunk and fell in the river and drowned?"

I breathe slowly in and out, as though the release of air will make it easier to let the truth out. "It didn't happen quite like that. Will abandoned his friend on the side of a logging road and drove on to the camp, which was another mile or so. It was dark, and Cooper was drunk." I hesitate before continuing. "But that's not the worst of it. Something else happened that night. A man died in a car wreck. Dana says Will killed him."

Andrea looks skeptical. "Why should we believe her?"

"Do you know the man's name?" Kumar asks.

"No. I tried researching accidents in the area where Will lived at the time, but I couldn't find anything that matched the date. It might have happened in a neighboring town."

Kumar scribbles a note to herself. "I'll have someone look into it. Any idea where Will might go to hide out?"

I shake my head. "We don't have access to a cabin or anything like that. Like I said, he's not a survivalist. He's not going to last long in the elements."

My eyes glaze over as I picture Will thrashing through the forest. That's what makes this so hard to understand. He's not an outdoorsman, by any stretch of the imagination. He doesn't even own a gun. The idea of him killing someone is beyond my comprehension. Then again, I don't know my husband like I thought I did. The police suspect he abducted VV — possibly the dead woman in his car, too. Was it because they were easy targets for a copycat killer with no real skills but a lust for power? Will has always had a controlling streak. It's terrifying to think what lay beneath it.

A call comes in on Kumar's radio and she steps out of the room to take it. When she returns, I can tell by the expression on her face that there's been a major development.

"Have they captured Will?" I ask, squeezing my fingers in my lap.

"No." She sets her lips in a grim line. "The dive team just located the bag."

CHAPTER 52

My breathing tapers to a gurgling rasp. I'm woefully ill-prepared for this moment now that it's here. I don't want to face the truth. I couldn't wait to get Dana out of my life, but I never wished her dead. I would do anything to rewind the clock — let her raid my refrigerator a thousand times over. I was a fool to escalate the situation, needling her and prodding Will. I had no idea what he was capable of. I let my emotions take over, and my rage devour my reason. This is where it got me in the end.

"I need you to accompany me to the morgue to identify the body," Kumar says.

I recoil at the thought. I have no desire to see Dana — either to gloat over my enemy in death, or cry over her. But what choice do I have? She has no family that I know of. She was my employee, she lived in my house — I owe her this much.

I turn to Andrea. "Can I ask you to watch the kids again?"

She gives a wary nod, a shell-shocked look on her face. I get the sense she'd rather extricate herself from the situation, but it's clear to her I'm out of options.

I gather up my purse and sweater and follow Kumar out to the squad car. My heart thumps erratically on the drive to the morgue. I knew it had to end this way. I knew there was a body inside that bag when it fell. The scene has played on repeat in my mind ever since, and I've only become more convinced each time. I feel sick to my stomach at the thought of the twins finding out that their father murdered their nana's caregiver. I'd almost rather he died than be captured alive. I can't believe I'm entertaining thoughts as disturbing as suicide-by-cop, but that's where my shattered heart is taking me.

When we arrive at the morgue, Kumar escorts me into an office and tells me to wait until they call me in. I lay my head on my arms on the desk and sob silently. Why did I ever invite Dana into my life? All I wanted to do was take good care of my mom and try to keep her at home with us as long as possible. Three weeks later she was dead. How did it all go so horribly wrong? I need her now more than ever. Even VV can't be here for me. My eyes spring open and I sit up with a jolt. I need to call and find out how she's doing. I dial her number, but she doesn't answer. I try Julia next. It rings several times before she picks up.

"You have a nerve calling me," she seethes.

"Julia, I—"

"Don't! I don't want to hear your pathetic excuses about how you didn't know what your husband was doing. You must have suspected something. You can't be married to a monster and be clueless about it, unless you're deliberately closing your eyes to the truth."

I heave a shuddering sigh. "I know it's difficult to believe, but I didn't suspect a thing. Will's always been reserved and a little on the secretive side, but he loved your mom — she's like family to us."

"Don't insult me!" Julia screams into the phone. "Is that how you treat family? Abduct her, drug her, tie her up in an abandoned barn with nothing but a couple of bottles of water and a bucket to relieve herself in? Don't ever call me or my mother again. The best thing you can do is get yourself the most expensive lawyer you can afford — you're going to need it!"

She hangs up, leaving me reeling, as though she's been raining down physical blows on me. I press a trembling fist to my mouth. I never expected Julia to turn on me, but I suppose I can understand her need to lash out at somebody. I'm Will's stand-in — an extension of the evil he perpetrated on her mom. I still can't wrap my head around his cowardly, despicable acts of abducting and terrifying defenseless women. Did it make him feel powerful or something? Did he know the woman who died in his car? Was she an easy mark, like VV?

The door opens and Kumar enters, her lips set in a strangled grimace. Acid curdles in my stomach. I'm second-guessing my ability to do this. Is it too late to say I've changed my mind?

To my surprise, Kumar pulls out the chair opposite me and slumps down in it. She rubs a hand over her brow before looking me directly in the eye. "I'm sorry to have to tell you this, Morgan, but your husband is deceased."

CHAPTER 53

The words spin inside my head like fragments from a meteorite that's just exploded. I knew there was a possibility the manhunt might end this way, but now that it's been confirmed, I can't quite take it in. My husband is dead. The father of my children is no more. Did he die in a shootout with the police? Or did he take the coward's way out and kill himself? I hide my face in my hands as I picture him hanging from a tree in the forest.

"Are you okay, Morgan?" Kumar asks. "Can I get you some water?"

"Yes, please," I mumble, reaching in my purse for a tissue. I dab at my eyes but there are no tears left, only a burning sensation on my eyeballs.

Kumar returns with a plastic cup of water which she sets in front of me. I take a shaky sip. "How did he die?"

"We're still trying to determine that."

I nod mutely. No final standoff with the police, then — just a cowardly departure from this life. It seems fitting. An image of Will laid out on a cold, steel table flashes before me. I scrunch my eyes shut to blot it from my mind.

"We believe he was murdered," Kumar says quietly.

The only sound in the cavernous silence that follows is my labored breathing. *Murdered?*

"Morgan, this is going to be difficult for you to hear, but Will's body was in the bag the dive team retrieved from the river."

I stare blankly at Kumar. I heard what she said but it didn't register. That's impossible. Will was on the run from the police, being hunted by a canine unit through the forest. Unless there's some kind of Houdini wizardry involved. My chaotic thoughts frantically flock together to try to make sense of this new, more terrifying reality. If Will wasn't driving his car, who was? If he didn't abduct the woman who died in the crash, who did? The West Coast Killer? Kumar had hinted at the possibility they were working together. Rattler would think nothing of disposing of Will if they'd had some kind of falling out, and he could very well evade capture in the woods. The monster has been covering his tracks for the better part of a year now.

"I don't understand. Was Rattler driving Will's car when it crashed?"

Kumar frowns. "It's speculation on our part that they might have been working together. We're reviewing CCTV to try to determine who the driver was."

She places her palms on the table in front of her. "Would you like to see your husband now?"

I swallow the jagged knot in my throat and give a jerky nod.

To my surprise, Will looks peaceful, almost as though he's drifted off to sleep in the hammock between the oak trees in our backyard. The only telltale sign that this is the kind of sleep he will never wake up from is the bloodless pallor of his skin. I hate what he's done to us, but I miss him already. My shoulders quake with silent sobs and I look away, overcome by a gnawing emptiness. Kumar is deep in conversation with the mortician. He leads her over to a tray of Will's belongings and reaches with gloved hands for a folded sheet of paper. Kumar opens it and reads it through, glancing once or twice in my direction.

After a few minutes, she escorts me out of the room and back to the small office I waited in earlier.

She places the paper on the desk between us. "Do you know a Jay Taft?"

My breath catches in my throat. "From what I understand, he was a friend of Will's from high school. I never met him."

"Did you know he passed away recently?"

"Yes. Will told me." My eyes flick to the paper in front of me. Kumar taps a finger on it and pushes it gently toward me. "You need to read this."

My stomach churns as I skim read Jay Taft's deathbed confession. Shock decimates through me when the full horror of what Will has done becomes clear.

CHAPTER 54

It's the elusive confession Will was so desperate to get his hands on. And maybe he did, only it didn't play out the way he'd intended. Did he enlist Rattler to help him get rid of Dana, only to have Rattler turn on him? Either way, it doesn't matter anymore. Because Dana was right about Will murdering another man that night — a cold, despicable act he laughed about, after which he continued his drunken rampage and left one of his friends to die needlessly. I feel like my insides have been scooped out and nothing remains but the hard truth of my new reality: *I'm a monster's widow.*

In my traumatized state, I barely register the fact that Kumar is driving me to the police station instead of home. She ushers me into an interview room and clasps her hands on the table in front of her. "Let's talk off the record for a few minutes. How much did you know about the murder that happened the night of Cooper Merkler's death?"

"Nothing." I give a despairing shake of my head. "Will never talked about it. The first I heard of it was when I overheard Dana accusing Will a few days ago. To be honest, I didn't believe it. I thought she was making stuff up."

I chew on my lip as I think about how unconvincing that must sound to Kumar. Will lied to me about how Cooper died

— why would I think he wasn't lying about the other man who died that night too? My stomach churns with disgust. At least Jay had some remorse for what he'd done. Will was prepared to take his secret to the grave — until Dana got in his way.

An officer knocks on the door and motions to Kumar. "Be right back," she says, rising to her feet. She's gone for a good twenty minutes before she returns with a recording device, which she sets on the table between us. "One of my officers found this in the wreckage of your husband's BMW. It was jammed beneath the driver's seat. Do you recognize it?"

I eye it with suspicion. "It isn't Will's." My lip quivers. How would I really know that? He had a whole other life when he was on the road. And a past I knew nothing of.

Kumar folds her hands in front of her on the table. "We suspect it belonged to the dead woman in his car."

"Have you identified her yet?"

"No, but we're working on a promising lead." Kumar tightens her lips. "I'm going to play back the recording for you. It will be uncomfortable to hear, but I want you to listen all the way to the end and see if you can identify the voices. I need to warn you that your husband sounds as though he was under some duress."

Goosebumps prick my arms. If Rattler was involved, that could mean anything. "What . . . kind of duress?"

"I can't speculate until we have more information. Tech is analyzing a copy of the recording as we speak." She raises a brow. "Ready?"

My head jerks in what she interprets as a nod, and she hits play.

"*You murdered Bradley and Alicia!*" The woman speaking has a shrill, verging on unhinged, tone. I don't recognize the voice. My heart thumps a frenzied drumbeat in my chest. Who are Bradley and Alicia? Exactly how many people did Will kill?

"*I didn't mean for anyone to die.*" I flinch when I hear Will's response. He sounds tired, broken, like he's been at this for hours. It's eerie listening to his voice after seeing him lying cold on a slab in the mortuary only an hour earlier.

"*You have two choices — record a confession or die!*" the woman goes on. "*You, your wife, and your kids! You don't deserve any of it! You should be rotting in prison.*"

I furrow my brow, recalling that Dana said something similar to him in the park that night. But it isn't Dana's voice on the recording.

Will mumbles a response, but I can't make out what he says. I tense at what follows — it sounds like blows raining down as he cries out, begging the unidentified woman to stop.

There's a muffled exchange in the background with a third person. I strain to hear the nuances of their intonation, but I can't catch it.

Kumar hits pause and raises her brows in anticipation. "Anything?"

I shake my head. "I don't recognize the woman talking to Will. It sounds as if there's someone else there too, but I can't hear anything they're saying."

Kumar gives a disappointed nod and resumes the recording.

"*You're running out of time,*" the woman says. "*I know where your wife and kids are staying. I've been there.*"

"*Leave my family out of this! I'm begging you. They had nothing to do with it.*"

"*You took my family from me, and you want me to show your precious family mercy?*"

"*I did something stupid. I was sixteen. I wish—*"

"*You wish?*" the woman screams. "*You know what I wish? I wish I could haul you up to that overpass and throw you over it so you could feel what it's like to crush a windshield, like the rock you dropped on Bradley!*"

I clutch my stomach as though I've been punched. My gaze connects with Kumar's — compassionate but shrewd, as though assessing how much of a shock this is to me, and how much I knew all along. She pauses the recording. "Have you heard the name Bradley Cash before?"

"No," I choke out, my throat too scuffed up with emotion to ask the questions swirling around inside my head. Jay

217

didn't name the victim in his deathbed confession. Maybe he was too far gone to recall it.

"Bradley Cash died the same night as Cooper Merkler. At around 6.10 p.m., local police started receiving calls about boulders being dropped from an overpass. It was dark and no one saw the vehicle that fled the scene. Cash was pronounced dead at the hospital."

I reach for the plastic cup of water and gulp enough down to coat my throat. "And Alicia?"

"Alicia Bernacki was Bradley Cash's fiancée. Their wedding was only three weeks out." Kumar's expression doesn't change but her shoulders sag slightly. "She committed suicide the day after he died."

CHAPTER 55

I sit there in stunned silence, trying to come to terms with the enormity of the devastation Will has wreaked on so many lives — mine included. Cooper Merkler died because of a senseless, cold-hearted prank. Bradley Cash was callously murdered only weeks before his wedding, and the coward who crushed his skull fled the scene, laughing like a maniac according to Jay's confession. Alicia took her own life out of despair. Instead of getting married, raising a family and growing old together, she and Bradley were buried within days of one another. Even Jay Taft and Tommy Hodgson were victims of the crimes that haunted them into adulthood and drove them to an early grave. Only my psychopathic husband was able to bury the ghosts of his past and go on to live out his dreams of a successful career, marriage, and a family. He managed to hide it all from me, which only makes him more despicable in my eyes.

Kumar motions to the recording device. "There's just a few more minutes, but it could be important, if you're up to it."

I give a reluctant nod, and she hits play again. The woman continues, her voice dripping scorn.

"Do you have any idea what it's like to find out your daughter hanged herself because she couldn't bear the thought of living life

without her fiancée? How would you like to find Ella hanging from the rafters with a rope around her neck?"

"Stop! Please! I didn't kill your daughter. I did some horrible things, but I'm not that person anymore."

"You're the very same coward. You never paid for what you did," the woman hisses. *"But your time has come."*

"No! Please! Put down the gun! I'll—"

Kumar pauses the recording and grimaces. "You don't need to hear the next part. He doesn't speak again."

I don't want to think about what happened next, but in my head, I hear the gunshot exploding anyway. I shiver at the thought that my husband's death has a timestamp on that tape.

Kumar fast forwards the recording, then leans back in her chair once more.

I wrinkle my forehead in concentration as the conversation becomes muffled, full of background noises, and snatches of an exchange between two women.

". . . in the car . . . need gloves . . ."

". . . where . . . the bag . . ."

My eyes lock with Kumar's. I'm guessing they're talking about putting Will's body in the bag. I dig my nails into the palm of my hand, recoiling at the thought.

"It ends there," she says. "They must have realized they were still recording and switched it off at that point. Do you recognize the second woman's voice?"

I rub a hand over the back of my neck. "Can you play it one more time? It's hard to make it out."

I position myself closer to the device and lean my ear to it.

". . . where . . . the bag . . ."

I repeat the words over to myself, a familiar habit that always orients me when I start to lose the plot. *Where . . . the bag . . . where . . . the bag . . . where . . . the bag . . .*

Dread crawls beneath my skin like a legion of ants. *Everything okay? You look like you're lost in thought.* It's the same voice that targeted me the day we met in the park — the woman who invaded my life like a virus and corrupted everything.

"It's Dana Becker," I whisper. "I'm sure of it."

Kumar gives a satisfied nod. "We suspected as much. She's Alicia's younger sister."

My jaw drops as the dots begin to connect. "Is Dana Becker even her real name?"

"Close. It's Danika Bernacki. We're waiting on DNA results, but we believe the dead woman is Stacey Bernacki, her mother."

I tent my hands over my forehead, trying to digest the horror of it all. Dana inserted herself into my life like a spider with a deadly bite, laying her poisonous eggs, waiting for the right moment to strike. Stacey was an integral part of the plot all along — stalking us as we went about our lives. A prickling heat travels slowly up the back of my neck. Is it possible she lured my mother out of the house the day she got lost? Maybe she put the note in her pocket — an ominous prelude to what was to come.

Kumar taps her fingers on the desk. "After you hired Dana, we believe they began to craft their campaign to destroy Will's life — the life he had deprived Alicia and Bradley of, as they saw it."

I can't ignore the uncomfortable nagging at the back of my mind. They weren't wrong. But somewhere deep inside, Will was broken too. His father's alcoholism and imprisonment had messed him up. Maybe he'd scared himself when he saw how low he could go — how much he enjoyed making others suffer. He'd buried that part of himself, but he never dealt with it by confessing to what he'd done.

"Will was never at peace," I say, voicing my thoughts out loud. "He didn't like getting close to anyone — he couldn't open up and share things. I think he found the deception exhausting. It was easier to retreat inside our little world and build walls around it."

"Until Danika Bernacki entered it," Kumar says.

I jerk my head up, racked with sudden fear. "Is she still alive?"

Kumar squares her shoulders. "We believe so. It's likely she was driving your husband's vehicle. We suspect she and Stacey were waiting for him in the early hours of Monday morning when he was about to leave for the airport. The coroner noted blunt force trauma to the back of his head. Odds are, they ambushed him at the house."

"But he called me from the bridge!"

Kumar's expression softens. "He was already dead by then. It must have been a recording they forced him to make before they killed him."

I rub my hands slowly over my face. I can't bear the thought of returning home after what happened there.

"The good news in all of this is that Will wasn't working with Robert Rattler," Kumar says. "The FBI are confident Rattler had nothing at all to do with this case. Or Veronica Valdez's kidnapping either. She gave a statement earlier and identified her abductors as Danika and Stacey Bernacki."

CHAPTER 56

At the hospital, I pin my visitor's badge to my lapel and head to the elevator. I'm desperate to see VV and tell her how sorry I am that she got dragged into the diabolical situation Will created, and for which I'm partly to blame. I exposed her to danger by inviting a maniac into our lives. She told me at the outset that Dana was a *bad lady,* as she put it. I should have listened to her. She's only ever watched out for my best interests, like a mother would. And this is how I rewarded her. We've all paid a heavy price for my impatience. I should have taken the time to go through a reputable agency — shortcuts are always booby-trapped.

The one thing I have to give Dana credit for is exposing the rot in my marriage. I don't agree with how she went about it — feeding off the venom of revenge — but some might say Will got what he deserved in the end. I'm not sure how I feel about that. I never had the chance to talk it over with him and decide for myself how remorseful he really was, or if he was more sorry that he'd been caught than anything else. I only have that sickening recording to go by. I'll never know the truth now, and I'm going to have to be honest about that when the twins are old enough to ask questions. We all have to make peace with the fact that some things remain unanswered in this life. I'll tell the kids their father swore off alcohol after that terrible night, but I won't hide the reality that he covered up what he did and lied about it. However difficult it is for them to hear the truth, I'm not going to try to redeem Will's reputation posthumously.

VV is sitting up in bed when I enter her room. She spreads her arms wide when she catches sight of me, matching the broad smile on her face. I hurry over to her and hold her close, sobbing like a child in her familiar arms as the pent-up emotion of the past few days cascades over me.

"Everything will be okay. I'm okay, Mrs. Morgan," she says, stroking my hair until my sobs subside.

"I should have listened to you." I brush my fingertips over my damp cheeks. "Did she hurt you?"

"She hold a gun to my head, but I tell her I am not afraid of her. She say she kill me for lying to police."

"I'm so sorry, VV," I say, my voice dropping to a shame-laden whisper.

She shrugs. "Is over now. Has the police caught her?"

I press my lips together and give a tight shake of my head. "She slipped through their fingers. They had a canine unit out looking for her, but the trail's gone cold. Kumar says there's a chance she could come after you again." I throw a quick glance at the door. "Do you know you have your own personal armed guard out there?"

VV nods enthusiastically. "I feel very safe here."

"Knock, knock."

I glance up as Julia breezes into the room. She hugs her mother and greets me with a sheepish smile.

"Julia, I'm truly sorry about—"

"No!" She holds up her hands. "It's me who should apologize. I can't imagine what this is doing to you. I feel awful about tearing into you now that the truth's come out."

"I don't blame you. I would have done the same thing if I'd as much as suspected your husband of doing something so heinous."

Julia grimaces. "You've been nothing but kind and supportive to Mom." She shifts uncomfortably. "Whatever Will was guilty of, I know he treated her with the utmost respect."

I nod. "He was good to my mom too."

Julia and VV exchange a loaded look.

"What?" I raise my brows in alarm. "Did he do something else I don't know about?"

VV takes Julia's hand and pats it gently. "*Está bien*! Tell her. She needs to know."

My heart knocks against my ribs. I don't think I can handle any more disturbing revelations about the dark side of the man I married.

Julia heaves a deep sigh. "When Mom was tied up in the barn, in and out of a drugged state, she overheard bits and pieces of Dana's and Stacey's conversations. Stacey was fully on board with the plan to murder Will — a life for a life, as she saw it. She'd been surveilling you for months before Dana ever approached you at the park. She acted as the fake references when you called, and she even lured your mom out of the yard on the day she went missing, and put that note in her pocket."

My skin prickles at the news. "I suspected as much."

"That's not the worst of it," Julia adds, her voice growing quieter. She turns to VV, who gives her an encouraging nod.

Icy tremors shoot through me. The air in the room feels dense, like thunderclouds are gathering. "What do you mean, *not the worst of it*?"

Tears well up in Julia's eyes. "I'm sorry, Morgan. Stacey told Mom she was going to be a lot more work to get rid of than Pamela was."

CHAPTER 57

I drive back to the Airbnb from the hospital in a leaden stupor. With this final blow, my heart has been beaten hollow. As hard as it is to accept that Will is dead at Dana's hand, it's even harder to come to terms with the fact that she murdered my mother — the woman I hired her to care for. Any lingering sense of sympathy I had for Dana's cause has evaporated. Part of me understood why she wanted to avenge her sister's death, but I can never forgive her for needlessly murdering an elderly woman who had nothing to do with any of this. Blind rage has eaten into Dana's conscience and devoured what was left of her heart. She's as cold and callous as the West Coast Killer in my eyes.

I take a moment to orient myself after I pull into the driveway and park under the carport. It's not just my own grief and anger I have to navigate. Somehow, I have to break it to my children that their father won't be coming home.

Andrea is sitting on the deck, clicking away on her laptop while keeping a watchful eye on Sam and Ella, who are running around in the backyard blowing bubbles at each other. When she sees me, she closes the lid on her computer and pats the white plastic chair next to her. "How's VV doing?" Her smile fades at my haunted expression.

"Will's dead," I say quietly, as I sink down in the chair.

"What?" Shock explodes over her features. "How? Was he resisting arrest?"

I shake my head emphatically. "The police didn't kill him. They think Dana and her mother did."

Andrea shoots me a startled look. "I don't understand. I thought Will was on the run from the police?"

"I thought so too. Turns out Dana was driving his BMW." I heave out a sigh, my eyes glazing over as I watch the carefree antics of the twins. "The police identified the older woman who died in the crash. She was Dana's mother, Stacey Bernacki."

A frown cleaves a deep groove in Andrea's forehead.

"Dana — her real name is Danika — staged everything. She and her mother put Will's body in the bag and threw it in the river. The coroner says he was already dead by then."

Andrea shakes her head slowly. "I don't get it. Why would Dana's mother help her kill Will?"

My stomach recoils at the thought of recounting the awful thing Will did that led to this whole nightmare, but I can't keep silent any longer. "Revenge for her daughter's death — Dana's older sister. The same night Cooper Merkler died, Will dropped a boulder from an overpass and killed a man called Bradley Cash. Bradley was Dana's sister's fiancée. The next day, she committed suicide." I gulp back a sob. "I think that's why Dana and her mother threw Will's body from the bridge — it was symbolic in a way. A pretty sick form of revenge, but I do sympathize with them for what they went through. I feel awful about it."

Andrea reaches for my hands and grips them tightly. "That's Will's guilt to bear, and he took it to the grave. You can't go through life carrying the weight of what he did. It's not healthy for the kids, and it's not healthy for you either."

My shoulders jerk with silent sobs. "I don't know how I'm going to tell Sam and Ella. I feel sick to my stomach every time I think about all the lives Will destroyed."

Andrea releases a heavy sigh. "What he did was abhorrent, but you need to forgive him and let this go, or it will eat you alive. We've all done things we wish we could undo. Some of us got lucky and our stupid choices as teenagers didn't turn out to have such dark consequences."

"The hardest part for me to forgive is not what he did — horrible as it was — it's that he lied about it. Will was a coward and a fraud — he never faced up to what he'd done. I don't know how I'm supposed to live with the fact that he wasn't the hero his kids think he was."

"Mommy, can we have some juice, please?" Ella asks, running up and panting dramatically in my face.

"I'll get it." Andrea rises to her feet and casts a knowing look at me. "I'll give you a few minutes to talk to the kids alone."

I offer a grateful nod in return, before lifting Ella onto my knee. Right on cue, Sam comes running over. "I'm thirsty."

"Andrea's getting you both some juice." I reach an arm around him and pull him close. "Mommy needs to talk to you about something very sad."

Sam's head swivels in my direction, his curiosity piqued. "What?"

"I don't like sad." Ella promptly buries her head in my chest and plugs her thumb into her mouth.

I smooth a hand over her hair. "I know, Ellie Jelly. But some days happy things happen, and some days sad things happen. Today is a sad day. Do you remember the nice police lady who likes macaroni and cheese?"

Sam nods enthusiastically. "Does she want some?"

I chuckle, despite myself. "No, sweetie. She told me that Daddy died, and it's very sad because he won't be coming home."

"Never?" Sam asks, after a moment's contemplation.

"I'm afraid not."

Ella wiggles upright in my lap and blinks solemnly up at me. "Did he went to sing with the angels, like Nana?"

CHAPTER 58

"I don't want to stay in the Airbnb tonight," I say to Andrea. "I need to take the kids home — they could use some stability right now."

Her face knots with anxiety. "What if Dana comes back?"

"She won't. She wouldn't dare. The police have launched a massive tracking operation to find her. She's going to run as far from here as she can."

Andrea gives a hesitant nod. "In that case, I'll help you pack up your stuff."

Sam and Ella are thrilled at the news that we're going home, and quickly set about gathering up their toys and backpacks. It hasn't registered, yet, that their father won't be waiting at home to greet them with a customary tickle fight. Andrea helps me load as much stuff as possible into my car, then puts the rest in her rental. She's picking up her Hyundai from the body shop tomorrow. A shiver runs across my shoulders when I recall the fateful night I watched Will put his hands around Dana's neck. One or the other of them was destined to die — it was only a matter of who would come out on top. I guessed wrong.

When we arrive back at the house, Andrea gives me a hand to unload everything from both cars and carry the stuff inside.

"Are you sure you're going to be okay spending the night here on your own?" she asks, her eyes crinkling with concern. "Do you want me to stay with you?"

"I appreciate the offer, but we'll be fine. You've done more than enough already. Go home to Tom. I'll make sure to lock the door behind you."

"What about dinner? Do you want me to bring you something over in a bit?"

"That's kind of you but I promised the kids I'd order pizza."

She exits the house with a tenuous smile. "Call me if you need anything. I'll leave my phone on, just in case."

When the pizza arrives, I set the twins up at the kitchen table with a slice each and a glass of milk. I pick at my food, wondering why I'm not hungry when I can't even remember the last time I ate. All I really want to do is sleep, but I know as soon as I close my eyes, I'll see the nightmarish image of Will laid out on a steel table. I should probably start notifying people, but what on earth do I tell them? My phone pings on the counter where I left it charging. I drag myself to my feet and walk over to check the message.

I still know where you live.

A knot of panic forms in my throat, leaving me gasping for breath. I run to the kitchen window and peer out at the studio, but there's no sign of life — no lights, no movement, no vehicle parked outside. How did Dana know I was home? Or did she? The timing could have been a coincidence — not that it's any consolation. She wants me to know that she's very much alive, and that she isn't finished with me yet. I don't know if she wants to kill me, or just terrorize me. Hasn't she got her fill of revenge already? My finger hovers over the text as I waver between deleting it or responding. The sensible thing to do would be to report it to Kumar. Maybe she can trace it. But that's probably wishful thinking on my part. Dana's no dummy. She's likely using a prepaid phone, which means she's made it safely out of the woods and is someplace with Wi-Fi — somewhere she feels safe enough to text me from.

I double check the front door to make sure it's locked, then call Kumar. Less than thirty minutes later, she shows up, followed by a second squad car. "I've assigned an officer to keep your house under surveillance tonight," she says. "We strongly suspect Bernacki hitched a ride and is already a long way from here, but we can't take any chances. We don't know her mental state. Until we have her in custody, you need to remain vigilant."

I fall asleep with the twins snuggled in my arms on either side of me. I envy their ability to close out a cruel world and retreat to the realm of refreshing slumber. For my part, I sleep fitfully, my eyes shooting open every hour or so in a desperate bid to disbelieve everything that's happened. Inevitably, it all comes flooding back. My brain synapses sift through the events of the past twenty-four hours, reminding me of my new reality, repeating it like a mantra. *My husband is dead. VV is alive. Dana is on the run.*

I can't help wondering how Dana is going to come to terms with the fact that she killed her own mother. If she's anything like Will, she'll refuse to accept responsibility for her actions and try to convince herself it was his fault. Maybe she wants to make me pay now that he's dead. Once you've crossed over to the dark side of retribution, it's hard to find your way back.

Despite my exhaustion, I rise the following morning with a flicker of hope brewing in the pit of my stomach. I made it through the first night of the rest of my life without Will. Even though the bedrock of my world has crumbled, I can still keep putting one foot in front of the other, muddling through the grieving process. I've lived through the eye of the tornado — now it's time to pick up the pieces and rebuild. The goodness of people like VV, and the kindness of neighbors like Andrea, will bolster me when the days are dark.

Dana might have slipped through the authorities' net for now, but she won't win in the end. Despite her pathetic text — a threat that rings hollow in the morning light — I refuse to live in fear. If she really intends to come after me, she wouldn't have alerted me to her plan. Her note was the parting shot of a woman who knows her days are numbered and wants to fire one last poison dart my way.

But vengeful darts are like boomerangs. They always return to their owner in the end.

EPILOGUE

Dana

In the hole-in-the-wall café Danika had stumbled across earlier, she stirred a sachet of sugar into her coffee — a much-needed respite from the adrenaline-fueled past hours. She glanced surreptitiously around at the other customers, relieved that none of them were eyeing her baggy sweats and Foothill High School hoodie with any degree of curiosity.

After the crash, she had evaded capture by swimming across the river and hitching a ride with a van full of potheads heading to a concert. They believed her story about getting high and falling in the river, which they thought was hilarious. They offered her another joint, and some dry clothes, then drove her as far as Bakersfield. The universe approved, apparently.

She sipped her coffee pensively, the past few days running through her head like a bad horror film. The minute Will Klein put his hands around her neck, the urge to kill him was overwhelming. She had given him the chance to own up to what he did, but his heart was as black as ever — maybe blacker. Jay's confession should have been enough to provoke Will's conscience. Instead, he fought harder to cover up the heinous crimes he had reveled in. So she'd followed the law of the jungle: *kill or be killed*. Her plan to wait for him in his garage Monday morning before he headed to the airport and whack him on the head with his own shovel had gone seamlessly. Tossing him from the bridge had seemed a fitting finale — a symbolic gesture of justice for Alicia.

It felt powerful to mete out retribution. Just like when that belligerent drunk Tommy Hodgson tried to convince her it was all Will's idea — calling him a sadistic sicko who enjoyed making people suffer. Will may have been the one who dropped the boulder on Bradley's car, but Jay and Tommy were right there with him that night, egging him on.

Danika's mood darkened as her thoughts turned to her mother. That's where things had gone horribly wrong. Her heart ached when she recalled spinning out on that hairpin bend and wrapping the car around a tree. She had never meant for anything to happen to her mom. Everything she did was for her. She couldn't even comprehend she was dead at first. She had tried shaking her, but her eyes remained stubbornly shut. It was only when she'd checked her pulse that she realized she was gone.

Danika grimaced, studying the dirt embedded in her nails from climbing up the riverbank. There was a certain irony in her reckless actions leading to a needless death — the very thing Will was guilty of. But she didn't blame herself. He had started this war. Her mother's blood was on his hands. And now it was on his family's hands. One of them would pay for her death — she would make sure of it, no matter how long it took. Her mom didn't deserve to die like that. She had been robbed of everything — her child, her future grandchildren, her joy in life.

A smile crept onto Danika's lips as she set her empty coffee mug down on the table. That's why killing Pamela had been so satisfying. It had given her back the control she'd been wanting after so many years of feeling helpless. She had made Will's family suffer — got revenge for what Will stole from them.

"More coffee?" a waitress asked, her glass carafe poised to pour.

"Sure, thanks."

The young girl tipped the pot up and sloshed the burnt dregs into Danika's mug before sauntering off to a neighboring table.

So now what? Danika couldn't return to her mother's house in Santa Cruz — the police were probably crawling all over it by now. But she still had a key to her ex's place in San Jose. He prided himself on being a prepper with plenty of stored food and water — even some cash and gold coins. Breaking in there while he was at work would be simple enough. She could take enough to buy a cheap car and disappear. Serve him right for cheating on her.

She pulled out the burner phone she'd found in one of the potheads' backpacks. Smothering a mirthless laugh, she typed in a familiar number. She couldn't resist texting Morgan one last time. She was such an easy target to taunt — weak, volatile, but spineless. Painting Sam's snotty little face that night and watching her punish him all week long for doing it had been immensely satisfying. And her childish attempts to force Danika out of the studio? Laughable. Danika thought for a moment, then typed a single line designed for maximum impact: *I still know where you live.*

Pushing her plate to one side, she threw some cash on the table. Time to go. She had a lot of ground to cover before it got dark. She pulled up her hood and plunged her hands into her pockets, bracing herself against a biting wind. At the edge of town, she tried hitching another ride. This time she wasn't so lucky. An endless parade of cars whizzed by without as much as a second look from the driver. In spite of the cold, she tried pulling down her hood in case she was putting people off by hiding her face. Hopefully, she would pass as a homeless bum and looked nothing like the mugshot they had almost certainly plastered all over the news by now.

Close to an hour went by before a black Mercedes sedan pulled over and the passenger window rolled down.

"Where are you headed?" the driver asked, his mirrored aviators glinting in the setting sun.

"San Jose."

He nodded. "I can take you as far as Fresno."

"Thanks." Danika climbed in and slammed the door behind her. The direct route up the I-5 was faster — but Fresno would get her halfway to San Jose. With a bit of luck, she could catch another ride before nightfall.

"Bakersfield not your cup of tea?" the man asked, as he merged with the northbound traffic.

Danika suppressed a smirk. "I need to disappear for a bit. Let's just say I did something I shouldn't have."

"Haven't we all?" He laughed, a low, caustic chuckle that smashed into her chest, knocking the breath from her lungs.

Her eyes traveled slowly over his face, taking in the silver scar that stretched from beneath his right eye to his curled lip.

Turning, he grinned at her, displaying a gold-capped front tooth. "Don't worry. I'm good at making people disappear."

THE END

AUTHOR'S NOTE

Dear Reader,

I hope you enjoyed reading *The Caregiver* as much as I enjoyed writing it.

One question I am often asked is where I get my ideas from. Building a story is kind of like mixing a recipe. I might see something interesting on TV, or read a riveting news story, and it prompts a gripping what-if question. Combine that with a fascinating character I spotted at the grocery store, or in an airport terminal, toss in a few surprising elements from my imagination, and hey presto — a story is born. It sounds simple, but the execution is a lot harder and requires discipline, which is where the struggle begins!

Thank you so much for taking the time to check out my books; I would appreciate it from the bottom of my heart if you would leave a review on Amazon or Goodreads, as it makes a HUGE difference in helping new readers find the series. If you enjoy fast-paced, well-crafted psychological suspense mysteries — clean enough to recommend to your mother-in-law, but compelling enough to keep you reading until two in the morning — I invite you to check out my website and join my newsletter to be the first to hear about my upcoming book releases, sales, and fun giveaways. You can also follow me on Twitter, Instagram, and Facebook. Feel free to email me at norma@normahinkens.com with any feedback or comments. I LOVE hearing from readers. YOU are the reason I keep writing!

All my best,

Norma

THE JOFFE BOOKS STORY

We began in 2014 when Jasper agreed to publish his mum's much-rejected romance novel and it became a bestseller.

Since then we've grown into the largest independent publisher in the UK. We're extremely proud to publish some of the very best writers in the world, including Joy Ellis, Faith Martin, Caro Ramsay, Helen Forrester, Simon Brett and Robert Goddard. Everyone at Joffe Books loves reading and we never forget that it all begins with the magic of an author telling a story.

We are proud to publish talented first-time authors, as well as established writers whose books we love introducing to a new generation of readers.

We won Trade Publisher of the Year at the Independent Publishing Awards in 2023. We have been shortlisted for Independent Publisher of the Year at the British Book Awards for the last four years, and were shortlisted for the Diversity and Inclusivity Award at the 2022 Independent Publishing Awards. In 2023 we were shortlisted for Publisher of the Year at the RNA Industry Awards.

We built this company with your help, and we love to hear from you, so please email us about absolutely anything bookish at feedback@joffebooks.com

If you want to receive free books every Friday and hear about all our new releases, join our mailing list: www.joffebooks.com/contact

And when you tell your friends about us, just remember: it's pronounced Joffe as in coffee or toffee!

Printed in the USA
CPSIA information can be obtained
at www.ICGtesting.com
LVHW041325210624
783650LV00009B/494